The Heroin Highway

By

Stuart Patray

BLACK FOREST PRESS
San Diego, California
December, 1996

First Edition

Book cover illustration by Jan Lowry

Disclaimer

This document is an original work of the author. It may include reference to information commonly known or freely available to the general public. Any resemblance to other published information is purely coincidental. The author has in no way attempted to use material not of his own origination. Black Forest Press disclaims any association with or responsibility for the ideas, opinions or facts as expressed by the author of this book.

Printed in the United States of America
Library of Congress
Cataloging-in-Publication

ISBN:1-881116-84-0

"To my father.

You remain a powerful presence in my life."

Chapter One

The office of the National Security Advisor to the President of the United States was spacious and comfortable. But the surroundings did not put Dr. Robert Wallace, professor of International Studies at Columbia University, at ease; far from it. He squirmed in the chair like a hyperactive school kid, continuously crossing his legs, trying to find a tolerable position.

He was tired and a bit irritated. His scholastic expedition began at an exhilarating pace but turned into a political football upon his return from Moscow with news of the startling discovery. Wallace took off the wire-rimmed eyeglasses and rubbed his eyes. He exhaled softly, put the glasses back on and peered around the room. Finally, the door opened and in walked Marlin Kwolski, National Security Advisor to President LaFleur.

"I'm sorry you had to wait Doctor Wallace. I trust your flight to Washington was comfortable."

"Yes, it was fine." Wallace rose from the chair and shook hands with Kwolski. A smallish man with a large, round head, Kwolski exhibited the stiff erectness and distant professionalism of a career bureaucrat. He settled behind a desk.

"It's a pleasure to meet you in person after our many telephone conversations. Your reputation as a scholar and researcher precedes you. Especially now with your discovery of the La Mai report in Moscow."

"Thank you for the kind words Mister Kwolski. But I must confess, I was hoping President LaFleur would be able to meet with me personally to discuss it."

"My apology. The president is unable to attend due to his busy schedule. However, as National Security Advisor to the administration, I have absolute jurisdiction in matters involving the United States' security interests and certainly, the La Mai report qualifies as a national security issue. Rest assured Doctor Wallace, President LaFleur has given me full authority to handle this matter at my discretion."

Kwolski picked up a copy of the *New York Times* from his desk and scanned the front page. "I was hoping we could avoid publicity until the document was fully analyzed by the CIA."

"A source from the *Times* intercepted a copy of my translation of the La Mai report I made to the Senate Select Committee on POW-MIA Affairs. An unfortunate circumstance."

"Perhaps Senator Jones leaked it."

Wallace smiled. "No doubt he's the most outspoken member of the committee regarding the POW-MIA situation. But really Mister Kwolski, the public needs to know if the possibility exists - and mind you - I say possibility, that Vietnam is still holding American prisoners of war."

"That's a matter of opinion Doctor Wallace when it's conducted through the media. This is a highly sensitive and emotionally charged issue. It must be handled with delicate care, especially when another country is involved, particularly a country that has had an unpleasant relationship with the United States during the last thirty years. We still have an embargo against Vietnam. I understand not all the members of the senate select committee are happy about this."

"Not at all. The only committee member receptive is Senator Jones. The La Mai document directly challenges the committee's research and contradicts its conclusions. I suppose it was quite embarrassing. It wasn't my intention. I'm only interested in academic research."

"Of course, Doctor Wallace. Ironic timing. The committee had just released it's final report after three years of costly investigation indicating no evidence of American prisoners of war existed in Southeast Asia. Then pops up General La Mai's calculations. However, the committee has decided not to dissolve until this matter is put to rest."

"Will there be more investigations?"

"Perhaps. It's only speculation at this point but the Pentagon has indicated the chairman of the committee, Senator Bainbridge, will call for hearings with Vietnamese officials in Hanoi."

"That's positive news Mister Kwolski. Because the American-imposed embargo was a result of North Vietnam not accounting for all American prisoners of war and missing in action, General La Mai's report may not seem as outrageous when taken in that light."

"Quite right doctor. That embargo has been in place since 1975 when the North Vietnamese violated the 1973 Paris Peace Accords which ended American involvement in the Vietnam War. That's a long time. But let's dispense with the peripheral matters and focus on the main objective. You believe General La Mai's report to be authentic, correct?"

"Yes."

"You're positive?"

"Yes."

"Perhaps the report is an elaborate hoax concocted by Vietnam and the former Soviet Union to embarrass the

United States. Perhaps La Mai was mistaken. How can you be sure Doctor Wallace?"

"I foresaw all possible contingencies. With the collapse of the Soviet Union and the democratic movement spurred by President Boris Yeltsin, the files of the Soviet Communist Party were declassified. There was literally hundreds of thousands of party documents I sifted through during my six months in Moscow on the grant I received from Columbia University. It was buried in vaults at the Kremlin no one had opened in years.

"It's not a plant," he continued. "This is an internal military document, classified national security, not for public inspection. It was top-secret, crammed in files of North Vietnam's Central Military Affairs Party Committee. But no one could foresee the eventual demise of the USSR."

"Even so, a report claiming the Vietnamese were holding 2,000 American prisoners of war is farfetched to say the least. We haven't seen a shred of evidence in two decades to substantiate La Mai's claims."

"It's 2, 586 POWs to be exact, distributed in prisons in North Vietnam, Cambodia and Laos according to La Mai. That figure is more than four times the number of POWS released after the signing of the peace accords treaty."

"That's about right. There were 591 prisoners of war released by North Vietnam in Operation Homecoming."

"I stumbled upon the report in the archives of the former GRU, the Chief Intelligence Directorate of the Soviet Red Army. It was dated September 12, 1972. General Ban La Mai was at the time the chief of staff of the North Vietnamese Army. If anyone knew about American prisoners of war, he did."

"The Vietnamese have reacted quickly to the publication of it. They claim La Mai did not hold that post in 1972 and the report is a forgery."

"Yes, well, unfortunately, Ban La Mai died in 1988 so we have no way of confirming its accuracy. However, his report was authenticated by an accompanying document. It was a summary of the general's report that was prepared by the GRU and signed by its chief, General Ivan Petrovich."

"For the sake of argument, let's say it is authentic. The most disturbing aspect of the report is that this La Mai character indicates the United States government was aware the Viet Cong had not revealed the exact number of prisoners."

"That's correct Mister Kwolski. General La Mai stated the U.S. could only makes guesses on the number of prisoners of war based on its losses. But the exact number was withheld from American forces in strict accordance with the instructions of the North Vietnamese Politburo."

"Hmm." Kwolski looked down at his desk for a moment and drummed his fingers. He looked back up at Wallace and spoke slowly.

"Doctor, I realize you have been thrust into an uncomfortable position; put up to ridicule by the national media. Your integrity has been attacked by fellow researchers when you went public with La Mai's report. Despite it all, you made the right decision. We appreciate your patriotism and courage in coming forward to disclose what you found. Keep in mind, we're skeptical but President LaFleur wants this matter resolved. If there's any chance American POWs may still be alive in Vietnam, we want to find 'em."

"So do I Mister Kwolski."

"I'm glad to hear it. Because the administration wants you to travel to Southeast Asia as an emissary on behalf of my office and the Senate Select Committee on POW-MIA Affairs."

"Why?"

"To investigate some leads."

"But why me?"

"We feel you're the perfect candidate since you have no ties to the U.S. government and can provide us with unbias, independent data. As an academic, it's the opportunity of a lifetime in international research. I took the liberty of speaking to the Board of Regents. Columbia University agreed to extend your paid sabbatical if you choose to accept our offer. Of course, all your expenses will be taken care of."

"What do I have to do?"

"We will fly you to Vientiane, Laos to meet with officials of the Joint Casualty Resolution Center for a debriefing."

"Why Laos?"

"There's a Laotian drug lord headquartered there, named Kuhn-Sah Duc. He's involved heavily in the Golden Triangle heroin trade. The National Security Agency suspects this Duc character is using an international front company called Pacific Equity to launder his drug cash."

"I don't understand. What does this have to do with the La Mai report?"

"We've received information that Duc may indeed know whether American POWs exist due to his thriving heroin trade in Vietnam. Apparently Duc has cultivated intimate ties with Vietnam's top-level communist party bosses. We've tried to infiltrate Pacific Equity but without success."

"This sounds more like some spy mission than an academic endeavor. I dunno. . ."

"Please hear me out Doctor Wallace. You can provide us with a valuable cover. We also want you to meet with an American named Jim Laramie, a former Vietnam veteran."

"What for?"

Kwolski shifted uneasily in the chair. "What I'm about to tell you is classified national security. It goes no further. If ya tell the press, we'll deny it and scrap the La Mai report."

"You have my word."

"Laramie commanded several covert missions into Southeast Asia looking for evidence of American POWs. Off budget missions, conducted by presidential administrations without the consent or knowledge of Congress. Laramie never found anything but threatened to go public when funding was cut off. He was discharged and fled to Southeast Asia and became a sort of a soldier of fortune. He's been there ever since, conducting independent investigations on his own with the help of sympathetic private citizens."

"You suspect this Laramie fellow may have personal knowledge of POWs?"

"He was trained well. We lost touch three years ago but he recently resurfaced. Reports from the U.S. Embassy in Bangkok indicate he's been very active. We think we can get you in touch with 'em."

"Is it safe?"

"Absolutely. You'll work in complete anonymity, under constant surveillance. Laramie may be a mercenary but he's still a patriot. His only purpose in life is pursuing that evasive myth of live American POWs in Vietnam. It's time to put this painful issue to rest Doctor Wallace. Either it's a sentimental legend or General La Mai has blown Vietnam's cover."

"What about this drug lord?"

"Safe too. Above all, he's a businessman. We can provide Kuhn-Sah Duc with powerful inducements to talk with you. Richard Armstrong, the deputy Secretary of State at our Bangkok embassy, will assist you with Duc."

Twenty minutes more of reassurances passed until Doctor Wallace left the NSA office. Kwolski pressed the desk intercom after he was alone.

"Bill, get in here."

A feminine looking man in his late twenties entered the office, dressed immaculately in a dark suit, carrying a pad and pen. He took a seat in front of Kwolski's desk.

"Doctor Robert Wallace has decided to accept our proposal. He leaves tomorrow for Laos. Make sure the trip is well publicized in the papers."

"Yes, sir." The young man began writing furiously on the pad in short hand.

"Contact all our agents in the media including radio and television. I'll have a press release ready for delivery to 'em. We want to especially play up Doctor Wallace's meeting with Kuhn-Sah Duc and Pacific Equity officials. The stories will be leaked anonymously from quote 'Pentagon sources' unquote. Understand?"

"Yes, sir, Mister Kwolski. One thing though, won't releasing information prematurely on Doctor Wallace's trip before he completes the task place him in possible danger?"

"Of course Bill. That's the plan."

Chapter Two

The suburban Virginia park was peaceful except for the clatter of sparrows in the pines and the hum of a gasoline engine. Six miles south lay the sprawling metropolis of the nation's capital, Washington, D.C.

The car motor was still running. The police officer bent over the slumped body, retrieving a piece of paper. He backed out of the driver's side, examining the paper in the sunlight, his eyes squinting as he fumbled for his bifocals.

"Pete, what'cha got?" said the other officer, approaching the vehicle.

"Looks like a suicide but. . ."

"But, what?"

"I dunno. There's something strange. Look at the gun."

Pete moved out of the way, still reading the note while the other officer leaned inside the car.

A revolver lay beside the body on the car seat.

"There's a syringe lying beside 'em. Apparently he was using drugs. The coroner and photo boys are on their way. Figure he's been room temperature, maybe two hours."

"I see what ya mean. It's weird the gun is so close to the body. Usually a shooter's gun will fall farther away. Maybe murder. Homicide will figure it out."

"Take a look at his shirt."

"What 'bout it?"

"No blood. No mess. No nothing. He shot himself in the mouth from what I can tell but hardly no blood."

Jack looked closer at the body. "Not only that, I don't see an exit wound. The bullet must still be lodged in his head. Autopsy can give us a better idea. Anything missing?"

"Can't tell. The park police called it in. I was the closest unit in the area. Been here only a few minutes when you arrived Jack."

"I found something."

"What?"

Jack kneeled under the front seat, taking out a pen light from his shirt pocket. He gently pushed out a small, plastic packet with the light, just underneath the feet of the corpse.

"Looks like heroin or something. Our boy with the golden arm had a penchant for the high-priced stuff."

"I'll be damn," Pete replied. "I didn't see that."

"ID?"

"Robert Wallace. A professor from Columbia University."

Jack puckered his lips and rubbed his chin. "Hmmm. This guy sounds familiar."

"Ya know 'em?" Pete asked.

Jack snapped his fingers and pointed at Pete. "Yeah, yeah. The professor working with the Senate Committee on POWs."

"Ya lost me."

Jack pointed to the body slumped in the front seat of the Lexus LS. "He discovered a document in Russia that indicated Vietnam had not accounted for all American

MIAs and POWs after the Vietnam War. Then he visited Southeast Asia on some fact-finding mission for the government just recently. I remember reading 'bout it."

"Really?" Pete pushed back his cap.

"Sure enough. I remember now. This Wallace fellow is suppose to be flying to Vietnam this week to testify at those hearings for the senate committee regarding POW evidence he found."

"Okay, yeah. I heard about that on the news last night. They're holding hearings in 'Nam to find out if POWs do exist and close the case once and for all. Well, looks like he won't make it."

"Nope." Jack reached in and turned off the ignition.

"Hey, the forensic crew aren't here yet."

"Ahh, forget 'em. It don't matter now. He's gone."

"I can't figure it. An Ivy League professor on drugs, shoots himself. He doesn't seem the type."

"Hell, these days, you can't tell. But this doesn't look natural, like it was staged. What's the note say?"

Pete pushed up his glasses on the bridge of his nose and squinted. "'I can't go on. The La Mai document is not authentic and I knew it. I've let everyone down, including myself. My academic career is ruined. Please forgive me.'"

Pete looked up from the note and shrugged. "Typed. That's it."

"La Mai document, La Mai document. I think that's the POW evidence he found in Russia."

"I dunno."

"It seems like Wallace discovered a bunch of controversial evidence."

"Like what?"

"I can't really remember. Something to do with federal government officials, during the war in Southeast Asia." Jack shook his head. "I want to say there were rumors Wallace was going to present incriminating evidence to the Senate Committee that put President LaFleur in a bad light."

"The president," Pete replied. "Can't be."

"Maybe not. Oh. Get his address off the driver's license and we'll search his home. Get out the crime tape and seal the scene."

"That won't be necessary." A tall figure appeared from nowhere, as if he materialized in front of the startled cops.

"This is a possible crime scene," Jack said, walking quickly toward him. "No one is allowed. . ."

"Brad Richardson, FBI." He whipped out a badge from inside a coat pocket and flashed the gold metal in their face. "We have federal jurisdiction. Get your commanding officer on the phone. Let me have that note."

Chapter Three

Two days later, across the Pacific Ocean, the figure crept silently up to the bamboo fence and began wedging his emaciated body between an opening in the ten-foot high structure.

He had worked on this portion of the fence for months, loosening the rope which bound the yellow bamboo poles together in a tight configuration. Slowly but methodically, he separated them.

The opportunity to exploit the unseen gap in the fortress fence had arisen during work detail. He had worked in the compound for years and built a degree of confidence among the hard-boiled guards.

Every day during harvesting, he would loosen the rope and poles with tools from the work shed. Now, finally, the time had come to free himself and escape from this hell he had been condemned to so long ago.

How long had it been? Twenty years? Thirty years? He had lost all track of time since that day he was captured by the Viet Cong and carried off in a bamboo tiger cage. He couldn't remember anything except his company called him major. Yeah, that's right, he was a major.

Was the war still raging? Guards told him American forces had withdrawn in disgrace, defeated, abandoning him. He didn't believe their propaganda.

The only connection to back home was a yellow-edged wallet photograph of his wife and child. The major derived much pleasure from showing the picture to the other prisoners. Everybody wanted to see it until the guards took the photo and burned it in front of him.

But he just laughed and shot them birds; they didn't quite understand the hand language but they knew it wasn't polite. He was thrown into solitary confinement. The prisoners would hear him singing all night long and giggling like a psychotic mental patient.

His scrawny body, thinned from years of hard labor and torture, sustained barely on rice cakes, allows him to slip through the fence gap with relative ease. The major, clad in gray pajama-type clothing and tongs, pushes through the fence head first. He stops periodically to look back and dodge the spot lights which scour the compound, lighting it up momentarily like a brief dawn.

His hands, scarred from cuffs and shackles, reach for the other side of the fence. He pulls his torso until the entire body is through the bamboo prison.

He remains low to the ground as he takes off running for the lush, tropical jungle under the cover of night. The Southeast Asian moon casts a erie, pale illumination as the major runs across the terrain like a wild dog released after years of confinement.

Suddenly, foreign voices can be heard. The spotlights flash over the fence and toward the jungle, following the pathetic figure as his running becomes erratic and desperate. Cracks of rifle fire ring out, disturbing the silent Eastern night. Patrols of guards open the gate and begin tracking the escapee with dogs.

He glances back in fear, stumbling through the jungle, striking shrubbery and trees while attempting to elude his captors. He falls down many times, his body weak from sheer starvation and neglect. But his will to live is strong. He gets up and continues to flee.

He hears the yaps of the dogs and shouts of the foreign tongue, a language he never adjusted to despite having to learn it by force. The patrols are getting closer. His feet are cut and bleeding from the harsh jungle floor. Tongs are nothing compared to Army boots.

Breathing is sporadic; the mouth wide open as he gulps currents of air. Desperation and panic are overtaking him. He runs faster and faster, his arms thrashing beside the body. He planned for this very moment for years; prayed to God it would come. Now it's here and he must make it. He can't go back. He will never go back.

Though the face is cut and lacerated by tree branches, he continues to run as hard as he can through the lush vegetation. He wipes the blood from his eyes. There it is! The Po-Tong River looks like an old friend. The Po-Tong ran just one-half mile southeast of the compound.

Now the Po-Tong River is between him and freedom. The dogs' barks close in. Once he crosses the river, his scent will be washed away and the dogs will lose the trail. He stumbles into the river, his chest heaving as he gasps for air. The Po-Tong is not too deep, probably about five feet in the middle. He jumps in.

His gray pajamas are dark and heavy from the water. The wet clothing reveals the outline of a skeletal body as it struggles across the moving water. The bank is close now. He reaches out for the grassy slope. The foreign voices are close. They yell out in protest but he pays no heed.

The dogs growl and run up and down the river bank. He struggles up the hilly bank, grabbing clumps of grass to pull himself out of the murky water. As he climbs out of the brackish swell, the years of grime and dirt are washed away from his body. It felt good.

He stands up, still trying to catch his breath, and begins to run. A sound, like an explosion, from across the river bank pierces the night. A puff of white smoke drifts down the Po-Tong current. He feels his back explode, paralyzing his movement. The major cries out as it cuts through his body and erupts out his chest, opening a gaping hole. But no one is there to hear him.

He stops running, just stands still. He looks down at the massive hole in the chest, blood flowing from the wound. He looks up at the night sky, tears running down his face. An entire canopy of stars greet him. He feels an odd relief.

He places his hand on the chest wound. It's warm and wet; then opening the red, bloody palm, he examines it. It looks strange. He falls to his knees and his head sways. Again he peers up at the night sky and thinks of home. Always home, the thought never left his tortured mind. He would not see his native land again but it didn't matter, nothing mattered.

Another gun shot rings out and the back of his head explodes like a pumpkin being dropped from a rooftop. He falls face first to the ground, motionless. The patrol crosses the Po-Tong to the other side. Flash lights illuminate the wasted body lying on the jungle floor.

The pack of dogs sniff the bloody corpse, biting at the rag-tag clothes, the bloody mass of brains exciting them into a frenzy. The guards kick the dogs back from the still body. The commanding officer takes his boot and pushes what is left of the man over on his back.

He couldn't allow the American prisoner to escape. Their captivity has been a top-secret agenda of the politburo for decades, not to mention the important role the POWs play for the American government merchants.

The officer breathes a sigh of relief. As commander of the prison, his communist superiors would have executed him if the American major had escaped. Such a blunder would not be tolerated by the Hanoi regime nor their American capitalist partners.

He flashes a light on the face of the dead major. Gasps and mumbling arise among the group, many guards bend down on a knee for a closer look.

The commanding officer decides the body should be left to the creatures of the jungle. The body was to be brought back and made an example of to other prisoners who dared think they could escape. But the dead man has disturbed him.

They prepare to leave the river bank and travel back to the compound. The dogs continue to sniff the body and gnaw on the fingers and arms. But the guards grab the leashes with a jerk and exit the river bank. The dogs whimper and peer back at the skinny figure as the patrol departs.

The lifeless body, sprawled out beside the river, gives the appearance of a mutilated ghost while bathed in the pale moonlight. His gray pajamas, splattered with bloody pulp, were too big and hang off the bony figure. The wet metal tag around his neck glistens in the lunar light.

His last moment on earth was enjoyable. He tasted freedom; at least for a few minutes. His spirit was released. A smile warms the cold, white face; a smile the guards were unable to change no matter how many times they kicked the major's face with their steel-toe boots.

Chapter Four

The jet touched down with a mighty screech, smoke boiling from its tires from the pressure of the descent. The cargo of passengers taxied toward the terminal.

Stephen Decatur wiped the perspiration from his brow and looked down at the Hawaiian shirt. The palm-tree layered clothing was stained with sweat.

"It's about damn time," he mumbled to himself as he unbuckled the seat belt, reaching for the garment bag and lap-top computer in the compartment above the seat.

He left Australia this morning and flew into Hanoi, the capital of Vietnam.

He had begun to wonder if the aircraft would ever find the desired destination, strung out over the Pacific Ocean and crossing time zones too numerous to recount. He felt the symptoms of a nauseous case of jet lag coming on.

He remembered leaving Los Angeles three days ago, flying into Honolulu for a night. Then on to Sydney for a night. The trip from the Hawaiian Islands to Down Under almost killed him; 16 hours of unadulterated boredom, stacked together like sardines in a can with people who became interesting only after consuming several Canadian Mists and Coke.

Stephen was use to air travel in his job but this trip had been unusually difficult. "I must be getting old," he told the flight attendant as he departed the plane with the bag in one hand and the lap-top in the other.

He was still in good shape. He had an athletic build thanks to four years of college football as a defensive back at the University of Georgia. But three surgeries later had saddled him with a gimpy knee.

Yet the workload had become monotonous, boring; it held no appeal anymore. That weary notion of unfulfillment had set in. He began feeling older than his thirty-four years of age.

A cheerful but cynical writer, Decatur cut his cub reporter teeth at the *New York Times* and *Washington Post* before making enough contacts to move into free lance circles.

The free lance journalist provided news stories for several U.S. national publications and international news services. He was on special assignment for Reuters News Service, covering the state visit of members of the U.S. Senate Select Committee on POW–MIA Affairs.

Stephen pushed his way through the crowd at baggage claims, emerging from the throng of people and beside the circular escalator which propelled the luggage around and around, disappearing into the wall and reappearing periodically.

He glanced briefly across claims, then down again to the escalator, then shot his head back up. He spied a familiar face - a pale, white face among the sea of yellow Asian faces. The face gradually revealed a row of teeth as it broke into a smile.

"Paul." Stephen took a couple of steps forward. "Jesus, Paul Mathis?"

"Stephen Decatur. My God." The man began walking toward him. "How long has it been? Six years?"

"At least," Stephen replied as he walked around claims toward the familiar face. "Probably seven."

They shook hands, then embraced.

Paul took Stephen by the shoulders with both hands and shook him furiously. "It's great to see yah man. Christ, of all places, who would have thought we'd meet again in Vietnam."

Paul Mathis was in his early fifties. Now a video journalist, Stephen had met him during his internship stint with the *Times* where Paul served as a beat reporter for the city desk.

A touch of gray over the temples and silver-rimmed glasses gave him the studious appearance of a college professor but the colorful background of his life defied such a category.

Paul joined the Vietnam War opposition movement in the late 1960s as a draft card burning student at Kent State, culminating with his participation and arrest at the infamous protest held during the 1968 Democratic National Convention in Chicago, a fact in which he took extreme pride.

He became swept up in the hippie culture, dropping out of life and joining a commune in New Mexico with fifty other people, mostly women, in an attempt to stretch the concept of free love to its limit.

Stephen remembered the exotic stories he told during their lunch breaks. Woodstock and Abbey Hoffman - the "glory days" as Paul referred to them.

But Paul Mathis withdrew from the flower child phenomenon after developing a rabid dependency on drugs, eventually joining a recovery group and becoming a dedicated member, as fervent about eliminating chemical abuse as he was about stopping the Vietnam War. He reluctantly settled back into the suffocating confines of conventional society.

"I guess you're here for the damn Senate Select Committee hearings," Paul said.

"Yep. Reuters gave me an all expense paid vacation. You?"

"CNN. We've gotta crew here to film the state visit. By the way, what time does it start tomorrow? I never picked up an itinerary in Atlanta. I was running late and almost missed my flight."

"Let's see." Stephen pulled out a piece of paper from his pants pocket. Directions from his editor. "Nine in the morning at the Central Government Directorate Hall in downtown Hanoi."

"Shit," Paul exhaled, expressing a sullen look. "Maybe we can get this mess over with and close the final chapter on this God-forsaken war."

"Yeah. I guess this has special meaning for you, what with all the protest stuff you used to bore me with at the *Times*."

"It was more than stuff. A lotta years of my life were consumed by the Vietnam War, even if I didn't serve."

❀ ❀ ❀ ❀ ❀ ❀

A Vietnamese kid tugged at Stephen's belt, jabbering in his native tongue and holding a long brown clump in a hand. He did know some English. "Fifty buck Bob. Fifty buck."

"What's that crap he's selling?"

"Dried Bengal Tiger genitals," Paul answered.

"What?"

"Bengal Tiger genitals. Considered an aphrodisiac in Asia. Highly sought on the black market."

"Fifty buck Bob." The kid shook the dried genitals at Stephen, wanting him to take it. The journalists noticed the child had no left arm, just a stump hanging from the shoulder.

"Uhhh. Jesus. Forget it kid." Stephen waved off the little gadfly who ran to the next tourist he saw.

"I hate saying no since the kid is deformed. But I got no use for tiger nuts."

"An Agent Orange baby."

"The toxic defoliant?"

"Yep. After the U.S. pulled out, Vietnamese women began experiencing an abnormal amount of birth defects in their babies. Still happening. Kids born with tumors, no arms, legs, pathetic."

"Damn. I know Agent Orange caused cancer in our soldiers but I didn't even think about Vietnam. I guess I shoulda given him some money."

"Don't worry about it. There's thousands of 'em, like the Amerasian kids. Nothing you can do about it."

Stephen paused, looking at the kid hustling an Australian tourist, waving the dried, brown genitals around with the one good arm, hoping for a handout.

At first he wanted to laugh, seeing a one-arm kid push tiger balls on unsuspecting passengers. The figure cut a comic scene.

But suddenly he was overwhelmed with a feeling of shame. Not so much for the kid as for himself, because of his inability to handle the situation. He wanted the kid away from him, so no one would see.

He decided to change the subject.

"So what's your gut feeling about the La Mai document? Any validity?"

Paul shook his head. "At first yeah, when I read the translation in the *Times* before Wallace's appearance in front of the select committee. But now. Nah. You heard about his suicide, didn't ya?"

"Sure. I tried to sell an expose' of it to *Time Magazine*. They balked. Wouldn't touch it."

"His suicide note said the La Mai report was bogus. Besides, Wallace was a drug addict. The cops found drugs on 'em. Believe me, I know. That stuff will mess with your mind."

"Yeah. . . but his death is suspicious. I mean, it happens right before he's going to testify. I interviewed his colleagues and they said Wallace never used drugs, didn't even drink. The local cops suspect foul play but aren't talking publicly."

"The FBI ruled it a self-inflicted gunshot."

"That's another strange thing about his death: why did the FBI move in so fast? It was clearly in the D.C. cops' jurisdiction. Suddenly, the crime scene is crawling with feds. FBI don't usually involve themselves in local police work."

"You think foul play in connection with the hearings here in Hanoi?" Paul asked incredulously.

Stephen shrugged his shoulders.

"Hell. And maybe Wallace was killed by the same shooter who was on the grassy knoll that day in Dallas when President Kennedy's car passed."

"Still a smartass," Stephen replied.

"La Mai's report isn't authentic. The Pentagon told the Senate Select Committee that back in Washington. The professor wanted some headlines. But he couldn't live with betraying his academic integrity, went on a drug binge, and blew his brains out. Simple as that."

"Probably right. This shit about live American servicemen still being held is starting to sound about as credible as UFO abductions."

"It seems something would have turned up years ago—a body, a dog tag, something. With that large of a discrepancy proposed by General La Mai, someone would have seen a POW by now. The senate select committee went over it with a fine tooth comb. Perhaps the Senate wasted its time forming the committee. Who knows."

Stephen saw his luggage and grabbed it up as it came by. "There's mine," Paul said, pointing to the garment bag. Stephen picked up the bag and handed it to him. They began walking down the terminal.

"Let me play devil's advocate for a minute."

"Go ahead."

"You didn't believe our government about the war during the Sixties. Why believe 'em now? Or the Hanoi communists for that matter."

"Listen, the war ended two decades ago. I've moved on. As far as Vietnam is concerned, we'll never know for sure. The committee concluded its probe and reported to Congress that no evidence existed of any American POWs alive or held in captivity in Southeast Asia. Period. End of story."

"You're right. Even if they're were some POWs, surely they're dead by now. The committee is here simply to implement damage control. Talking tough in the media about Hanoi's complicity."

"Exactly. All for show. Circumventing embarrassment caused by Wallace's escapade in Moscow. Just a little PR for the voters back home, then it's business as usual back in Washington. Yah know Senator Bainbridge. He always wants good press. He's such a goddamned media hog."

Stephen stopped to tuck in the bright Polynesian shirt into his jeans. "Got that right. I just want to get this bullshit over with and get back home. This place gives me an uneasy feeling."

"Why?"

"I dunno. I had a rough flight."

"Hell, maybe the politicians will give us some straight answers about the MIAs for once."

"Even if it's 20 years too late."

They walked out of the cool airport into the oppressively humid Asian air, hailed a taxi and headed for downtown Hanoi.

The first day of committee hearings with Vietnamese government officials began with the usual pomp and ceremony accompanying state visits including repetitive but sacred rituals of handshakes, bows and nervous laughs—for media photo sessions—as each group tried to feel the other out while presenting the appropriate appearance to the press.

Prior hearings between both groups had been cordial and almost buddy-buddy. Such benign meetings, characterized by elaborate junkets—wining and dining by the Vietnamese government—had produced no new information on American POWs, only well-fed and suntanned Senators.

The Vietnamese delegation was aware of General Ban La Mai's report and knew the Senate Select Committee wanted answers.

Stephen entered the Central Government Directorate Hall and found a seat in the auditorium among a teeming phalanx of other journalists representing various nations of North America, Europe and Southeast Asia. He got out his pad, pen and tape recorder and readied himself for action.

The American and Vietnamese delegations sat across from each other at a large conference table equipped with microphones so the gallery could hear the dialogue.

Committee Chairman Walter Bainbridge and the Vietnamese Foreign Minister spoke on behalf of each group through interpreters.

The two-hour session was uneventful for the journalists; a bland meeting peppered with the usual diplomatic lingo which rendered little useful or revealing information on the plight of American soldiers missing in action.

However, one sharp exchange of words did emerge from the political propriety between Senator Bainbridge and the Foreign Minister regarding the La Mai document. It caught Stephen's attention.

The Vietnamese Foreign Minister vehemently denied the existence of live POWs, dismissed the La Mai document as "Soviet propaganda aimed at discrediting Vietnam" and refused a request by the committee to inspect the military records of the late Chief of Staff of the North Vietnamese Army.

The hearings hit an impasse and a recess was called to allow both parties to gather their thoughts. The media pool broke.

Stephen walked over to the section of the auditorium designated for video cameras. Paul was readjusting his camera tripod.

"Sitting in the Central Directorate Hall makes me think the Cold War isn't over after all," Stephen said. "How 'bout the words between Bainbridge and the minister."

"Yeah, that tickled me," Paul said. "Got it all on film. It's on satellite feed back to Atlanta. Americans will get some laughs out of that when it airs tonight. What'd you think of the first day?"

"Nothing spectacular. But the foreign minister certainly was irritated about General La Mai. Didn't want to cooperate. The original committee report to Congress clears the way for the elimination of the trade embargo. But now, I'm not so sure."

"Doesn't matter. The committee will stick by its original recommendation to eliminate the embargo."

"How do you figure? That verbal exchange may not play well for veterans and POW families back home. May hold things up for a while anyway."

"Nah. The committee is under a lot of pressure to end this POW matter for good so the U.S. can normalize relations with Vietnam."

"Of course Vietnam is pressuring them."

Paul smiled and shook his head. "No. I mean pressure from the United States."

Stephen gave the video journalist a funny look. "What are you talking about?"

"Are you hungry?"

Stephen nodded.

"Let's see if we can find a decent meal in this town."

The journalists left the Central Directorate Hall and entered the congested streets of Hanoi, filled with people on bicycles, motor bikes and rickshaws. They found a comfortable cafe located below a huge billboard of Fuji Film.

A diminutive Vietnamese waitress—jet black, straight hair and a pale yellow complexion—took their order. Paul ordered for both of them.

"What'd you order us?"

"I'm not sure. Some Asian mystery meat. You'll like it. I've had it before."

"You been to Vietnam before?" Stephen asked as he settled down into the booth in a dim-lit corner of the cafe as local patrons stared at the two Westerners.

"Been to Southeast Asia several times on assignment."

"So you know the place fairly well."

"Fairly well."

"Now what's this stuff about pressure from the United States."

"Corporate business," Paul replied, squinting through his glasses as he looked the joint over. "They want the trade embargo lifted so they can invest in Vietnam, specifically the multi-nationals headquartered in America."

"My editor at Reuters told me the National Security Advisor personally met with Wallace about the La Mai document and arranged his trip to Southeast Asia. Obviously, he's interested in resolving the POW matter before touching the embargo."

"Don't buy it. The LeFleur administration is under intense pressure to lift the trade embargo and allow U.S.

corporations to conduct business in Vietnam. Oil companies are eager to begin drilling operations off Vietnam's coast. Petroleum has been discovered in the coastal regions of the country but Vietnam needs the technology of these companies to take advantage of its natural resources."

"Uh-huh."

❁ ❁ ❁ ❁ ❁ ❁

"Of course Vietnam also wants this embargo lifted badly. It's damaged their domestic economy. I've heard that Hanoi officials have already held informal meetings with some of the CEOs of these oil companies in anticipation of the embargo being lifted. So not only is the White House being lobbied by the Vietnamese but American big business wants the embargo gone."

"Huh. I hadn't heard."

"Wait. It gets better. Mobil hasn't even waited for the lifting of the trade embargo. The company has aligned itself with the Arabian Oil Company, a Japanese petroleum outfit. Apparently Arabian has a contract with Vietnam for drilling rights and Mobil wants to get in on the action under the cover of Arabian."

"Is that legal?" Stephen asked. "It seems an American company like Mobil is violating the sanctioned embargo."

"Well, in legal terms, I guess Mobil is covered since Arabian owns the oil rights. You see, oil has been discovered in regions under the South China Sea. Vietnam is scrambling along with China and the Philippines to develop those oil rich fields under that body of water. I understand Vietnam plans to lease areas it claims as territory in the South China Sea to U.S. Oil companies once the embargo is gone."

"That might be true but Reuters reported that President LaFleur advised Senator Bainbridge about this meeting after the La Mai report surfaced. I think the president is committed to getting down to the bottom of it."

"Maybe. But those corporations have access to him because of their campaign contributions. I mean let's face it, he's gonna listen to them. LaFleur needs their financial support for re-election."

"I can't argue that."

"Personally, I think this state visit was planned to placate American families of POWs and MIAs when La Mai's report became public. Calm their fears. That's all."

"Well, this whole situation is wishful thinking. I believe the POW legend is just that—legend. But still, even if La Mai's report is fake, we've gotta obligation to check all possible leads before shutting the door. We're talking about men's lives, men who fought for our country."

Paul's eyes narrowed. He adjusted his glasses and rubbed his chin, staring at the beaded curtain which lead to the cafe's other dining room. Thick cigarette smoke hovered around the lights.

"You really mean that?"

"Of course."

"Then perhaps you'll be interested in this. I've been cultivating a relationship with an ex-military intelligence officer over the last couple of years. Been a good source when it comes to the Vietnam War POW issue."

"Yeah, so?"

"This is just between you and me. Okay?"

"Okay."

"I'm meeting this guy tomorrow."

"He's here? In 'Nam?"

"Yeah. Been in Southeast Asia looking for POW evidence for years. He was in the war. Kinda a renegade type. He claims to have evidence of American POWs."

Stephen's eyes got big and his head dipped in disbelief.

"I know, I know," Paul said, raising a hand. "You gotta approach it with an open mind. You said we should explore all possibilities before shutting the door, right?"

"Uhh. . .yeah, but I didn't think. . ."

"This is legit Steve. This ranger led expeditions into Southeast Asia sanctioned by certain sections of the federal government."

Stephen crossed his arms and leaned back into the booth. "Everybody claims to have evidence like Professor Wallace. Remember those photos of POWs that turned out to be fakes. I thought you didn't believe any POWs exist."

"I don't. But this has the making of a good story. Believe me, this guy isn't a Rambo crack-pot."

"Where'd you hear about 'em?"

"Some of my sources at the Pentagon got me in contact with him. I hear he has an incredible story to tell. Now let me tell you up front, the Defense Department thinks he's nuts but my sources slipped me his dossier. He's got an impressive background in the American intelligence community."

"Even if this fellow has credible information, why are you interested? You've been skeptical of this entire affair from the start."

"This guy has contacts Steve, right up to the White House. This could be a great career opportunity, the story of a lifetime, whether POWs exist or not. He's ready to tell what he knows since the Senate Select Committee is here."

Stephen was silent.

"What'd ya think?"

He shrugged. "Mmm. . . yeah, sure. Why not? I guess it won't hurt."

"You don't sound so positive."

"It's just a surprise, coming from you."

"Granted, his info may be misleading. I'm not saying it's gospel. But if there's a shred of truth in his story, it could be a major scoop, the break I've been looking for. He led covert missions that were never made public. Who knows what he can tell us, not just about alleged POWs but secrets of the U.S. intelligence community."

"What's his name?"

"Jim Laramie."

"Why bring me on?"

"You're my friend. Besides, I rather not go alone."

"That makes me feel secure."

The tiny waitress brought the food: tenderized meat on sticks accompanied with rice and bean sprouts.

"But seriously, this ranger is okay. It's safe. So, are you in?"

"I'm in."

"Great. We'll go after tomorrow's committee hearing."

❀ ❀ ❀ ❀ ❀ ❀

Following adjournment, Stephen word processed an account of the second day of the Hanoi hearings on his laptop computer. He was comfortably seated in the auditorium of the Central Government Directorate Hall as a crowd of journalists filed out in a single line.

The committee and Hanoi officials had departed and would resume talks the next day. Paul walked up, hauling camera equipment around his shoulder.

"Ready?" he asked.

"Almost. I've gotta press time to beat."

Stephen hit the send button, transmitting the data from the laptop through a fax modem across several time zones to Reuters in Washington, D.C.

He reached behind the rear panel of the laptop and pressed the power button. A sound like the buzz of a tiny engine going dead was emitted. The liquid crystal screen went dark.

Stephen closed the laptop and walked out of the building with Paul. They crossed the street and the video journalist motioned a man seated in a small, Malaysian-made car.

The car pulled up to the curb. Stephen jumped into the back seat while Paul got into the passenger side.

He pointed to the Vietnamese driver. "Stephen, this is Chin.

"Hello."

"Ha-low," Chin replied in broken English.

"He's going to take us to Ho Chi Minh City."

"Oh. Huh? Wait! What city did you say?"

"Ho Chi Minh," Paul answered.

"What the hell's going on? That's hundreds of miles away in South Vietnam. Shit Paul, you didn't tell me Laramie's there. I can't go. I've gotta cover the hearings."

"No. I didn't tell you."

"Get serious. This isn't some damned prank fraternity road trip. I'm getting out."

Paul frowned and gave his fellow journalist a stern, disappointed look.

"Stephen, I didn't have to let you in on this trip. I set it up all by myself, with my own money and time. I thought you'd jump at the chance to go."

"I would. But you didn't tell me. . ."

"Do you really want to do your job as an investigative journalist or just feed off the scraps thrown by the Senate Select Committee? But hey, it's okay if you want to play it safe and print press releases from the committee's spin doctors, like all the rest of those intellectual prostitutes pretending to be journalists. Chin, stop the car."

The Malaysian vehicle came to a abrupt stop. Paul pointed to the door.

"Well, what're ya waiting for? I'm sure the committee will have some interesting press releases tomorrow. You can rewrite that drool, put your byline to it and get a big ego trip seeing your name in print coast to coast."

Stephen opened the back door, hesitated for a moment, then slammed it shut.

"Shit. I hate it when you're so damn sanctimonious. I want to puke when you get on your soap box and preach journalistic ethics."

"You in?"

"Let's go," he said in a reluctant tone.

The trip took about six hours before the little car pulled into Ho Chi Minh City, formerly Saigon, the former capital of the defunct Republic of South Vietnam.

The city was renamed after one of North Vietnam's leaders following the fall of South Vietnam in 1975 and unified into a consolidated but communist Vietnam.

Stephen felt like he had been through a sand storm traveling the pockmarked dirt roads. Despite the dust, open windows were necessary because the car was not equipped with AC.

He complained about potholes in the streets of Washington, D.C. but these looked like bomb craters left over from the war.

They finally reached black top on the outskirts of Ho Chi Minh while night muffled the remaining streams of daylight. Dirty and tired, Chin drove them to a small bar located on the perimeter of the thriving, industrial city.

The seedy club, built out of primitive bamboo and tiki wood, housed an assortment of social outcasts—criminals, prostitutes and general malcontents. The journalists entered the dim-lit establishment through a curtain of string beads.

U2 blared out that "She moves in mysterious ways" from a dilapidated juke box in the corner—one of the West's esteemed exports. Mysterious was the operative word for Stephen, who wanted to be anywhere but this Third World, low-rent, backwater dive. He entered timidly, trying not to attract attention to his movements.

Patrons seemed to not notice, attending to their pleasures of drinking, opium smoking and whores. Asian women danced on the tables of high-paying customers, wearing nothing but tasseled nipple cups and a smile.

Pornographic videos played on the television above the bar—nude Oriental women dancing around an ox. Stephen turned his head; he didn't want to see what happens.

Paul pointed to a large man sitting alone in the back of the bar room. He was seated at a rustic wood table. A lit candle in a bottle, stationed in the middle of the table, provided most of the light. He wore camouflage pants, black t-shirt and a four-day beard growth.

The man cast an immense shadow which fluttered against the back wall, illuminated by the candle's flickering flame. It gave him an ominous presence.

The journalists noticed his shoulder holster, containing a Colt .45 caliber semi-automatic pistol—the "Double Eagle" model—and notorious "man stopper" preferred by U.S. military men. It demanded attention.

Stephen felt uneasy. Paul, self-assured and focused like a missionary on a crusade, led them to the table and spoke.

"Jim? Jim Laramie?"

The man looked up from his drink and, without a word of greeting or blink of an eye, requested media identification.

They produced their picture ID media cards. After examining them, he stood up from the table and held out a hamhock-of-a-hand to shake, satisfied as to their journalistic validity.

"Sorry for the inconvenience but you can't be too careful 'round here. I'm Jim Laramie."

"Nice to meet 'cha. I'm Paul Mathis. We spoke on the telephone several times as you know. It's good to actually put a face to the voice. This is my associate Stephen Decatur. He's an independent journalist concerned with the plight of the POWs."

"Hello," Stephen said, extending a hand.

"Uh-huh," Laramie replied, shaking his hand firmly.

He was a hulk of a man, way over six feet and at least 270 pounds, with broad shoulders, large chest and thick arms.

He carried a black, powder-burn scar on his left cheek. Stephen noticed the numerous tattoos that discolored his forearms, one displaying a dragon, another a knife with a snake wrapped around its blade.

Jim Laramie smoked a large brown cigar, Asian-made, inhaling puffs and exhaling rings of white, acrid-smelling smoke. He was an intimidating specimen even without the Double Eagle.

A topless waitress approached their table. Jim ordered another refill on the bourbon while the journalists, mind on business, demurred. Paul wasted no time getting down to business.

"Tell me what you know about POW sightings?" he asked.

"Wait a minute," Stephen interjected. "I don't mean to be rude but I'd like to know some background about Mr. Laramie before we get started. He apparently checked us out, or at least you. I want to know about him if you don't mind."

Paul laughed nervously. "Jim and I talked on the phone and exchanged letters now for about 24 months. Believe me, with his record, he's a Who's Who of military valor."

"It okay," the soldier said, flipping cigar ash on the floor. "I don't trust anyone either. You need a healthy skepticism, especially when dealing with the government."

He looked straight into Stephen's eyes with a blank expression.

"I'm retired from U.S. Army special forces, did four tours of duty in 'Nam as a ranger. Was a member of Delta Force and performed infantry operations against the Viet Cong using primarily indigenous troops. Delta Force trained South Vietnamese troops called CIDG—Civilian Irregular Defense Groups. I've been decorated several times, including four Silver Stars for Gallantry and the Congressional Medal of Honor. I was getting ready for my fifth tour when my CO gave me some startling news. No... make that advice."

"What advice was that?" Stephen asked, his curiosity sparked by the words "Congressional Medal of Honor" spoken so nonchalantly by the Vietnam vet.

"That we weren't gonna win the war. To forget about another tour."

"Why?" Paul asked.

"He never explained himself, got killed two weeks later by a mortar. But I learned this bloody conflict, costing more than 58,000 American lives, wasn't suppose to be won. When I realized what highly-placed CIA and military intelligence was involved in, using the struggle between North and South Vietnam as a cover, I washed my hands of it."

"What were they involved in?"

He looked at the brown bourbon, rolling the drinking glass in his big hand, then shot it up and down with a quick flip of the wrist. Laramie gritted his teeth, making a seething sound, as the liquor went down.

"Not enough time to explain. I was nothing but an ignorant, patriotic puppet, getting my strings pulled by Washington. All that flag waving condemning communist encroachment was nothing but bullshit. Neither the White House nor Congress gave a damn about us. Hell, now we know Lyndon Johnson planned the Gulf of Tonkin incident. You guys remember the Pentagon Papers being published, don't 'cha?"

"No," said Stephen.

"*The Times* published the Pentagon Papers," Paul said, turning to Stephen. "It detailed among other things that President Johnson faked the Tonkin Gulf incident to drag the U.S. into the Vietnam War. Never had a media flagship like *The Times* so skewered the Washington establishment, except maybe when it published the translation of the La Mai report."

"Exactly. It was a bitter lesson to learn but I realized modern war has nothing to do with differing political ideologies. Ideologies are just intangible emotions used to incite the masses into fighting a war for their masters. The masters reap the profit. Anyway, enough of the philosophical crap."

"What about your post-Vietnam activities?"

"I remained in special forces and led several covert military operations into Southeast Asia as the behest of the federal government. Our mission was to gather evidence of captive prisoners of war since Vietnam had never accounted for American MIAs in violation of the Paris Peace Accords. It was strictly off the books, records shredded ala Ollie North style, funded by the Pentagon and White House. It's what intelligence agencies call classified information."

"How many?"

"I supervised five missions of elite para-military professionals into Vietnam, Cambodia and Laos beginning in 1980. The lid was blown off the operation in 1992 when our last mission somehow leaked out in the press. The White House and CIA tried to use me as a scape goat, saying I organized the expedition independently outside military parameters. By then I had become a vocal critic of the government's inaction on POW-MIA accounting."

"Tell Stephen what happened."

"I was officially retired following the press leak. But those bastards in the CIA and White House tried to finish me off for good, they didn't trust me. Didn't like me knowing so much. The Justice Department filed charges of government conspiracy and espionage against me. Can you believe that? Here they sanctioned the missions, then after it's made public, the assholes deny it and try to hang it on me."

"Why did they choose you for the missions in the first place?" Paul asked, waving the cigar smoke from his face.

"Because of my unique knowledge of Vietnam, having served there so long, and my special forces expertise. I didn't want the missions to become public either because it might harm our chances of getting back any POWs. But once it came out, I didn't mind. The public has a right to know what their government is doin'. Unfortunately, the American people have no idea and the government will lie to keep it that way."

"What about the charges?"

"Dropped. They didn't won't to put me on a witness stand under oath and risk exposing their clandestine operations. When the U.S. Attorney slapped me with the charges, I began to talk loud in the local media. Buddy, they dropped 'em in a New York minute. The sons-of-bitches had no case and they knew it. They wanted to intimidate me, a preemptive strike to shut me up."

❁ ❁ ❁ ❁ ❁ ❁

"Who specifically in the government tried to do this to you?"

"Not sure exactly but it came from the upper levels of the Pentagon, Central Intelligence Agency and White

House. Those branches provided the resources for our missions into Southeast Asia."

"Why try to shut you up? Why not deny it happened like politicians in Washington usually do."

"Congress knew nothing of the expeditions, kinda like the Iran Contra affair. The missions had no unaccountability and was financed by a Pentagon slush fund with the blessing of the CIA and White House. But that changed when LaFleur was elected."

"What changed?"

"The entire POW recovery program was scrapped. The White House dropped it like a hot potato."

"Why?"

"I don't know."

"You said you knew too much. What do you know that the government doesn't want public?"

"We brought back evidence of American prisoners of war. Much of that evidence is stored in the POW-MIA files in the U.S. Embassy in Bangkok and at CIA headquarters in Langley."

"Why would that upset the government?" Paul inquired. "You accomplished your mission."

"That's a good question. As I said, things changed when LaFleur took office. CIA leadership also did an about-face."

"What kind of evidence did you bring back?" Stephen piped up, his curiosity aroused.

Laramie sipped the bourbon and popped the chewed stogie back into his mouth. "Our group witnessed American POWs in Vietnam prisons. We saw 'em working in fields."

Paul and Stephen's mouths dropped open. They turned and stared at each other in astonishment.

"Are you sure?" Stephen asked in disbelief.

"Positive. I saw 'em. We took reconnaissance photos of them at work details, which is stored at Bangkok, away from the American public. We also took high-tech video equipment and filmed their movement within prison compounds. That video was seized by customs officials the moment we landed back in Los Angeles and has never been seen again.

"There's something else you should know before we get any deeper," he continued. "There was twelve of us on the last mission, all elite military personnel. Since then, nine have died in mysterious deaths ranging from car crashes to unexplained suicides. Someone definitely doesn't want the public to find out what we saw."

"If you really saw POWs, why didn't the group try to break 'em out?"

"We were given strict orders by our superiors that should we encounter POWs, we could only gather intelligence of their whereabouts, document the evidence and submit it to them. Under no circumstances were we to attempt a military rescue."

"So what have you got for us," Paul asked.

"Ten days ago, I led an expedition into Laos with some military friends—ex-ranger buddies and other Vietnam vets who stayed behind after the war. We went into the Muong Hom district. Ever heard of it?"

"Yeah. I understand it's a big-time drug manufacturing area. Part of the so-called Golden Triangle."

"You better believe it. The Muong Hom district in Laos is in the heartland of Southeast Asia's Golden Triangle, where the opium and heroin trade thrives and makes up a large portion of illegal narcotics shipped into North America. The Lao Sung tribe lives there and has long been a major cultivator of the opium poppy."

"Why go there?" Stephen asked.

"We went to meet Kuhn-Sah Duc, the drug lord of the Lao Sung tribe."

"Yeah, I've heard of 'em," Paul noted. "We got some reports over the wire service about his drug activities."

"He doesn't get much press over in the states but believe me, everyone knows the name Kuhn-Sah Duc here. He heads the largest heroin cartel in Asia. He has his own private army and fortress in Laos. Makes Manuel Noriega look like a nickle-bag, street pusher."

"So what 'bout him?"

"We made some friends here during my government expeditions. We received reports from them that Kuhn-Sah Duc had knowledge of American POWs. Of course we noted this in our reports to the Pentagon but they told us under no circumstances would American military deal with a drug dealer. So I organized this mission into Laos.

"Hell, any chance was worth trying in order to save American men," Laramie continued. "We were at the end of our rope. We contacted him through his distributors, told 'em our intent, and arranged a meeting. It wasn't easy. It took 18 months before he would agree to see us."

"Why talk to him?" Paul asked. "You know where some of the POWs are from your government missions."

"Duc has current information of their location. You see, the Vietnamese move the POWs around the country so they won't be discovered. Over twenty years after the war, they're still paranoid Americans will find out about the prisoners."

"So what did this drug lord tell you?" Stephen asked, excitement beginning to brew inside him.

"You gotta promise to keep this under your hats until the opportunity is right to go public. If you target me as the source, I'll deny it. Kuhn-Sah Duc would kill me if his name was used. I want this info put into the national media but we must be discreet and patient. If we're premature, the government will shut us down and the POWs will be lost forever. I need your cooperation and trust."

"Of course," Paul answered quickly. "We're here to help."

"Good. I need someone like you who has access to the press when the time is right. With the proper timing and publicity, the media attention can force the White House to do something about Vietnam's refusal to account for the missing servicemen. But it must be planned strategically with step-by-step objectives in mind. I've been stopped too many times. It must be right."

"You got it," Paul said.

Jim put his right elbow on the table, pointing his large index finger at both men. "I mean it. This information puts you in jeopardy. We must be careful and quiet."

"You've got our word Mr. Laramie," Stephen said.

"Call me Jim."

"Okay Jim. We don't want to risk POW lives or ours. We want to break this when the appropriate time arrives."

"Okay. Kuhn-Sah Duc's men found a body, partially decomposed of a clearly Caucasian prisoner of war. Been shot. They found him near the Po-Tong River in northern Vietnam, figure he'd tried to escape recently. Here's his dog tag."

Laramie dropped the metal tag and chain on the table. Stephen picked it up and scrutinized the ID, like a jeweler examining a precious gem. "Edward Po. . Lin. . sky."

"Yep. Major Ed Polinsky. Third Battalion, 26th Marine Regiment. My sources in the Pentagon checked his military record. Stationed in Northern I Corps—South Vietnam's northernmost military region bordering North Vietnam. On July 2, 1967, his Marine battalion was involved in Operation Buffalo. They were attacked by an NVA regiment south of the DMZ near a hill called Con Thien where a Marine combat base was located."

"Wait. NVA? DMZ? What's that?"

"North Vietnamese Army, Demilitarized Zone. Three other Marine battalions counterattacked the NVA force. The fighting lasted until July 14. About 159 Marines were killed, 345 wounded and 1,290 black pajama bastards killed. Polinsky was never seen again, missing in action."

Stephen handed the tag to Paul.

"One more thing. Duc told me specifically where some of the POWs are located."

The journalists again looked at each other in disbelief.

"How does he know?" Paul queried.

"Duc has heroin connections in Vietnam, does a lot of business in poppy harvesting there. The Vietnamese government is on the take and gets a percentage of the drug trade from Duc. He's seen many POWs in remote regions where prison camps are located. He told me he's seen Americans alive in Vietnam prisons during the years he has transacted business with the Vietnamese government."

"This all sounds incredible," Stephen said.

Jim reached into his back pocket, pulled out a photograph and placed it on the table. The journalists glanced at it, then at him.

"Go ahead. Look at it," he insisted. "I took that with a high-powered telephoto lens during one of my missions. Kept the negative."

It was a clear color photo of white and black men working in a field during the afternoon. In the background, Vietnamese guards dressed in military uniforms patrolled with guns.

"My group's planning another excursion but this is definitely not government sanctioned. It's strictly freelance and this time we're gonna bring home the real McCoy. No more diplomatic jawboning like what's going on in Hanoi. It's time for action. No more speculation."

"What are you gonna do?" Paul asked.

"Break out some of the POWs in a covert operation. If you two are interested, you can come along and document it. We want proof."

"Maybe this Duc character is setting a trap. Maybe he's lying. You said he works with the Vietnamese government. Drug pushers aren't known for their honesty and integrity."

"Duc doesn't know exactly which prison we'll hit. He gave us multiple locations. But it doesn't matter. He had a falling out with Vietnam regarding their drug arrangements. He blatantly told me it would please him to see us break Americans out. Of course I took this with a grain of salt but my sources in Southeast Asia tell me relations are indeed strained between Duc and the Hanoi communists. Vietnamese military incursions into Laos and Cambodia have upset his heroin operations."

The Vietnam vet opened his large hands, palms out. "Well, what do ya say? I don't have to tell experienced reporters like yourselves the dangers, like getting killed, do I?"

"When?" Paul asked. Stephen turned and looked at Paul with glaring eyes.

"Are you crazy? You not really considering this?"

"We leave in three days."

"We'll think about it and get back in touch with you."

"Yeah, that's a good idea," concurred Stephen. "We'll get back with you. By the way, you said the embassy in Bangkok has documented evidence of POWs."

"That's right," said Laramie. "They have the most detailed and accurate information on Vietnam War POWs including the intelligence my group gathered. Reconnaissance photos and live sighting reports. Things like that."

The journalists left. As Stephen walked through the string of beads, he looked back into the smoky bar. An Asian stripper had set her naked butt on Laramie's knee, her arms around his neck while he poured the woman a drink in one hand, his other hand was on her hip.

"What'd ya think?" Paul asked, stopping outside the bar and inhaling the thick, humid air.

"I dunno. Frankly, I'm overwhelmed by what he said. I need some time to think it over."

"See, I told you Laramie has credible evidence. He just didn't pull that dog tag out of a hat. Stephen, this could be our Watergate, like Woodward and Bernstein."

"Not so fast Paul. That dog tag could be fake. This stuff about breaking out POWs we don't even know exists scares me."

"This is one way to test the accuracy of the La Mai report."

"Too risky. Too dangerous."

"Laramie knows more than he's saying."

"What makes you think that?"

"I can feel it. He knows who closed the government operations down. He knows who tried to shut him up."

"Maybe we should take another road trip."

"Where?"

"The embassy in Bangkok," Stephen replied.

"Why?"

"Check out Laramie's story before agreeing to go on this little safari."

❁ ❁ ❁ ❁ ❁ ❁

Stephen and Paul flew out of Ho Chi Minh City the next day on a chartered single-engine wreck of a plane which looked like it had been used primarily for crop dusting.

Though uncomfortable and crammed with boxed cargo, it was the only available aircraft to be had on the journalists' limited salary.

"This ain't first class but we got outta Vietnam in a hurry," Paul said, peering out a window in the back of the cramped plane. Lush vegetation of a rain forest decorated the terrain below.

"Do you really believe what Laramie told us?" Stephen asked, cradling the laptop. "It was so bizarre, as if I dreamed the entire episode last night."

"That photo and dog tag wasn't a dream."

"Flimsy, circumstantial evidence at best for what he's claiming Paul. Laramie may be delusional. Shell-shocked from the war. Whatta they call it? Post-traumatic stress disorder."

"Before we pass judgement, let's take a look at those POW-MIA files at the U.S. Embassy. Then we'll go from there."

❀ ❀ ❀ ❀ ❀ ❀

The plane touched down in Bangkok, the capital of Thailand, a country that boasts of prostitution as one of its national industries. The flight took about four hours and the passengers were frazzled and weary.

But the low altitude of the plane flight allowed them to see spectacular portions of Southeast Asia including Cambodia and the body of waters comprising the Gulf of Siam.

Stephen unloaded their baggage while Paul hailed a cab.

"Are we goin' to the embassy now?"

"Absolutely," Paul replied. "We can't sit on this."

"I hope were not chasing a ghost. My editor will be wondering where the hell I am."

"It was your idea to come to Bangkok. Hey, there may be a Pulitzer Prize stashed away in those embassy files."

The trip to the U.S. Embassy seemed to take forever. Bangkok's road system is entirely inadequate to handle the volume of traffic produced from the capital's surge in economic development due to the international investment of corporations in search of cheap labor.

At times, the cab would come to a complete stop on the interstate due to motorist congestion. At the end of the afternoon, they arrived at the U.S. Embassy. The cab drove them under the embassy portico to the doorstep. The building, made of a grey stucco exterior, was comprised of two stories.

The journalists paid the driver and walked into the building. They were greeted by an American in a dark blue suit, who seemed nervous and upset.

"Hello, my name is Felix Berger. I'm the administrative aid for the embassy here in Thailand. May I help you gentleman?"

"Yeah. I'm Paul Mathis and this is Stephen Decatur. We're journalists covering the Senate Select Committee hearings in Hanoi. We would like to look at the embassy's files on American Vietnam War POWs and MIAs."

The weak smile disappeared and the blood left his face. His weasel-looking eyes darted back and forth, as if scrambling for an excuse. "Uh, that will be impossible right now. Can you gentlemen come back sometime later?"

"Why can't we look at 'em now?" Stephen asked.

"We've had some problems and the files aren't available right now. Perhaps arrangements can be made for another visit in the future."

"Mr. Berger, we just got off a plane from Ho Chi Minh City. We've come a long way to see the files and we're not gonna leave until we do."

Berger looked perturbed. "Let me talk to Mr. Armstrong and see what he advises."

"Who's he?" Stephen asked.

"He's the Deputy Secretary of State coordinating activities here in Southeast Asia," Berger said in a haughty tone.

"Whoa. Sounds impressive to me," Paul said. "Why don't you do that. We'll wait right here until you get back."

Berger departed abruptly, miffed at Paul's lack of respect for authority.

"Paul, why don't you go upstairs and see if you can find any of those files. It seems to me they're stonewalling. They may not release 'em until the committee issues another report. What do you think?"

"That's a good idea. You talk to this Armstrong and I'll go upstairs and take a look. Tell Berger I went outside."

"Alright but stay outta sight. Plan it where you can reappear without being noticed. It seems this place doesn't have much staff."

"Okay. If I'm not back when you're ready to leave, stall for time."

"You got it. Good luck."

Paul departed and crept upstairs to the second floor of the embassy. Approximately ten minutes passed before the squirrely Berger returned.

"Mr. Armstrong will speak to you if you'd like."

"I would like that very much."

"Where's your companion?"

"Oh, he suddenly felt sick and had to go outside for some fresh air. The flight didn't agree with him."

Berger looked at Stephen with a frown of disgust and led him down a hall to some double doors on the right. "This is Mr. Armstrong's office. You may go in."

Stephen opened one of the doors and entered. A man eloquently dressed in an double-breasted Italian suit, smoking a cigarette, was seated behind a large black metal desk. He appeared to be in his late-fifties, balding with short brown hair around the sides and back of his head with a sprinkle of gray.

The humid conditions seemed to not bother him despite the clothing though sweat beads decorated the bald, tanned head.

A fan placed on a credenza blew air toward him, rustling the few papers on an otherwise immaculate desk. He was reading a copy of the local newspaper with his feet elevated on the desk corner. He looked up from the newspaper and greeted the journalist.

"I'm Richard Armstrong, Deputy Secretary of State for the U.S. State Department." He stood up and offered a hand.

"Hi, Stephen Decatur. I'm a journalist with Reuters News Service covering the Senate Select Committee hearings with the Vietnam government concerning American POWs."

They shook hands. Stephen took a seat in front of the desk.

"Yes, well, we always want to help the press. The government never can have enough good press, now can we?"

He smiled, folded the newspaper and threw it in the waste basket. "What can I do for you Mr. Decatur?"

"Mr. Armstrong, an associate and myself are interested in researching the embassy's investigative files on Vietnam War POWs and MIAs to augment our stories on the committee hearings. We understand the U.S. Embassy has an extensive record of POW sightings and such."

"I'm afraid that information is classified under the National Security Act. We would be violating federal law if we allowed public inspection of those files. When you get back to the states, try the Freedom of Information Act. Perhaps you can get some data if you access the proper government channels."

"I've never heard of that law. Of course I'm no lawyer. But I can't understand why it would jeopardize national security for the public to know what evidence exists of American POWs."

"I understand your concern Mr. Decatur but this is a very sensitive matter involving other governments. We don't know any evidence of POWs exists. However, if it did, which has never been substantiated, we would not want to put POWs in harm's way by publishing reports of their possible existence in the news media. It could endanger their lives and aggravate the Vietnam government."

"Excuse me but I think there is plenty of substantiated evidence of their existence and I understand the embassy files contain such evidence. How much more in danger could they be in? Theoretically, POWs have been in Vietnamese jails now for twenty, thirty years. What does it matter if we put pressure on the Hanoi government through the press? Maybe if there was media pressure, coupled with existing public support, the U.S. government could force Vietnam to turn 'em over, if indeed they exist."

Armstrong's eyes narrowed and his tan brow became wrinkled. He leaned across the desk and spoke slowly in a hushed tone.

"I get every piss-ant reporter in the world coming in here, claiming media privilege under the guise of righteous causes, when all they want to do is stir up trouble. You think you're the first reporter who wanted the scoop on American POWs. Well, it doesn't exist. It never did. You parasites have no idea what the military has gone through. You don't understand what the Vietnam War cost, not only in terms of lives but in national confidence.

"It destroyed the American military and eroded public confidence in its government," he continued. "And all you media vultures can do is pick over the dead bones of the soldiers who died in that war. You louses keep dredging up the past, reopening wounds. Now get your ass outta here and don't come back. I've got no time for sensationalist reporters like you draining the life blood of our country."

Stephen sat stunned. He was at an utter loss for words. Embarrassed, he didn't think pushing the POW issue deserved such a verbal assault. He had interviewed many an arrogant, bloated bureaucrat but this guy redefined the term.

Armstrong put out the cigarette and immediately lit another one. "You heard me," he said, leaning back in the chair.

"I don't understand," Stephen replied, confused.

"Get out. Get the hell out. Or do I have to throw you out?"

Stephen couldn't believe the animosity boiling out of the deputy secretary of state. It was unreasonable.

"One other question," Stephen said as he got up from the chair, trying to stay cool and collect.

"No more damn questions. Now leave!" Armstrong put the cigarette in his mouth, got up from the chair and began walking out from around the desk. Stephen was shocked at his behavior. This so-called reputable, high-ranking government official was about to physically throw him out of the office.

"Have you ever heard of Kuhn-Sah Duc of Laos?"

Armstrong stopped dead in his tracks, his eyes got big.

"Where'd you hear that name?"

"That's classified information kinda like your POW files. You understand, I have to protect my sources. There's a lot of foreign governments involved here and its a sensitive matter. We don't want to put my sources in harm's way, now do we?"

It was not lost on him that the name of the Laotian drug lord completely altered Armstrong's mood. Suddenly, his anger subsided and his mood radically changed, almost to fear.

"Have you ever heard of him?"

Armstrong hesitated momentarily; apparently Stephen's question caught him by surprise. "No!" But his facial expression betrayed his response. "Now for that last damn time, get the hell outta here!"

"Certainly Mr. Armstrong. I'll get out of your way. I can tell you're a busy man. It gives me a real sense of security seeing our tax dollars at work."

But Armstrong didn't hear Stephen's verbal jab. As he opened the office door, he glanced back and saw Armstrong sitting again at the desk, staring at the wall and taking long draws from the cigarette.

Paul Mathis walked down the hall of the second floor and ducked into an office. The four walls were covered in file cabinets. The video journalist walked over to a wooden desk and opened the top drawer, withdrawing a metal box.

He opened the metal box, took out the tray, placing it on the desk, and removed a key. He walked to a corner cabinet, pushing the key into the top lock of the wall cabinet. The lock popped.

Paul bent down and pulled out the lower drawer. He reached in and removed three manilla folders. One was stamped "STATE DEPARTMENT." Another was labeled "DRUG ENFORCEMENT AGENCY" while the last was stamped "UNITED NATIONS."

"Here it is," he whispered to himself. "Just like it's suppose to be."

Stephen walked through the hall and back into the lobby. Berger was sitting at a desk, his arms folded and a leg rocking up and down.

"You certainly have a lotta nervous energy Felix.'

"It's Mr. Berger. I couldn't help but hear Mr. Armstrong shouting. Is everything alright?"

"Yeah, tell me about it. I couldn't help but hear him too, unfortunately. No, Felix, everything is not alright."

"I knew it, God, I knew it. I can't believe I'm in the middle of this." He dropped his head on the desk. "I had nothing to do with it. I knew the press would find out. You can't keep something like that a secret."

Stephen tried to hide his surprise and played along with the distraught administrative aid.

"Listen Felix, why don't you do yourself a favor and get it off your chest. Tell me your side of the story."

"I told you it's Mr. Berger. I dunno. This whole mess is not my fault. I had nothing to do with. I was ordered to comply by my superiors. That's all."

"Yeah, yeah, I understand. But yah gotta tell me the whole story so the press won't get it confused. We certainly wouldn't won't to name any innocent people in our stories."

"Good God, no! I don't wanna see my name in any story regarding this incident. As I said, I had nothing to do with it. I didn't even know they were going to hit the embassy. They just came marching in here three days ago and began shredding everything. God, it was a mess."

"Who, Felix? Shred what? Start from the beginning slowly and tell me every detail so when we do a story, it'll be accurate to ensure your name doesn't appear."

"As I said, it's Mr. Berger. Well, I guess I can if you promise not to use my name. I suppose Mr. Armstrong gave you the details."

"That's right. So you won't get in any trouble by telling us. I promise I won't reveal my sources."

"Alright, from the beginning." He took a deep breath. "Three days ago, Tuesday, I was doing my usual work here at the embassy when a group of CIA agents burst in and basically took the place over. They claimed they had executive orders from President LaFleur's National Security Advisor to operate the embassy temporarily and destroy all files relating to American Vietnam War POWs and MIAs."

"They got rid of all the files kept on POWs and MIAs?"

"Yes. They destroyed the entire POW-MIA case load which filled about 30 feet of wall cabinets, all the research and work for the last 25 years. The files contained refugee live sighting reports of American POWs and MIAs and numerous reports from the Joint Casualty Resolution Center liaison offices in Ho Chi Minh City, Vietnam; Vientiane, Laos; Phnom Penh, Cambodia; and here in Bangkok. The files included handwritten notes from field investigators."

Berger took out a white handkerchief from a back pocket and dabbed his forehead.

Stephen tried to act as if he already knew what had occurred at the embassy. But Berger's revelations simply numbed him.

"Over two decades of government work on Vietnam War POWs and MIAs up in smoke, huh," he said. "I'm sure those files were indispensable to current investigations into the fate of missing Americans. Now there will be no evidence, no link, no trail to follow. Did you appeal to your superiors and try to stop it?"

"We didn't have any time. They took us by surprise and began shredding everything without warning. Mr. Armstrong ordered us not to interfere."

"He did, huh? Did the U.S. Ambassador to Thailand go along with it?"

"No. That's what makes it so strange. He wasn't notified about the National Security Advisor's directive. When he learned of it, he tried to stop it but it was too late. The files had been destroyed."

"What about the Senate Select Committee on POW and MIA Affairs? Were they aware of the National Security Advisor's directive?"

"I don't know. The files had been declassified so the select committee could view them. I really don't know if the committee members are aware of the shredding or not. You would think the National Security Advisor would have informed them, wouldn't you?"

"Yeah, you would. So Felix, the files are gone. They'll never see the light of day."

"It's Mr. Berger, please. Yes, it's all gone."

"Don't you think it's a strange coincidence this happened just as the senate committee is meeting with Vietnamese leaders on the POW issue?"

"Very strange. Perhaps it's connected to the burglary. I don't know."

"What burglary?"

"Three weeks ago, an employee of the embassy, a Laotian man, stole some files. Well, we think he stole them. He had access and disappeared after the files were discovered missing. Terrible looking fellow with a mangled facial expression. But a good worker, spoke English fluently."

"What were in the files?"

"Financial transactions of a United Nations economic development program implemented here in Southeast Asia."

"Was it important?"

"I didn't think so. But Mr. Armstrong was terribly distraught about it."

"Did Mr. Armstrong seem upset about the national security advisor's order?"

"Well, no. He just told us to assist the CIA agents in anything they needed and he went back to his office. I understand the U.S. Ambassador is furious with him. I also heard through the grapevine, that, well, maybe I shouldn't say."

"Go ahead Felix. I'm all ears. It's safe with me."

"Well, I heard the ambassador contacted the Pentagon about the shredding and the chairman of the Joint Chiefs of Staff has ordered a secret investigation. Apparently the joint chiefs didn't even know about it."

Paul appeared at the top of the stairs, waving files, trying to get Stephen's attention.

"Uh, Felix, I forgot to tell you. When I was leaving Mr. Armstrong's office, he told me that he wanted to see you pronto."

"Why didn't you tell me sooner?"

"Oh, I guess his temper tantrum disturbed me and it slipped my mind. You better get in there."

"Oh my God. He's gonna be pissed. You remember, my name doesn't appear in your story."

"You got it Felix."

"Mr. Berger, dammit," the administrative aid called out as he scurried down the hall toward Armstrong's office.

Stephen motioned Paul to descend the stairs. He came down with the files under a arm and both men quickly exited the U.S. Embassy.

❁ ❁ ❁ ❁ ❁ ❁

The journalists made their way to the nearest restaurant. Fighting pedestrian traffic and smog, they observed an open tavern on a side street in the Thai capital and quickly made a b-line for the establishment.

They hopped bar stools and Paul placed an order. Stephen eagerly filled him in on the shredding of the files as told by Felix Berger.

"You know, I did see two big industrial paper shredders upstairs. And Berger said CIA was ordered by LaFleur's national security advisor to do it?"

"Uh-huh," Stephen replied. "He thought it might be connected to some embassy files stolen on a United Nations program. He said Armstrong was upset about it yet when the CIA shredded the POW-MIA files, Berger said Armstrong was not concerned at all, let 'em do it."

"Strange. Why shred? The only reason I can think of is someone doesn't want any evidence of Americans missing in action to surface."

"My conclusion too. Berger said the joint chiefs were investigating it. Something else strange happened. Armstrong reacted when I mentioned Kuhn-Sah Duc. It altered his mood completely, like I shocked him. It was weird man. First he went absolutely ballistic, tried to throw me out, then he gets docile when I drop Duc's name. I think the guy is unstable."

"Most bureaucrats are. Now I understand why I couldn't find any POW files. I was frantic and just began grabbing files out of the cabinets."

"Let's take a look at 'em."

Paul opened the file folders and handed Stephen some of the papers.

"I've got something here."

"What is it?"

"Uh. . . various reports covering the United States and the United Nations' attempts to curb illegal narcotics commerce from the Golden Triangle. Looks like it details the government's drug interdiction programs here in Southeast Asia and federal law enforcement's attempt to stem the tide of opium and heroin."

Stephen skimmed through the papers.

"This is a Drug Enforcement Agency memo. Says the official figure for the 1995 federal drug-control budget was $11.9 billion, of which a large portion went into drug fighting here. But get this, that doesn't even include the additional prisons built to house the swelling tide of cocaine, heroin and marijuana offenders in custody, now estimated at over 700,000 nationwide. Nor does the budget reflect the cost of mass incarceration, now around $150 a day per prisoner.

"Other expenditures off record include the invasion of Panama, funding of drug enforcement in 49 foreign countries and public health costs," Stephen continued. "According to this DEA memo, if we include the expenses I mentioned, since 1980, American taxpayers have spent more than $300 billion on drug enforcement."

"Jesus, that's ridiculous."

He flipped the page over.

"Listen to this. Attached to the DEA file is a report from the Brookings Institute. The report states that drug abuse is now a global epidemic. It says the production of heroin, cocaine, cannabis and synthetic drugs is at an all-time high and new drug producers are emerging in Central and South America, Africa, Central Europe and Asia. It concludes by stating, 'The seeds of widespread drug consumption exist practically everywhere.'

"Now check this out," he continued, opening the State Department file. "Here is a recent narcotics survey from the U.S. State Department. The survey states the invasion of Panama directed by President Bush in order to oust dictator Manuel Noriega and cripple Panamanian drug commerce was a failure. The survey states that Panama remains a major narcotics, money-laundering and illicit drug-transhipment nation."

"Geez. We're spending all this ungodly money on the drug war and losing."

A young Thai girl placed their food on the counter.

"What'd you order us?" Stephen asked, a bit apprehensive.

"It's a fried dish."

"What kinda fried dish?"

"Cobra."

"Excuse me?"

"I said cobra."

"That's what I thought you said."

"Deep fried cobra. Considered a delicacy here in Thailand. Try it."

Stephen poked at the chucks of fried meat while shuffling through the United Nations file.

"Here's another state department memo. All this stuff concerns narcotics. It says the United States is participating and helping fund a global drug interdiction program implemented by the United Nations using economic development programs to upgrade the standard of living in Third World countries so the peasants won't depend so much on poppy cultivation for their living."

"Keep goin'," Paul said, swallowing a piece of the Thai delicacy.

"Okay. According to a House of Representatives transcript, the Secretary of State testified last year in front of the international operations subcommittee of the House Foreign Affairs Committee. Alright, he was asked what the LaFleur administration plans to do about the failed war on drugs. The Secretary of State responded that the narcotics problem would now be brought under a newly created international post through the United Nations because the administration wanted to address drug control on a global basis in the future.

"According to the Secretary of State, the LaFleur administration has already committed $500 million in taxpayer money to continue the global drug eradication program maintained by the United Nations called the UN Drug Control Program. He said the program was aimed at areas like the Golden Triangle and more specifically, the Muong Hom district in Laos."

"That's the area Jim Laramie penetrated when he visited Kuhn-Sah Duc," Paul interjected. "Duc is the drug lord of that tribe there."

"Uh-huh. The transcript says the Lao Sung tribe has long been a major cultivator of the opium poppy. The

Secretary of State testified that in order to wean the Lao Sung away from the lucrative cash crop, a consortium of world agencies such as the International Fund for Agricultural Development, under the umbrella of the UN Drug Control Program, has provided funds to these areas in the Golden Triangle for economic development.

"Through this global fund, roads were built, livestock imported, irrigation projects funded and local farmers were offered cheap planting credits on the condition that they grow something other than opium poppies. Maybe this is connected to the UN files Berger said were stolen."

"Hah. Fat chance of that."

"That the stolen embassy files are connected?"

"No. That the UN program has weaned them away. The financial incentive of the poppy is too powerful."

"Okay, here we go," Stephen said, turning the page. "The Secretary of State indicated other drug producing regions throughout the world were also targeted by the UN Drug Control Program such as the Bekaa Valley in Lebanon. However, members of this international operations subcommittee were presented depositions from U.S. customs agents who dismissed the UN experiment and said such an eradication program would be cost prohibitive in major drug producing countries like Lebanon, Columbia or Laos because cocaine, heroin and marijuana trade now generate 15 percent of each country's entire gross domestic product."

"God, that's amazing. Sounds like this UN Drug Control Program is another rat hole swallowing up tax dollars. Do you see anything about POWs or MIAs?"

Stephen thumbed through the remaining files.

"Nothing. I'm afraid they shredded everything."

"I wish we had visited the embassy a little earlier. Dammit, we were that close to getting those files," he exclaimed, raising his right index finger about a half-inch above the thumb.

Stephen placed the files in a brief case he had brought along. "We better keep outta sight. Once the embassy discovers these files gone, they may come looking for us."

"No problem," Paul replied, wiping his mouth. "We'll be out of Bangkok in two hours. Our pilot is flying us back to Ho Chi Minh tonight."

"Good. We don't need to hang 'round here."

"Anyway, we've gotta rendezvous with an Army Ranger."

"Huh? You're seriously considering goin' with him?"

"Yep. The entire files on Vietnam War POWs and MIAs just went up in smoke thanks to our own officials. I'm not talking Vietnamese commies here Steve. I'm talking our own damned public servants. Something's wrong, bad wrong."

"I don't trust that Laramie. I know he's a Congressional Medal of Honor winner and all that shit but still, we don't know enough about 'em. Once we're out in the middle of some jungle in Vietnam, no one can find us. We won't be able to get help. It worries me. People could get killed."

"Steve, this is the chance of a lifetime. Do you realize the opportunity that is knocking on our door? We've got to seize that opportunity. Sure it's dangerous but you've gotta take chances for anything worthwhile."

"I know. But I gotta bad feeling. First the La Mai document, then Wallace's suicide, now the POW-MIA files are shredded just as the Senate Select Committee is meeting in Hanoi."

"Whatever is goin' down, whether it has to do with POWs or not, we could be staring at the potential scoop of the 20th Century. And with Laramie, we've got an exclusive."

"Not exclusive. Someone else knows but they aren't talking."

"Okay, it's settled then. Now eat your snake. We've gotta plane to catch."

Chapter Five

While the journalists were in Bangkok, Hanoi had become the focus of the international community. Vietnam's capital was buzzing with talk of the shooting. The dull hearings between the Senate Select Committee on POW-MIA Affairs and the Vietnamese government had suddenly become exciting – too exciting.

A distraught Vietnam veteran had interrupted one of the meetings; unfortunately, he used a 9 millimeter pistol to do it, squeezing off six shots before he perished in a gun battle with Vietnamese law enforcement. A member of the foreign minister's staff was killed when two bullets ripped through his neck and face.

Stephen, looking sullen and frustrated, met Paul at the Central Directorate Hall carrying a copy of the *London Times*.

"Take a look at this," he growled, handing the newspaper to Paul.

"Yeah, what?"

"The international media is bellowing about the shooter's rampage. The London paper quotes the Vietnamese foreign minister as saying the shooting was another example of the West's decadence and capitalistic imperialism."

Paul scanned the paper.

"Typical. He's placing the responsibility of the official's murder squarely on the United States government. Well, the foreign minister called for the hearings to end. He got his wish."

"He did?"

"I was talking to the AP reporter a minute ago. Senator Bainbridge declared the hearings over. Apparently the shooting shook him up pretty bad. The committee is leaving for Washington today."

"Did they make a decision?"

"AP is reporting the committee will make a decision after evaluating the information provided by the foreign minister. We've been scooped badly. The entire globe knew about the most tragic event to take place in foreign policy history while we were in Bangkok searching for files that no longer exist."

Paul folded the newspaper and threw it down.

"Tell me about it," Stephen said. "I'm finished."

"But it's not the end of the world."

"For me it is. I just got off the phone with my editor. He wants to know why the hell I didn't have anything written about the shooting. He's been trying to call me for two days. Every other damn newspaper and television station on earth had it except for us."

"I know. I got chewed out when I called Atlanta. Ted Turner doesn't like being the last to know."

"That's easy for you to say. I didn't get chewed out, I got fired."

"Jesus, Stephen, I'm sorry buddy."

"Oh, the hell with it. It doesn't matter. I wanted to go to Bangkok and we did. Of course, wouldn't you know the good stuff would happen here while we're gone."

"I wouldn't call it good stuff. The committee won't be back, ever."

"I can kiss off my file shredding story. Maybe if I offer it to my editor for free, with an apology, I can get my job back."

"Forget Reuters man. You can sell that story anywhere, to the highest bidder. Once we complete the trip with Laramie, the entire international media will come crawling to us on their knees begging for our stories. I can feel it. This is big time. We're sitting on something important, something that's about to explode and Laramie's gonna take us to it."

"I just wanna make it back in one piece."

The journalists met Jim Laramie at a remote location outside a little village in Northern Vietnam. Laramie was accompanied by ten ex-military veterans who favored remaining anonymous, refusing to speak at all to Stephen and Paul. They distrusted the press as much as Viet Cong, grudgingly excepting them only as a necessary evil.

Two had participated in the government sanctioned covert expeditions of which Laramie had spoken. They and Laramie were the only officers left from the original elite para-military group.

The remaining soldiers had returned to Southeast Asia after the war. God only knows why they came back, Stephen wondered, perhaps trying to bury some ghosts from their past.

Paul brought along his video equipment, compliments of a beguiled CNN. Stephen noticed Laramie's group carried a spectrum of weapons and gadgetry. It included automatic firearms, grenades, shoulder held stinger missiles, flares, infer-red scopes, night vision goggles and other high-tech military equipment too complicated for the journalist to describe.

"Where'd you get all this stuff?" Stephen asked.

"I got friends," Laramie replied. "There's still a lot of sympathy and support that exists among the American public despite the government's sentiments."

The journalists brought along the bare essentials as instructed by the Army Ranger. Food items and sturdy clothing for traversing difficult terrain. Laramie's group would provide the tents and camp ground needs.

Stephen took Paul by the arm and pulled him off to the side, away from the group. "I don't like this. Did you see all the weapons they brought?" he whispered. "We don't know what these G.I. Joes are gonna do. They might sniff some napalm, go berserk and kill us."

"Steve, don't panic. Getta hold of yourself."

"None of 'em will talk to us except Laramie. I think they're a bunch of paranoid psychopaths. Probably got shrapnel in their heads. I've seen those 'Nam movies like *Platoon* and *Full Metal Jacket.* Lots of blood and guts. Did you see the way they looked at us? I don't like it. I don't like it one bit. These guys are crazy. They don't want us here. Once we're out in the jungle, they'll cut our throats."

"Laramie cleared it with 'em before he invited us. They're hard-ass soldiers, that's all. They're weary of outsiders. You can understand that. They need weapons to break POWs out for God's Sake. What do you think they're gonna use? Sling shots. We've got to be willing to take risks. We aren't going to find the answer sitting behind a desk in some comfortable, air-conditioned editorial room staring at a PC."

Stephen drew a long breath and looked up, squinting at the blood-red, Asian sun. Something inside felt uneasy, a sickening feeling was overtaking him. "It's just that ..."

"Just what?"

"We don't know what's waiting for us out there in the jungle."

"Right. We don't know and never will until we go. It's too late to bale out now Steve. C'mon, as I said, this is the journalistic opportunity of a life time."

Laramie informed them the group would travel through rough country—jungle and mountainous terrain. He said the prison they would penetrate was located west near the Laotian border, where Kuhn-Sah Duc's men had found the POW body.

It was situated below a mountain range under deep jungle cover, a hundred miles from the nearest village. He estimated it would take the group three to four days to reach the fortress on foot.

"This prison gotta name?" Stephen asked.

"Dach Lu," Laramie answered.

"If we do get lucky and rescue some POWs, we still aren't home free. We've gotta somehow get out of the country."

"I've taken care of that," he replied. "We've tracked out a route to the coast where a boat will be waiting to take us to the Philippines."

"Another ex-military ally?" Paul queried.

"As I said, I got friends. There's been an underground movement existing in Southeast Asia for years with the purpose of liberating POWs left behind. I'm a card-carrying member of it."

The group embarked at dawn. The hot Vietnamese sun coupled with the jungle humidity made Stephen and Paul feel like they were trapped in a sauna. Thirty minutes into the trip, they were drenched in sweat. The physical exertion of carrying back packs and hauling camera equipment made the excursion difficult.

❁ ❁ ❁ ❁ ❁ ❁

They camped the first night beside a muddy river somewhere in the heart of a Southeast Asian rain forest.

Vietnamese women, both young and old, on their knees, panned the water along the river edge. Periodically, one would hold up something in her fingers skyward, too small to see, then place it inside her mouth.

"What're they doing?" Stephen asked as he lent a hand pitching camp.

"Panning for precious gems," Jim replied, pushing up a pole inside a tent.

"Is that what they're putting in their mouths?"

"Yeah. Every once and a while, the peasants find a small ruby or sapphire. They hold 'em in their mouths to discourage idle chatter, helps 'em concentrate on work."

"Is it safe for them to see us?"

"Sure. We're miles from any authorities. These people are totally isolated, lucky if they come in contact with anyone in a year."

"Jim, why are ya doin' this?"

"Doin' what?"

"This mission."

"I told ya, the POWs of course."

"No. I mean what happened to you during the war. What made you so distrustful. I think it has to do with what you told me and Paul about CIA and military intelligence being involved in something."

Laramie crawled out of the tent and stood up. He pulled a cigar from a shirt pocket and lit it. He took a few steps toward the river and stopped, puffing on the cigar, watching the peasants pan.

"Understand. I have nothing against the Vietnamese people. They're honest, hard-working people. Americans are honest hard-working people. It's the governments that get in the way."

Stephen walked up beside him and stared at the river. The gurgling motion of the running water made a soothing sound.

"Okay. I can see that."

"Back in '68, the communist forces launched their Tet offensive, conducting a series of attacks on cities throughout South Vietnam. Tet is the Vietnamese lunar new year, their holiday of holidays. A cease-fire truce was in effect but the enemy struck with their largest offensive of the war in violation of that truce. I was ordered to lead a battalion of CIDG forces against a village located in a marshy Viet Cong refuge known as the Tram in the delta terrain of the Mekong River.

"We had orders to terminate because it was filled with VC sympathizers who were stockpiling a cache of weapons. Aiding and abetting Charlie. We flew in on Hueys. A battle broke out. I was wounded. We killed everybody—women, children—anything that breathed. Then we leveled the village with blocks of C-4 explosives. Funny thing was we didn't find any VC. Only a few weapons were found—just a couple of Soviet bolt-action carbines used by the villagers."

"I understand mistakes happened a lot in 'Nam," Stephen said quietly, trying to sound comforting. "Confusion happens in war. You were following orders. You couldn't help it."

"It's not how it happened, it's why it happened."

"I don't understand."

"Special Forces recruited a lot of Vietnamese from the lowland delta areas. Most CIDG were of the Hao Hao religion, a peculiar sect antagonistic to the VC and seemingly everyone else in Vietnam. We also had a minority of Chinese and Cambodians. Occasional violent disputes would break out between these groups, nothing unusual except a dispute erupted about our mission. Many of the Cambodians and Hao Hao sect refused to attack the village."

"Why?"

"After I got medivaced out, I found out the village wasn't a VC stronghold but an opium facility. The Hao

Hao sect and Cambos knew this, they had worked in the opium trade. It was their livelihood. The CIA provided the so-called intelligence about weapons and Viet Cong sympathizers. But it was misinformation. They cunningly used the commotion of the Tet Offensive to eliminate a competitor."

"What are you saying?"

Laramie turned and looked at the befuddled journalist. He harbored a strange expression—one of pity yet pierced with pain. Pity for who Stephen did not know.

He tossed the cigar in the dirt and ground it down with a boot.

"High levels of CIA was involved in Golden Triangle drug trafficking. But they began to lose control of Southeast Asia in the early 60s. Local opium lords began encroaching on their markets. The Vietnam War disrupted the opium lords and helped re-establish CIA as a major trafficker."

"Jim, you're not telling me the war was fought. . ."

Warm raindrops began to fall.

Laramie turned away from the river and hurried toward camp. The journalist followed.

"Let's pitch these tents quickly," he yelled at the group. "The rain'll settle in for the night."

Jim turned to Stephen. "Typical monsoon climate. Heavy rainfall between April and October and dry the rest of the year. Typhoons are fairly frequent."

"Typhoons? Great!"

He had no idea where he was, as far as he knew, Laramie could be leading them to Tibet. But the ex-ranger seemed to carry an air of authenticity; it calmed his fears.

The first day's travel almost killed the journalists. They weren't use to such physical exertion while the soldiers seemed to thrive on it. Their muscles ached from carrying the equipment. The soles of their feet were developing blisters, despite thick padding in the soles of their boots.

Laramie utilized a compass and other navigational instruments to track the progress of the group. He acquired maps of the region including a topographic map of the terrain taken from reconnaissance photos, compliments of sympathetic air force buddies.

The group broke camp at dawn for a second day of travel. The Asian mosquitos, which seemed the size of humming birds, bit them relentlessly despite the net hats and heavy clothing. Leeches attached themselves to limbs, requiring Laramie's lit cigar to release the bloodsuckers' grip.

"You remember what you said about not finding the answer in a comfortable, air-conditioned editorial room?" Stephen asked, wiping his sweaty mouth with the back of a hand.

"Yeah, I remember," Paul moaned as he began to ascend a steep hill, camera equipment tugging at his aching back.

"I rather not have the answer and be comfortable and cool than die from a heat stroke in this pestilence-ridden, Third World hell-hole. I'm waiting to see vultures flying lazy circles above us."

Paul tried to smile but he didn't have the energy.

"Oh yeah, this is really my idea of searching for the truth," he continued, adjusting the weight of the pack as he followed behind Paul, who was climbing the hill at a snail's pace. "What truth are we gonna find out here? Shit, maybe that POW died of heat exposure. Hey, why do I have to follow you? I'm tried of looking at your broad ass."

"Life is like a sled dog team," Paul yelled back at him. "If you're not the lead dog, the scenery never changes."

❁ ❁ ❁ ❁ ❁ ❁

The third day of the expedition continued on foot. The group emerged out of thick jungle terrain and entered a vast mountain range. Civilization seemed a million miles away; it certainly had never touched this region of Vietnam.

The group stopped to rest before taking on the next mountain. Paul, sitting on a fallen tree, took off his boots and two pairs of socks to look at his blister-ridden feet. He took out a canteen and poured water over each burning foot.

Stephen suddenly appeared through the underbrush, shouting and waving his arms.

"Guys...you're not gonna believe this! I found a road, a big, damn road! Just over the hill there," he said, pointing furiously. "C'mon. Take a look."

Laramie and the others followed. Paul quickly began to put back on the socks and shoes.

"You see. There it is. Right smack in the middle of the jungle. Look at the size of it."

Laramie pushed back his cap and scratched his forehead. The entire group was still, speechless as they stared over the hill.

Outstretched for as long as the eye could see was a dirt road penetrating the deep jungle landscape, built directly into the mountain range. Made of a yellow soil, it was graded immaculately and appeared to be constantly maintained.

There were no discernable pot holes or rain erosion often seen in dirt thoroughfares. It's width was also remarkable. The dirt road could easily accommodate five lanes like an American interstate. Paul finally appeared, limping gingerly, and joined the silence of the group.

"I don't understand it," Jim said. "There's no such road on any of the maps. I was never told about this road by my Vietnamese sources or military friends."

He conferred with his companions but none could explain the existence of the road. He reached into his back pack and began searching through a pile of maps.

"Maybe they don't know about it," Stephen said. "The road seems to be fairly new." He walked on it and reached down, feeling the yellow soil.

"Yep. It's definitely new. These layers of dirt were recently constructed, probably in the last six months or so. See how the road has been built up, layer by layer. Look over there. See the pits. This soil was recently excavated from those pits to build the road."

"It's so damn huge," Paul pointed out. "It must have taken a long time to build it through the jungle and these mountains. It seems to go on forever. I wonder what it's used for? Whatever it is, it's big."

"Yeah, what is it used for?" Jim asked, looking up from one of the maps. "And what the hell is it doing here in the middle of nowhere?"

Suddenly, the group detected a rumbling under their feet. It began to shake the ground's surface. They heard the faint hum of an engine, coming closer.

"Hurry, take cover over here," Jim yelled, pointing to a thicket of palms. Stephen and Paul hobbled to the cover, bitching about their blisters every step of the way.

The engine hum became a roar until a cloud of dust enveloped the road. Through the dust, the group spied two 16-wheel tractor trailer trucks traveling the yellow dirt road. Paul pulled out a Pentax and snapped some photos behind a palm. He stopped and peered over the lens.

"What is it?" Stephen whispered.

The semi-trucks disappeared behind the cloud, the engine roar diminishing into a faint hum in the distance.

"Those were damn Mack trucks. American-made diesel trucks. And they looked brand-spanking new."

"They sure did," Jim said. "All shiny and bright. But they shouldn't be out here. According to my maps, the nearest village is about a hundred miles away. There isn't suppose to be a road system anywhere in this region."

"Who is using brand new American made trucks on a brand new road in a Vietnamese jungle?" Stephen asked. "What are they hauling out here?"

"The road leads in the direction of Dach Lu, so let's hit it," Jim ordered, ending the break. "We'll follow along the road to avoid jungle underbrush. We should make good time until we have to take a different direction. Keep an eye and ear alert for coming traffic."

The group spent the remaining day traveling the dirt road, periodically dodging semi-trucks coming and going. They camped that night in the jungle near the road but far enough out so no one could be spotted.

The next day was the same agony of heat, blisters and a plethora of biting insects. The fourth day of the trip was filled with weary anticipation. The group was cautious in their movement, expecting anytime to come upon the much sought-after, legendary POW prison.

"I don't get it," Jim said, taking off the cap and wiping his brow.

"Get what?" Stephen asked, walking up to the ranger.

"I thought we'd have left the road by now. But it seems to run right in the direction of the prison."

"Maybe it does lead to the prison. The facility needs a road to transport men and supplies, doesn't it?"

"Not like this road. They have some paths but most supplies are transported either by helicopter or pack-mule. There isn't suppose to be a system of roads in this region because the Vietnamese government wants the prison hidden and inaccessible. A road this size leading all the way to ..."

Laramie's voice trailed off. He turned his head, listening for something.

"What is it?"

"C'mon, everybody, into the bushes!"

The group left the road side and gathered in the thick foliage of the jungle.

"Okay, the prison is located just down the road, in the valley of this mountain chain."

"How do you know?" Paul asked, taking cover in the thicket.

"I heard the Po-Tong River roaring in the distance. It's about a mile from Dach Lu prison."

"I don't hear a river," Stephen said.

"It's there. Now listen up. The group follows me. We'll go through the jungle and up the mountain to have a look. Stay down and be quiet. If you want to speak, use sign language. When we're safely up on the mountain, then maybe we can whisper. There could be guards patrolling the outer perimeter of the compound, so be alert. Be on the look out for wires and booby traps. Understand?"

"Booby traps?" Stephen exclaimed. "Wait a minute. Nobody said anything about booby traps. Why don't you go ahead and I'll..."

"Shut up," Laramie interrupted. "We don't have time for bullshit. We're on a strict time schedule. That boat on the coast will leave if we don't make it back within three hours of the designated time. Move out."

The group stealthily made its way across the jungle and scaled a small mountain cropped above the valley. The trip took about an hour. In the distance, the steady roar of the Po-Tong River was now easily discernible.

Below in the valley an entire compound was exposed. Though the dreadfully hot sun was beginning its descent, Dach Lu prison was still visible to the naked eye.

The group saw a complex of numerous buildings surrounded by what seemed like a 20 foot fence crowned with barbed wire. The maze of buildings inside the fenced area was apparently cells to house inmates.

Beside the fenced compound, prisoners, dressed in gray clothing, were constructing some kind of building with mortar and blocks under the watchful eye of several armed guards.

In the distance, the group spied more gray-clothed figures working in what appeared to be tilled fields. Some of the fields were being plowed by tractors while an elaborate irrigation system was operating, providing life-sustaining water to the tilled soil.

"Their water source for the irrigation system must be the Po-Tong," Jim whispered to the group. "Look, here comes one of those semi-trucks."

Another large Mack pulled out of the compound, heading north on the yellow dirt road.

"That damn road was built right up to the prison," Jim pointed out. "I wonder what they're doing? A road that large, built through difficult terrain, for hundreds of miles, must have cost the Vietnamese government a fortune. They don't usually go in for things like that. It must be pretty damn important. This entire compound, including the cultivated land, is probably several hundred acres or so."

"Something is definitely up," Stephen whispered. "Maybe we can go down a little closer to get a better look."

"Yeah, maybe I can photograph the inmates out there in the fields," Paul added.

"Okay, lets go," Jim replied. "But remember, be quiet, stay down."

He motioned to some of the veterans. "Ted, you and Luke stay here and be on the look out. If you see anything suspicious, signal us."

They descended the mountain slowly and made their way to the bottom of the valley. The group moved among several rock formations and eased their way toward the fields.

They perched on a knoll just above the fields, camouflaged by lush vegetation. Jim peered through binoculars at the field workers while Paul inserted a telescopic lens on the 35-millimeter camera.

"Bingo!" whispered Jim under his breath.

"What is it?" Stephen asked anxiously.

"We got our men. Some of those prisoners working out there are Americans. I see several older white guys out in the field. And there's some black guys operating the irrigation system. Here, take a look."

Jim handed the binoculars to Stephen.

"Christ! It does look like Americans."

Paul began shooting pictures with the camera. The clicking sound excited Jim.

"Quiet Paul," he snapped. "The guards may hear the camera."

Paul stopped, nudged Stephen and handed him the camera. "Take a look through the telescopic lens. You'll see 'em better."

The journalist held up the bulky lens and peered into the Pentax. He slowly moved it around, then jerking it back, stopped suddenly. "My God. I don't believe it."

"What?"

"I'll be damn."

"For Christ's Sake, Stephen, tell us what you see," Paul mumbled in a hushed tone.

"It's Armstrong."

"Who?"

"Richard Armstrong, Paul. He's out there in the fields talking to one of the guards."

"Armstrong, Armstrong. Wait a minute. You mean the embassy guy who pitched a fit when you mentioned the POWs?"

"Yeah, that bastard."

"Oh, my God!"

"Who in the hell is Armstrong?" Jim asked.

Stephen put down the camera and turned toward Laramie, a serious look etched across his face.

"He's a U.S. deputy secretary of state stationed at the American Embassy in Bangkok. We met him a few days ago. He refused to let us look at the POW-MIA files you told us about. He just about threw me out of his office. Now I see why. He's somehow involved in all this. He's responsible for shredding the files."

"Shredding POW files? When?" Jim asked.

"We'll tell you later."

"I knew government officials were involved up to their asses in this," Jim whispered, gritting his teeth in anger.

"That sorry son-of-a-bitch is talking with the enemy while POWs in shackles work out there in the fields."

"Uh-huh and I see what our POWs are growing," Jim said, peering through the binoculars. "It's poppies. American POWs are being used as prison labor to plant and harvest poppies for heroin production."

"Shit!"

"The trucks are hauling drugs," Jim interjected. "That's why they built this road up to the prison, in order to transport the cultivated poppies for heroin production. I bet they've gotta laboratory set up in that compound to extract the opium from the poppies. Then they ship it via the road."

"Armstrong is involved in the heroin trade?" Paul asked.

"Yeah. And the POW coverup," Stephen countered. "That's why he went ballistic and shredded the files. He doesn't want POWs coming home because they'd reveal how American government officials like him are involved in Golden Triangle narcotics trafficking."

"And reveal how these parasites used them as slave labor," Laramie said, putting down the binoculars. "Our own servicemen left behind, forced to work in poppy fields."

"Man, get this," Paul whispered, peering through the camera lens. "You remember those Mack trucks?"

"Yeah."

"The tractors out there plowing, they're American-made too. I see the words International Harvester on 'em. They're using American built agricultural equipment. The irrigation system is American made. Geez, the chemicals the POWs are spreading out there on the poppies says Gold Kist on the bags."

"What the hell is goin' on? I mean, where are they getting all this American-made stuff from?"

"No more talk," Jim said. "I'm gonna take a closer look, scout out the compound. You guys go back up the mountain. We'll talk later. Paul, did you get some pictures of our illustrious secretary of state?"

"I've got his pretty little face on film talking with the Vietnamese guard."

"I'll meet 'cha back on the mountain in two hours."

❁ ❁ ❁ ❁ ❁ ❁

The group assembled at the top of the mountain. Laramie informed the journalists that he and his ten compatriots would hit the compound tonight under the cover of darkness, hopefully catching the Vietnamese by surprise.

They planned to set time regulated explosive devices throughout the compound, detonating them simultaneously to create a distraction while liberating the POWs. Laramie insisted Stephen and Paul remain behind.

Dressed in black clothing with blackened faces and carrying every imaginable type of weapon, the commandos descended the mountain and toward the prison.

The journalists watched the well-armed group disappear into the night.

"I've gotta bad feeling in the pit of my stomach," Stephen said. "There's so much that can go wrong. If something happens to 'em, how are we gonna get the hell outta here?"

Paul looked worried but didn't reply. He crossed his fingers and stared down into the dark valley, watching the sporadic illumination as prison spot lights darted back and forth. The night was peaceful with only occasional chatter from wild monkeys and other jungle residents.

But the tranquility was shattered as gun fire pierced the darkness. From their view at the mountain's peak, they could see flames of gun battles inside the fenced compound while voices yelled and sirens blared.

The prison spotlights, anchored at the four corners of the compound's perimeter, converged at the center, illuminating figures fleeing and shooting at each other. The journalists heard more gun fire, then screams.

Eruptions of fire lit up the night and large "ka-booms" echoed in their ears. Stephen shielded his eyes as the bright flames from the explosions leapt up into the night, scattering building debris in every direction.

The maelstrom of explosions leveled the compound. They wondered if anyone could survive the fiery holocaust. Bloodcurdling screams rung out into the night; Paul grimaced as more gun fire rattled through the prison. The commotion finally quieted, leaving only burning buildings down in the valley.

An hour passed. They heard the distant murmuring of Vietnamese voices and yelps of tracking dogs ascending out of the valley and up the mountain range.

"They must be tracking Laramie's group. Someone must have made it."

Paul nodded and chewed his fingernails. Stephen pulled out the .45 -caliber revolver Laramie had given him before leaving. He checked the gun's chamber. Paul looked at him, then the pistol.

"Or maybe they didn't make it. It sounds like the dogs are getting closer. Maybe we should leave now Paul."

"No. Jim told us to stay here and that's what we'll do."

The sound of footsteps permeated the jungle, erratic but coming closer. Someone was running hard.

Stephen snapped the gun chamber back in place and placed a finger on the trigger, preparing for whatever stepped out of the bush, bracing for the worst.

A blur came rushing through the thicket and fell to the ground in front of the startled reporters. It was Laramie. His chest moved up and down sporadically, gasping for breath.

"Jesus, Jim! You've been shot," Paul screamed.

"It's bad," he gasped, trying to catch his breath.

"What happened?" Stephen asked.

"We got caught by surprise. Some guards. . . uhhh. . . waiting for us after we set the explosives. Six. . . . of my men were killed. If we. . . uh. . . if we hadn't detonated, they would've had us."

"Where's the rest of the group?"

Laramie coughed up blood. "I dunno. Uh, separated in gun fight."

"Did you get any of the POWs?"

Laramie smiled weakly. A trickle of blood ran from the corner of the mouth and down his neck.

"Yeah. . . ahhh"

"Take it easy now."

"Many ran. . .for the jungle."

"Okay," Stephen said. "We've gotta get you outta here. Paul, help me pick him up."

"No," Laramie insisted. "I'm gone. Go ahead. The Vietnamese are following. I'll slow ya down."

"We can't do that," Paul said. "You're going with us."

"That's right," Stephen countered. "We can't leave you here."

"Forget it. Now go dammit. They'll be. . .uhh. . . here soon."

He began to cough, grabbing his chest. The blood from two bullet wounds in the chest flowed more rapidly. Laramie was dying before their eyes.

"Damn Jim, we can't leave you."

Laramie pointed to his back pack, which had fallen off upon impact with the ground.

"Look...papers."

Paul opened it and found a manilla envelope.

"Valuable information. I wanted to... uhhh... show you but needed to trust you. Spies wanted to get me. Take it, from Kuhn-Sah Duc. It explains everything."

The dogs were approaching; their barks becoming clearer. The journalists saw the glare of flashlights penetrating the dark jungle foliage.

"Jim, we can't go..."

"Dammit, go! I'll stay. The dogs. . . will come straight to me. Give you, uh. . . time to cross the Po-Tong. Go!"

Stephen looked at Paul. The video journalist nodded, grabbing his arm and pulling him along. They reluctantly left the fallen soldier lying there on the jungle floor.

They ran hard through the jungle, grimacing as their blistered feet burned. Vines and tree branches slapped them in the face but they couldn't feel it; the adrenaline was pumping. In the distance, the roar of the Po-Tong River was becoming louder.

Stephen fell. "My damn knee," he groaned.

"C'mon. No time," Paul yelled, pulling him up by an arm.

Laramie gasped for breath. He could feel life oozing out of him. Lying on his back, he could see the canopy of stars above, twinkling their message to earth.

Despite the pain, despite the ignominious end to his life in the jungle of a foreign country, a queer feeling of satisfaction gripped him. He helped his fellow countrymen; some of them escaped at least, to maybe taste freedom again, even if for only a few days.

He had done all he could. He was willingly giving his most precious possession—his life—for what he believed; there was nothing else.

The dogs were close; slowly, he eased the pistol out of its holster, leaned up, bracing himself on an elbow and aimed toward the direction of the sounds.

Those familiar foreign voices were closing in; the same incomprehensible voices he heard during his tours of duty. Laramie steadied his arm, taking careful aim. Vietnamese guards, reigning in German Shepherds on leashes, approached.

The soldier began discharging the handgun, striking several guards and dogs. They fell like dominos.

The pistol emptied and the remaining guards returned fire, striking him numerous times. Laramie groaned and fell hard on his back, motionless.

The guards, mumbling among themselves while keeping careful aim on the body, released the dogs, who rushed up to the body, biting and sniffing it. It didn't move.

Satisfied he was dead, an officer walked up to him and kicked the body in the side. Nothing. Then he leaned down on one knee, running a hand into the left side pant pocket, looking for valuables.

The Vietnam vet opened his eyes, grabbing a Bowie knife from his right pocket, and plunged the blade into the eye socket of the Vietnamese soldier. He screamed and fell back dead. The other soldiers fired, riddling the ranger's already bloody body. He dropped the knife, still. He was gone but not defeated.

Stephen and Paul reached the Po-Tong and crossed it without a hitch. Laramie's will power had delayed the patrols so that the reporters, on foot, had a good head start.

After three hours of traversing the jungle darkness, they came out on the yellow dirt road. Cut and bloody from the undergrowth, sweaty and exhausted, they slowed to a walk, following the road south from where they came.

Dawn began to break. The Eastern sun peaked over the mountains as a pale, grayish day began to emerge. Stephen tapped Paul's shoulder and pointed down the road. A jeep was parked on the shoulder.

The driver was at the edge of the jungle relieving himself. The reporters quietly made their way to the side of the jeep, out of the sight of the driver. The keys were in the ignition. Paul slipped into the driver's seat while Stephen sat in the passenger's side.

Paul stepped on the clutch, started the engine, and attempted first gear. The startled driver spun around and began running toward them, yelling in Vietnamese.

"Hurry up," Stephen screamed. "What the hell are you waiting for!"

"I'm not good at stick shifts!"

"Oh shit, this is a good time to tell me!"

The journalist made a U-turn in the middle of the road. The driver, screaming obscenities in a tongue not understood by the reporters, ran up to the passenger side of the vehicle. He had not buttoned his pants and the clothing fell down to his knees as he lunged toward Stephen.

He kicked the driver, striking him squarely in the face. The stunned man fell back on the road and rolled. Paul jammed the jeep into second gear, then third, as they picked up speed.

Stephen looked back. The Vietnamese man emerged from a cloud of yellow dust stirred up by the jeep. He was shaking a fist, yelling at them, standing there in underwear, his pants now down around his ankles.

Chapter Six

Fearful from witnessing last night's carnage, Paul insisted they leave the country immediately and drove toward the nearby Laotian border.

He said Vietnamese authorities would be scouring the country, looking for the perpetrators who attacked the POW prison. They had to get out.

The thought of American prisoners of war forced into laboring in the illegal narcotic trade at the behest of American and Vietnamese officials sent chills down Stephen's spine.

He couldn't get that scene out of his mind: Deputy Secretary of State Armstrong standing by a poppy grove, talking to a Vietnamese guard as Americans worked.

Paul recommended returning to Bangkok. They would find some kind of passage out of the country. He seemed to instinctively know the way. Stephen, still in shock, did not argue.

Paul said media credentials would facilitate the crossing of borders within the Southeast Asian countries. Just as the video journalist predicted, customs seemed impressed with the colorful American cards imprinted with each journalist's photograph. They entered Laos simply by flashing their media IDs, access into Thailand was just as easy.

"Laramie saved our lives," Stephen said. "He held up that patrol long enough for us to escape. He died trying to rescue those POWs. We owe him, let's make sure his death wasn't for nothing."

The video journalist did not answer.

"Let's make sure Armstrong doesn't walk. I want that bastard behind bars."

"Yeah, well, let's think this out, and make sure we got enough evidence. We have to pin those shredded POW files on him and make it stick."

"You've got the pictures of him and the POWs out there in the poppy fields. Maybe we should turn it over to American law enforcement authorities like the FBI or Attorney General."

"I dunno who we should trust in the government Steve. I mean if a deputy secretary of state is on the take, there's no telling who else is."

Stephen kept his eyes peeled to the road but the wheels in his mind were turning faster than those on the jeep. Eight hours earlier, a botched raid had turned his life upside down.

"Let's just get to Bangkok and play it by ear," Paul said, gripping the steering wheel. "We need to review the stuff Laramie gave us. He never told me anything about papers from Kuhn-Sah Duc."

"Do you think any of the POWs made it?"

Paul looked off into the Thai rain forest as the jeep sped toward the U.S. Embassy. He looked worried. "Maybe."

The pair reached Thailand's capital the next day. Exhausted, dirty and unshaven, they were in no mood to confront Armstrong. They crashed at a seedy motel.

They had hardly slept during the four-day trip into the interior of Vietnam. They got a single room with two beds in order to save money. Their new found free lance work had not yet provided funds.

Both fell into a deep slumber for the next 14 hours.

Stephen awoke the next day. Lying in bed, he opened his eyes and focused. He spied cracks in the ceiling, stained yellow from water damage. He remained in bed for several minutes, trying to recall the events of the last few days. It had been an emotional roller coaster; like a bad carnival ride that makes you sick, yet you can't get off.

He got up from the bed and sat on the side, looking around the smelly motel room, trying to acquaint himself with the surroundings. His knee was swollen and sore due to old football injuries.

Sweat beads arose on his forehead and ran down his face. Thailand's cheap motels were not equipped with air conditioning, only miniscule fans which blew the hot Asian air from one side of the room to the other. Forget running water. There were no showers. No washing off perspiration or grime, he would have to suffer.

Panic seized him, he realized Paul was gone. His bed was empty. He hobbled across the room and put on blue jeans and a t-shirt. He gently slipped into a pair of Reebok running shoes instead of boots, careful not to inflame the bloody blisters.

He peered into the jagged piece of mirror hanging on the stained wall, examining the dark circles under the eyes and lacerations decorating his face. He was about to leave when the lock on the door popped and the handle turned; in walked Paul, carrying cartons of food.

"Good, you're up. I got some food. I'm sure you're starved. I know I am. I woke up this morning and my stomach was hurting."

Relieved, Stephen pulled the manilla envelope from a nap sack and opened it. Paul popped open the cartons; steam rose from the contents. He handed one to Stephen, who stabbed at the food with chop sticks while removing the envelope's contents.

"So what have we got?"

Stephen put down the carton of rice and examined the documents with intense curiosity. He read up and down the columns carefully, his lips quietly moving.

"Hmm. It looks like a ledger of accounts receivable and payable, a spread sheet like an accountant uses. A record of business transactions; I guess belonging to Kuhn-Sah Duc. But it's got some staggering numbers."

"Like what?"

"Like $5 million here, $12 million there. God, it's incredible. Wait, this doesn't belong to Duc."

Stephen grabbed another sheet.

"Who then?"

"This belongs to the U.S. State Department. Here's the department's official seal." He held up the stationary for Paul to see. "An internal memorandum detailing payments from the United Nations, funds dispersed over a five-year period in increments of millions of dollars to countries in Southeast Asia—Vietnam, Cambodia, Laos, Thailand and Burma."

"How did Duc getta hold of U.S. government records? Maybe Laramie wasn't straight with us."

Stephen looked up from the ledger sheet. "Now listen to this." His eyes bounced back to the ledger.

"Those funds came from the United Nations Drug Control Program. Remember that program?"

"No."

"The House of Representatives transcript on this UN program we took from the embassy. Remember?

"Oh yeah, to wean peasants in the Golden Triangle away from growing poppies."

"Exactly. Our government's efforts to curb illegal narcotic trade on a global basis."

"What the hell does Duc want with U.S. records detailing this U.N. Drug Control Program?"

"I dunno. Richard Armstrong's signature is on these loan installments financed by the U.N. Also a. . . " Stephen strained to read the signature, "Marlin Kwolski has signed off on the UN loans. Kwolski, Kwolski. Where have I heard that name?"

"Simple. He's President LaFleur's national security advisor. You should know that."

Stephen snapped his fingers and pointed at Paul. "Felix Berger said the national security advisor ordered the shredding of the embassy's POW files. Damn, I never put the name with the position."

"What are you talking about?"

"Marlin Kwolski. I remember him now. He retired from the CIA and headed their Asian Covert Operations Division."

"How do you know?"

"Because he was expected to succeed Smith as CIA Director but got passed over. President LaFleur opted to install Norton as director when he took office. Kwolski raised hell in the press about how it was unfair because of his many years of service in the agency. So LaFleur named him to direct NSA to pacify him."

"Uh-huh."

"I remember a story that came over the wire regarding Kwolski's rejection for the CIA directorship. The story said President LaFleur was concerned about a checkered past Kwolski had from his service in Asia. He didn't want a full scale investigation into Kwolski's background. LaFleur wanted to avoid spending political capital in the early days of his administration."

"Did the story ever say what exactly the controversy concerning Kwolski's past was about?"

"No. It never stated specifically. But apparently the president was aware of it and afraid enough to pass him over. By all accounts, Kwolski should have been CIA director because of his years of service and expertise. But LaFleur felt his resume was too hot to handle, even for the White House. But Kwolski had enough influence and friends in D.C. to pressure LaFleur into giving him the NSA post.

"Ya know, mentioning the CIA triggered my memory," Paul said. "Richard Armstrong, if I'm correct, was a contract employee for the CIA before he moved on into the state department."

"Are you sure about that? You never said you knew Armstrong."

"I don't. But when I was working at *The Times,* one of our regional correspondents received a chart detailing agent hierarchy of the CIA's international covert and clandestine operations. Our correspondent was working on a series of stories about renegade CIA agents involved in criminal activities. It was given to him by a source at Langley who wished to remain anonymous. He made copies for several reporters because we were interested in CIA involvement in the overthrow of so-called hostile governments."

"And?"

"One of the names of the CIA agents stationed in 'Nam during the war was a Richard Armstrong. This has gotta be the same guy who is now deputy secretary of state here in Bangkok. It's common for government workers to transfer to other departments."

"Why didn't you tell me this before?"

"Because I didn't connect the two until you told me that story about Kwolski. Then it all came back. You've gotta remember, that was back in the mid 80s. I had forgotten about all that CIA stuff. But I do remember a

Richard Armstrong. I'd bet the farm it's the same person."

"So we can presume Armstrong and Kwolski probably worked together in the CIA over here in Southeast Asia. Our deputy secretary of state must have taken his orders from Kwolski, when he was head of CIA operations for the entire Asian region. Somehow they're connected to the Golden Triangle and POW coverup. President LaFleur knew something about Kwolski that bothered him."

"But I don't get why Duc would have these records."

"Me either. Unless the program was hurting his drug business and he wanted to stop it. The UN loans authorized by Armstrong and Kwolski indicate the money was used to finance infrastructure improvements and economic development programs. Encourage the people to stop growing poppies."

"But if we're assuming Armstrong and Kwolski are involved in trafficking, wouldn't it hurt their business also?"

Stephen shrugged his shoulders. "Yeah. But since Armstrong is stationed over here as a deputy secretary of state, probably it's his job to manage the portion of American money that goes into the UN program for Southeast Asian countries. Kwolski, since he's the NSA, would oversee global drug control programs like that anyway."

"It still doesn't explain Duc's possession of government records. Or how Jim Laramie convinced Duc to give 'em to him and why he wanted 'em. Laramie said these documents would explain everything but I don't get it."

"I don't either. The answer died with him."

✿ ✿ ✿ ✿ ✿ ✿

"There's more."

Stephen shuffled through the pile, spreading papers across the bed.

"Here's more payments but this looks like it might belong to Duc. I don't see any government identification. More ledgers with millions of dollars funnelled into something called Pacific Equity."

"A business?"

"Perhaps. Maybe Duc bought a legitimate business to launder his drug cash. The rest of these records look like Pacific Equity's corporate bylaws, annual income statements and so forth."

"The drug lord is a busy capitalist."

"But like you said, assuming this portion is Duc's personal business records, how in the hell does Laramie get him to hand 'em over, and what does it really mean regarding the POWs? After all, that was Jim Laramie's priority. Someway, all this is related."

Stephen stopped reading. He heard something, like footsteps outside the motel room door.

"Paul, the door," he whispered urgently.

A loud "boom" erupted, the door crumbled, collapsing inward and two Thai men, faces masked to where only their oriental eyes shown, entered, brandishing Chinese made AK-47 automatic firearms.

Stephen was struck in the head with the butt of a gun. He fell back on the bed. Paul jumped up but was hit in the stomach. He doubled over and dropped to the floor on knees.

One of the men gathered the papers spread across the bed and placed them back into the manilla envelope.

The other Thai man motioned the journalists with a firearm to leave the room. A motel employee came running down the hall as they were exiting.

The masked man opened fire, piercing the Thai woman with several bullets. She fell back in a pool of blood. They were led out the back entrance of the motel.

There in the alley, a Mercedes with tinted windows, was running with another assailant at the wheel. The journalists were prodded with the barrel of a gun toward the back of the automobile, where one assassin held open a door and pointed a finger inside.

As Paul was entering the back seat, Stephen summoned all his might and flung his right elbow backwards, striking the assassin in the side of the face.

He grabbed the envelope from his hand while pulling the pistol from his waist band. The other assassin came around the open car door, taking aim with a machine gun.

Stephen ran behind the back of the Mercedes as he fired. The bullets ripped down the trunk of the expensive car. He popped back up, squeezing the pistol trigger, striking the assassin in the shoulder. He let out a scream, falling back, firing the gun as he fell.

Stephen ran around the side of the car, dropping the pistol and picking up the AK-47. The driver of the Mercedes opened the door and jumped out, firing a pistol as he rolled along the ground.

Stephen swung the machine gun back and forth, holding the trigger down as bullets ricocheted along the pavement and the spent cartridges spewed out the chamber, plinking on the ground. The driver stopped rolling and lied motionless. The journalist saw a line of red on his back; he was dead.

The stunned assassin regained his footing and began reaching for the gun lying on the ground. Stephen ran furiously down the alley and toward freedom.

He heard the squeal of tires and looked over his shoulder; the Mercedes was coming toward him at a high rate of speed. There was a wooden fence at the end of the alley. Stephen could hear the roar of the engine approaching, closer and closer. He braced himself to leap up and grab the top of the fence.

Just as the bumper nipped the back of his legs, he jumped. The car went under the rising body and crashed into the fence. He caught the fence top with one hand but the structure collapsed from the automobile collision; he fell to the ground among the debris.

The momentum of the speeding Mercedes carried it through the fence. He looked up and saw the red brake lights. The car had stopped with a squeal. Then the white reverse lights appeared and the car began to speed toward him again.

He raised the machine gun, closed his eyes and fired. Bullets blasted out the car's back lights; he raised the-barrel higher and bullets riddled the back window, causing the glass to shatter. The Mercedes stopped abruptly, changed direction and exited the alley.

He thought he repelled them, at least for now. He felt something wet on the back of his neck. He reached back with a hand and felt it: blood; cut from the fence debris.

He noticed flashing blue lights reflecting off the back windows of the motel building. He turned around. Thai police officers were stationed strategically behind their small patrol car doors, handguns aimed at him. Stephen dropped the AK-47 and envelope. He raised his arms in the air.

❀ ❀ ❀ ❀ ❀ ❀

Sirens blared as patrol cars rushed their captured prey to the city jail. Despite being handcuffed and thrown in the back seat of a patrol car, Stephen received a little extra-curricula activity from Bangkok's finest.

He wasn't sure if the punches were meaded out democratically to everyone arrested by the Bangkok Police Department or reserved for those special occasions when foreigners visited.

Once inside the jail, he was stripped naked and searched, including a degrading interrogation of his private parts.

Following the humiliating treatment, his clothes were returned. He put them on and was led to a briefing room where he was fingerprinted and photographed. After several minutes of trying to communicate with an officer, Stephen finally convinced one to give him his wallet.

He took out the media ID card and showed it to the officers. The group examined it, mumbled among themselves in inexplicable Thai, then one left. He came back with what appeared to be a higher ranking officer. The man wore a different colored uniform with decorative chevron strips and epaulets indicating a superior rank.

He looked at Stephen's picture ID, then at him. He smiled, crumbled the identification and threw it into a waste basket.

Stephen yelled and tried to stop him but was slammed to the floor and struck several times with a baton. He coiled into a fetal position, grimacing in pain. The commanding officer belted out some orders, then spit on Stephen. The group broke out in laughter.

Two policemen picked the journalist up, dragging him down a flight of stairs. His sides ached from the baton blows; he was slipping into unconsciousness but the officers grabbed him by the hair, shaking his head furiously.

The stairs led into a room of dark cells which appeared ancient and decrepit. The dank chamber resembled a medieval dungeon; the overwhelming stench of urine, sweat and feces made him almost vomit.

One of the officers took off a key ring from his belt and opened a door to a jail cell while the other held him. Stephen was thrown headfirst into the cell; unable to break his momentum, he slammed against the back wall, gashing an eyebrow.

The officers laughed at the ease in which they tossed him like a rag doll, slammed the metal door shut with a "clang" and left.

Stephen remained on the floor, propping his head up against the stone wall. He tried to catch his breath, attempting to inhale pouches of uncontaminated air but there was none to be found. Only a warm, dense fog of human pollution filled his lungs.

He wiped the back of his neck with a palm. He examined his hand. The cell was dark except for minimal light coming from a kerosene lamp at the entrance of the stairs. He noticed his hand was moist. It was blood. The cut he received from the wooden fence was still bleeding.

Medical care was not a priority with Bangkok's police department and such service for jail residents must be found outside its confinement.

He rested his aching head and felt his ribs—nothing was broken. He wondered what would happen to him. His first brush with Thai law had not been encouraging.

He placed a hand on the floor, it was sticky and grimy. He withdrew the hand immediately and looked at it. The brown ooze was years of human sweat, dirt and excrement.

"Yech." He wiped the hand on his shirt and got up from the floor, examining the ground closely. It was like being in one of those old movie theaters where the grimy floor sticks to your shoes except worst.

The smell and filth made him nauseous. He walked over to the cot smashed up against the wall. It was tiny and dented with no covering. He saw something moving on the thin, dirty mattress. He kicked the cot and brown little creatures scurried off and down to the brown floor.

"Roaches" he moaned. His eyes adjusted to the dim light. He looked around the miniature cell and saw all types of insect life inhabiting the space, obviously drawn to the odors and human waste which decorated the floor and walls.

Stephen wouldn't sit on the cot. He would rather stand. The putrid odor filled his nostrils, the brownish muck before his eyes was appalling. He felt his stomach churn. He couldn't hold it any longer. He bent over with hands on knees and retched. Then retched again.

After several minutes, satisfied all matter had been emptied from his stomach, he wiped his mouth with a shirt sleeve. Fatigue overcame his desire for cleanliness and he collapsed on the cot.

Laughter emanated from adjoining cells. Apparently his inability to retain bodily fluids had amused other inmates, at least he wasn't alone in his misery.

His body needed recuperation from the beating he took. Despite revolting surroundings, he fell asleep. But slumber was quickly interrupted, the same two officers returned and physically tossed him off the cot as he slept.

He hit the grimy floor face down, smearing the smelly muck all over his face. The officers picked him up and placed him on the cot with his back against the jail bars. They extended his arms over his head and chained them to the metal bars. He couldn't move.

Stephen tried to plead with them but he was too exhausted. They left but not without giving him a swift kick to an already queazy stomach for good measure. The chains cut into the skin and circulation began to diminish in the raised arms.

The inhuman treatment continued for days except for 10 minutes twice a day when an officer would unchain him long enough so Stephen could gulp down the clammy gruel he had brought. He begged the officer not to chain him up again but the brute ignored the foreign appeals.

His arms bled and turned blue, he began to lose feeling in them, almost paralysis. First prickly sensations, then total numbness. He screamed for the police to release him but was only greeted with the echoes of his own voice, resonating through the dark chamber, accompanied by cackle calls from other prisoners.

Stephen tried to concentrate on pleasant things, if only he could get his mind off the physical torture he was enduring. But the chains cut deeper. His arms felt like useless appendages, white and bloodless.

His mind was bereft of pleasant thoughts, except for Paul, yes Paul. Where was he? Was he dead? Probably. If only he had tried to save him when he had the opportunity.

But he was a coward. He ran away, down the alley and into oblivion, leaving his friend at the mercy of thugs. His morose mind was spinning: Why did the thugs want the manilla envelope? How did they find them?

Stephen cursed himself for allowing them to take Paul. He cursed his plot in life, the rotten, stinking jail, the lost POWs; he cursed God. After screaming and cussing, exhausted from anger and utter disappointment, he mercifully fell into sleep, forgetting for a moment he was racked with pain.

He awoke from the nightmarish coma. Light pierced the cell, burning his swollen eyes. Halfway between dead and alive, he felt faces peering at him. He stirred, mumbling to himself. Cold water hit his face, jolting him into consciousness.

He lifted his head and tried to open encrusted eyelids. Tears welled up as he attempted to focus on the figures, illuminated from the light of the open stairwell. Breathing erratically, he leaned forward to see if the figures were real or just ghosts of a tortured imagination.

One figure reached above his head, unlocking the chains. The arms fell to his side like dead tissue. Movement in them was nil but the sensation of being beside him felt wonderful.

He coughed while looking at the cuts and abrasions on the arms; he had not seen them in days. He wondered if he would ever use them again. He turned to his benefactor and attempted to filter through the light—two Thai police officers but there was a another face—paler, white, not yellow.

"I hope you've enjoyed your stay here in the Bangkok Hilton, Mr. Decatur," a voice came from the pale face. "I trust the accommodations were to your liking. The Thailand authorities roll out the red carpet for visitors. But since you're an American being held against your will in a foreign country, this is a jurisdictional matter for the U.S. Embassy. So we'll look after you now. Unless you want to claim political asylum and stay here."

A bellicose laugh broke out of the pale face and Stephen detected tobacco smoke, a new odor, different from the usual dung heap. A cigarette was in pale face's mouth.

The face came closer and spoke. "Do you hear me? Do you understand what I am saying? You can leave but only in my custody." Stephen smiled deliriously at the thought: freedom!

Then pale face became clearer, he saw the narrow eyes, balding head and impeccable suit. Richard Armstrong!

The bastard had somehow found him in the pit of a Thai hell hole. Stephen rested his head in numbed hands, trying to sort out the situation. Was this deliverance, he thought, or more agony?

Armstrong snapped his fingers at the officers and pointed to Stephen. They picked up the reporter under each arm, exited the cell and carried him up the staircase.

Upon entering the first floor of the police department, the bright light stunned him. He shaded his eyes with hands, groaning at the intense sunshine peering through windows.

He didn't lift one foot, the officers dragged him along, out the building and into the back seat of a limousine parked in front of police headquarters.

Stephen noticed another Thai man, dressed in a black suit, sitting in the back seat, and holding a now familiar

AK-47. Armstrong hopped in behind the journalist and instructed the limousine driver to leave.

The haze clouding his mind began to dissipate, his eyes were becoming sharper. He sat still, sedated, conserving precious energy.

"I hope you like the limo," Armstrong said. "It's usually reserved for the U.S. Ambassador but we use it quite liberally when he's away on business."

The Thai man laughed at Armstrong's anecdote. Apparently an inside joke. He tried to move his parched lips and form words. The lips were cracked and arid. He swallowed his cotton mouth and attempted once more.

"Yes, yes, what is it?"

"Food, water," he whispered.

"No. You haven't been cooperative Mr. Decatur."

The Deputy Secretary of State leaned back in the seat, inhaling his cigarette, exhaling a ring of smoke that drifted into Stephen's face.

"What'd ya want with me?" Stephen mumbled, regaining some stamina, becoming more lucid.

"Not you. This." He held up the manilla envelope. "Anyway, you saw me at Dach Lu. We can't have you going home to the states and spreading lies about POWs. Rational people know such things are just the imaginations of distraught families of MIAs or loony soldiers like Jim Laramie."

Stephen's swollen eyes widened. "How'd you know about Dach Lu? About Laramie?"

Armstrong did not answer but continued enjoying the pleasure of tobacco.

He couldn't see where the limo was taking him. The windows were tinted extreme dark and only the movement of the automobile foretold a trip to somewhere. But the ride was bumpy, indicating a dirt road which probably led out of the city limits of Bangkok. He rubbed his arms, sensation was returning, the blood circulating.

"What happened to Paul?"

"Paul?"

"Paul Mathis. My friend at the motel. Is he. . ."

"Yes."

His worst fears were confirmed. He lowered his head and took a deep breath.

Suddenly the car turned, then came to a stop. The bumpy ride was over.

❁ ❁ ❁ ❁ ❁ ❁

The Thai man opened a door and exited the limousine first, followed by Stephen and Armstrong. The sun was bright and the day bore a thick air of humidity. Off in the distance was a lush rain forest accompanied by echoes of teeming animal life.

The car had brought them into a deserted area with no sign of civilization—just vines, shrub and blue skies. The only evidence of human life was a large metal building which reminded Stephen of the tobacco warehouses he worked in during his youth in Southeastern Georgia. The limousine had pulled up beside the structure, which was located in a cleared field.

He estimated the building to be at least a 100,000 square feet with substantial height, possibly a 20 foot ceiling or higher. Fabricated out of a gray metal substance, the structure appeared square in shape with metal exterior panels. A large docking bay was built on the side to accommodate the trucks.

But nothing else remotely resembling man's presence existed. It was built in the middle of a jungle.

He spied another yellow dirt road in the distance, apparently the road which the limo had been traveling on when it turned off toward the building. The road's construction and appearance was similar to the road he encountered in Vietnam which led to Dach Lu. Again, another large road constructed in a remote area, this time in Thailand.

The journalist was pushed along with the barrel of the AK-47.

"What's this building?" he asked.

"One of our refineries," Armstrong replied, walking toward the entrance of the building.

"For poppies?"

"Refining opium from poppies. Wong, take Mr. Decatur over to that thicket of palms. Watch him closely. If he tries to escape, shoot him. I'll be out in a few minutes."

Armstrong opened a metal door and disappeared inside.

Wong led him toward the palm thicket, then pushed him to the ground. Stephen tried to get up but was met by Wong's boot, so he decided to stay on the ground. The Thai man leaned up against a palm tree, pointing the gun at him.

Ten minutes elapsed before the building door opened again. Armstrong stood at the entrance talking to another white man, possibly an American. He gave Armstrong a glassine envelope containing a white powdery substance. The deputy secretary of state opened the semi-transparent envelope and dabbed the powder on his pinkie finger.

He raised the finger to his mouth and tasted the contraband. Stephen couldn't make out what they were saying but Armstrong nodded and seemed pleased with the taste the powder produced.

They shook hands and Armstrong left. The other man, wearing a white lab coat, paused to look at Stephen, then slammed the door shut. Armstrong strolled up to the palm thicket.

"Well, Mr. Decatur, how do you like our regional laboratory? Impressive, don't you think?"

"You bring poppies here to get the opium?"

"The opium is refined from poppies into morphine and morphine into heroin. This is one of several regional laboratories we've established in the Golden Triangle countries of Laos, Thailand and Burma. We've invested in sophisticated equipment and technology to produce the most cost efficient refining in the world. With these regional labs strategically located in our areas of poppy cultivation, we can facilitate the refining process quickly and access transportation effectively, with minimum cost."

"Who's we?"

The deputy secretary of state did not answer. He placed the packet of white powder into a coat pocket.

"As a journalist, I assume you're aware that huge amounts of opium are cultivated in these countries for several reasons. Opium is a long-established part of the native cultures of the Golden Triangle countries. Political, cultural and ethnic divisions make it difficult for the central government of supplier nations to maintain control of drug production within their borders. We exploit those divisions."

"Is the CIA involved in the Golden Triangle?"

"The major reason for heroin trafficking is not me, Mr. Decatur, nor rogue CIA agents. It's poverty. All countries where opium poppies are grown are poor, economically-depressed, Third-World areas. Opium brings growers and laborers more money than any other crop, sometimes four to five times more, and it's easy to grow.

"Poor peasants who tend poppy fields are unwilling to give up their profits even though the product causes pain and suffering throughout the world. Middlemen like myself organize the growing and smuggling. Sometimes the government is in partnership with us, like in Vietnam. Even if an illegal operation is stopped for some reason, traffickers can start operations elsewhere, enticing growers and laborers with ready cash."

"Why locate this refinery out here in Timbuktu?"

"Opium is typically grown in remote areas far removed from government power centers by harsh terrain. In that way, neither police nor soldiers can locate them, though we've bribed most."

"How much money do *we* make?"

"An acre of poppies can yield about 22 pounds of opium. From a local grower or international broker like myself, villagers receive in advance the equivalent of a few hundred dollars per acre, tax-free. At harvest time, 22 pounds of opium can be refined into 2.2 pounds of morphine, which can be easily transported. Morphine is further refined into 2.2 pounds of heroin. Refining can be done in a simple shed but with a state-of-the-art facility like this, we process millions of pounds quickly."

Wong seemed anxious, nervous. He walked over and whispered something to Armstrong. The deputy secretary of state made a hand gesture, waving him off. He seemed to enjoy holding court with Stephen, pleased with his knowledge of and participation in narcotic smuggling.

"Local growers smuggle small bags by pack animal or on foot to our refining labs. But now with the road system and truck transportation, we're making that obsolete. We transport tons of heroin quickly. A load then reaches a sea port or airfield. At that point, 2.2 pounds is worth $90,000 to the principal merchant who has bought it and represents millions of dollars in market value to American buyers. And that's just one acre. Private planes and boats carry it on a final leg across the Pacific to America. But most often, heroin is smuggled out on commercial planes or ships.

"Unless customs is tipped off, their chances of intercepting is slight," Armstrong continued. "Police would have to tear apart every kind of commercial and personal cargo to find even a few caches of drug. Police dogs are trained to sniff out heroin and it sometimes works. But heroin doesn't have a strong odor. We hide it away in commercial shipments of manufactured goods like cars or TV sets. Sometimes, even body searches are useless because smugglers swallow small elastic balloons stuffed with it. After passing through customs, they either vomit or excrete the smuggled drug."

Beyond the palm thicket, two individuals stirred, watching the three men. No one noticed. They crouched on knees, hiding underneath the foliage, listening, waiting for the right moment.

❀ ❀ ❀ ❀ ❀ ❀

"Which reminds me of an amusing story. One of our smugglers was a terrible heroin addict. Businessmen like me or Kuhn-Sah Duc never sample the goods, it's bad for business. He pilfered from us all the time, costing hundreds of thousands of dollars. He arrived in L.A. and got through customs by swallowing a heroin balloon. But the balloon burst later and he got more heroin than even he could handle. He died of a overdose. Poetic justice, don't you think Mr. Decatur?"

"Your sense of justice is twisted."

"Hmm. Journalists are so cynical. Don't ya think, Wong?"

The assassin took careful aim at Stephen in a mock show, pretending to shoot him.

"Not much for words. Anyway, once heroin arrives to importers in America, they dilute the pure drug with white powders such as quinine or milk-sugar, sometimes even rat poison, which resembles heroin. Now only 50 percent pure, heroin is resold to a distributor for as much as five times the purchase price. Distributors set up so-called factories in their residences and hire people to work around the clock to cut the product's purity even more. Then the heroin is packaged in foil or plastic quarter bag units of five percent purity.

"A kilogram, or kilo, of pure heroin can become 40,000 of these bags and each one is sold on the streets to addicts for $50 a pop. I think you can appreciate the mathematics involved here, Mr. Decatur; as little as $500 of raw opium from a poppy field can yield $2 million of street heroin. And some addicts must consume several quarter bags every day to avoid withdrawal. The tons of heroin that enter the United States annually reaps billions of dollars in tax-free profits."

"I know you and Kwolski shredded the POW-MIA files so the Senate Select Committee wouldn't see 'em."

He smirked. "Don't be ridiculous. The senate committee had nothing to do with it. Besides, our human asset easily ended the Hanoi hearings."

"Human asset?"

"Our deluded agent who shot the Vietnamese official."

"He was a CIA plant?"

"Had the right background, served in the war, a real patriot. We convinced him it was a covert operation to force Hanoi to account for American POWs. He was instructed to assassinate the foreign minister but the imbecile shot his aid instead. Didn't matter. Had the same desired effect. We exploited his loyalty and appealed to his sense of duty. He thought he had backup and an escape route. Boy, I'd loved to have seen the look on his face when security opened fire."

"You're a sick man Armstrong."

A sly grin broke across his wrinkled face. He looked at Wong and winked, then back at Stephen, more amused than angered at the reporter's comment.

"You have a preference. The old Viet Cong method: sharp bamboo shoots under the fingernails, in the eyes or Wong's machine gun. I suggest the latter. It's quick and relatively painless. Wong is quite proficient. Just a month ago, a POW escaped from Dach Lu and almost made it. Wong shot him as he reached the outer bank of the Po-Tong. Squeezed off a marvelous shot. Reminded me of my CIA days during the war.

"We'd take suspected peasants up in a helo and threaten to push them out if they didn't confess involvement with VC," he explained. "Unfortunately, many were innocent but we tossed 'em out anyway. Gooks were a dime a dozen in 'Nam. Certainly they're more valuable in peacetime. I can still remember those screams, watching them fall to earth. It's amazing what's done in the name of national security. The education I obtained in the CIA has been invaluable in my new career."

Wong spoke again to Armstrong in his native language, unintelligible to Stephen. "Alright" said the deputy secretary of state, glancing at his wristwatch. "We've gotta get back to Bangkok. Mr. Decatur, Wong asked to prolong your death a bit. I've consented."

The deputy secretary of state placed the manilla envelope under one arm and began walking to the limo.

"Wait," the reporter screamed. "I've got information... I can help you. Armstrong. . . wait! Listen! Armstrong!"

Wong took careful aim at Stephen's leg. The overwhelming presence of the barrel was unbearable. He couldn't look. Sweat beads formed on his forehead. His breathing became erratic.

"Please," he begged. "I...know people. I've got money."

The Thai man squeezed the trigger and a bolt of white-hot lightening struck his leg, piercing a hole in the calve. He screamed and grabbed his leg, withering on the ground.

Never had he felt so helpless; tears ran down his face as the burning sensation inside the red-stained leg grew worst. He waited for death, convulsing there on the ground. It wouldn't be peaceful; he would not go easy.

In that split-second of fear, Stephen realized the overwhelming feeling of abandonment POWs endure every day of their miserable lives.

Wong pressed the light-weight stock of the gun to his shoulder and took aim at Stephen's mid-section; first the stomach, then maybe the head.

Grasping the leg tightly, he looked up and saw the barrel of the gun looming. He closed his stained eyes and grimaced, preparing for the unknown that lie ahead.

A shot rang out and his body immediately jolted, racked by nerves, but he felt nothing, except the excruciating leg injury. He opened his eyes. Wong was holding his side with a hand. Then he released the hand and Stephen saw blood.

He aimed the AK-47 toward the palm thicket and fired several times, moving the gun barrel across the vegetation, showering bullets into the brush. He stopped momentarily. Another shot pierced the air, striking him in the shoulder. He dropped the gun and stumbled.

Stephen couldn't see where the gun fire was coming from but he harnessed all his power and began crawling toward the gun Wong had dropped on the ground.

Wong took a few steps back, trying to recover his equilibrium but it was too late, another gunshot pierced his temple, exploding out the back of the skull.

The journalist, panic-stricken, crawled to the gun and grabbed it. Armstrong's response had been delayed, thinking the shots had come from Wong. He ran toward the palm thicket and saw Stephen on his stomach, brandishing the AK-47 right at him. He reached inside of his coat and pulled out a pistol.

The reporter began firing but missed, scraping the limousine instead. The limo driver stepped out of the automobile with a handgun. Another shot ruptured his arm. The driver dropped the gun and got back into the car. Armstrong ran toward the limo while firing over his shoulder.

Another phantom shot rang out, striking Armstrong in the leg. He screamed and instinctively reacted by gripping the leg, dropping the manilla envelope to the ground. He limped toward the car and opened the back door.

Again, another mystery shot missed his head, fraying the roof of the limo. Armstrong jumped into the back seat. Stephen unleashed the machine gun in a hail of bullets, striking the limo door. The car backed out, gunning the engine, tires spinning in the sand, and spun out down the yellow dirt road.

Still on his stomach, he watched the limo disappear in a cloud of dust, resting his head on the gun. The journalist had slipped through the fingers of death by the narrowest of margins.

But who was his guardian angel? Someone had cut the noose from around his neck, just before it was about to close for good. He noticed a pair of worn-out tongs standing beside him.

He looked up and saw the ghost sniper: an emaciated, hollow-eyed man wearing gray clothing, too big for his thin body. He smiled at Stephen, revealing a gap of two missing front teeth and a lower row of cavity-infested black gums.

Unconsciousness was creeping up on him. Precious blood was leaving the leg wound while the physical fatigue from the jail incarceration had taken its toll. He felt the frail phantom pick him up by one arm while another set of hands grasped the other. They began carrying him into the palm thicket.

"The envelope" he mumbled, trying to fight from blacking out, pointing to the ground. One pair of hands released him.

He saw a small, oriental man run toward the manilla envelope, bend over and pick it up. He wore a broad straw hat, smock with draw-string opening, knee-short pants and tongs.

He sprinted back, draping Stephen's arm around him again. They began carrying him through the palm thicket.

The reporter felt he was floating above the ground as delirium set in. Palm leaves brushed his face as he was magically transported by his benefactors.

Occasionally, he would hear voices of encouragement, telling him to "Hang in there" and to "Pick it up, it's just a little further." His eyelids were too heavy, he couldn't keep them open. Blackness descended.

He awoke to a strong aroma filling his lungs. Opening his eyes, he spied palm leaves cris-crossed uniformly, tied with vine fibers, to form a thatch ceiling of some kind. He stared at the brown leaves, trying to determine where he was, what had happened.

Memories of Armstrong, the shootout filled his head. He wasn't dead. Or was he? He raised up, trying to move, waves of pain washed up the left leg like high tide at the beach. He looked down and saw a bandage wrapped around it. He remembered: Wong shot him but was himself killed.

He felt dead but he was definitely alive, the pain proved that. Stephen looked left, then right. He was lying on a bamboo cot at floor level. The pungent odor caught his attention again.

It reminded him of boiled pig intestines, what locals in his rural, Southern hometown referred to as "chitlins." He raised his aching head and looked around. He was in a small hut-like home, made of what appeared to be mud walls with a dirt floor. It was primitive, with bare essentials like a rustic table and chairs made of tikiwood.

The space was not partitioned off; no separate rooms, just one large one within four walls. Another set of cots was located at the other end, while a cloth curtain separated the beds from the remainder of the room.

In the middle of the room was a depression where a fire burned, sort of like a fireplace. Above the fire was a caldron suspended by chains attached to a metal tripod. Some kind of soup was boiling in the caldron, emitting the strong smell. Smoke rose from the fire and was released through a vent cut into the thatch roof.

A young Thai woman stirred the pot with a wooden spoon. She was preparing some kind of food. She observed Stephen stirring, watching him for several minutes.

She walked out the hut's entrance and returned with two men, one native, the other a white man clad in gray clothing. It was the ghost who had rescued him at the refinery. He walked up to the cot and sat down beside him on the dirt floor, crossing his scrawny legs.

"You're alive. We didn't know if you were gonna make it. Lost a lotta of blood but you're lucky, the bullet went right through. How ya feel?"

"Uhh. . . terrible," he whispered.

"It's gonna take some time. Rest. That stay in the Bangkok jail didn't help any."

"How. . . did I get here?"

"Quang and me carried you through the palms to an ox and wagon he uses to carry hay to livestock. We put ya in back of the wagon, carried you to his village here, about two miles away from the refinery and doctored the leg wound; it stopped the bleeding. I got medical experience during the war, so don't worry."

Though he spoke English, it was accented by a strange clip. More Asian than American.

"You're the one who shot Wong?"

"Yep. Me and Quang followed the limo out to the refinery and hid. Quang knew the refinery's location and figured Armstrong was headed there. When we saw his thug was gonna kill ya, I opened fired. Dammit, I missed Armstrong by a hair. An inch further down and that son-of-a-bitch would have bought it."

"How'd you know about the jail? How. . . do you know Armstrong?"

"Easy fella. Take it easy. I'm an American prisoner of war who escaped Dach Lu prison about eight days ago. Somebody broke us out. God knows who. I got through the fence during the commotion of the gun battle, fled across the Po Tong. I escaped into Laos, then into Thailand. I know Armstrong from Dach Lu. I came to Bangkok to kill 'em.

"But I got captured by the police for trying to steal some food, got thrown in jail," he continued. "I was there when they brought you in. I overheard your conversation with the cops. But I didn't dare talk to you with 'em listening. They released me the day before Armstrong came to see ya. The dumbass Bangkok police never connected me with the prison break in Vietnam. I staked out the jail and waited for you to be released. And what do my eyes see, but Richard Armstrong taking you out."

"Who are you?"

"Colonel Blake McDermott, United State Air Force. I was shot down over North Vietnamese air space in 1971, captured by North Vietnamese and imprisoned at Dach Lu. Me, hundreds of other American MIAs and local prisoners were forced to grow and harvest poppies around the prison. I vowed if I ever escaped, the first thing I would do is kill 'em, not the VC bastards."

"Him?"

"Armstrong."

"Oh, yeah."

"It just so happens you brought 'em to me sooner than I expected. Never in a million years did I think that being in that shit hole of a jail would deliver Armstrong to me on a silver platter. Damn, if only I'd aimed a little lower."

Blake coughed abruptly, holding his side with one hand and placing the other hand over his mouth.

"How'd you get captured?"

"We'd completed a bombing mission over an ammo dump. We were reconnoitering a road and found a tank alongside it, camouflaged with brush. I was so high the enemy didn't know I was there. I descended, almost supersonic and give the tank a good long burst. As I pulled up, I was hit three times by 23-millimeter rounds in the gas tank right behind my cockpit. The engine shuddered, followed by several explosions which filled the cockpit with smoke.

"My wing man shouted to get out, said I was burning all over. But I was staying with the airplane until I was either over the water or blown out. No way was I gonna get captured. I went to afterburner and gotta surge of power. I was in a right pull up, two or three miles from the ocean. The nose was coming up when the damn engine quit."

"What happened?"

"My stick suddenly came right back in my lap and the aircraft pitched forward, throwing me against the shoulder straps toward the canopy. My options were gone. I reached for the handle to eject the canopy. After it went, I squeezed the trigger and ejected. I hit in some rice paddies. I didn't have time to deploy my survival kit which was part of the seat in the airplane. I pushed the emergency quick-release switch to my parachute and. . . shit!"

"What?"

"I took a couple of steps and was pulled down hard. The electric cord between the battery and emergency radio in my pocket was wrapped around the damned parachute strap. By that time I was surrounded by North Vietnamese rifles. I said I'd never be captured and here I was in enemy territory. And I'd just dropped a load of napalm on 'em."

He rubbed his head and coughed again. "What 'bout you?"

"My name is Stephen Decatur. I'm a journalist."

"Nice to meet 'cha. Why does Armstrong want you dead?"

"I saw him at Dach Lu but I don't know how in the hell he found out. He's already murdered a good friend of mine."

"You were at Dach Lu?"

"Yeah. I was part of the group that broke you out. Well, I stayed behind but a group of American soldiers raided the prison. But I think most were killed."

"Damn. I owe you my life."

"No. I owe you. Jim Laramie saved you, not me."

"Who's he?"

"He led the operation. But we had to leave him behind and. . ." Stephen's voice trailed off.

"I wish I coulda met him."

"Me too. Armstrong wants the records Laramie gave me. But I dunno why."

"The papers in the envelope?"

"Yeah. You have 'em, right?"

"We got 'em. They're safe."

"Good. They mean something."

"Listen, Mi Ling is fixing some soup. Eat some. You need to get your strength back."

"Is that what smells so bad?"

Blake smirked. "Yeah, it's made from a bush root that grows wild in these parts. It's really quite good except for the smell."

The young Thai woman brought over a bowl, steam rising from its contents. He took a few reluctant sips of the broth. Better than jail gruel. The odor quickly left his mind and he consumed three bowls.

It felt good to have something on the stomach even if it was from a wild Thai shrub. His ferocious appetite seemed to please the woman. He lay back on the cot and rested.

"I figured you hadn't eaten in a while," Blake said, putting down his bowl on the dirt floor. "Back in Dach Lu, we'd go days without food. It got rough sometimes."

An elderly Thai man sat in a chair at the table, smoking a pipe which burned a substance that radiated a new pungent smell. The young woman sat in another chair, raising a bowl of broth to her mouth.

"How do you know the man?"

"Oh, Quang? We met at Dach Lu. He was arrested and imprisoned just for being from Thailand. They trumped up some charges, got some good years of slave labor outta him. After I got out of the Bangkok jail, I contacted him. He was more than happy to hide me out. He insisted I stay with him. That's his daughter Mi Ling. He's a widower. He lives in this rural village, a few miles outside of Bangkok."

"I can't believe I'm looking at a live Vietnam War American POW."

"It's been so long I've forgotten what or who I am. All I remember about Colonel Blake McDermott is that I was flying a mission in '71 and was hit, had to parachute out. After being captured, my life as an American ceased. From then on, I worked in the poppy fields. What year is it?"

"1996."

"Let's see. God, I've been in prison for 25 years." He shook his head, then rubbed his eyes, overwhelmed. "Jesus, 25 years wasted, down the tube."

"How old are you?"

"If it's 1996, then I'm 62. They took the best years of my life."

It was tragic. McDermott looked like he was at least 75, an elderly, decrepit man. The drawn face, pinched from starvation, etched with lines, leathery from working out in the hot sun, gave him the cadaverous appearance of a corpse.

The torture and neglect he endured at Dach Lu had taken its toll. He coughed constantly, stopping momentarily to spit out a slimy, reddish ball of congestion upon the dirt floor. Stephen wondered if death would not have been a more equitable solution than his present condition.

"What's your friend smoking? That stuff is strong."

"Opium. A favorite of the villagers. They can't live without it. It's their whole way of life. Look, it's getting late. We'll talk more tomorrow. You get some rest. I'm gonna hit the sack too."

"Okay. I could use some. Thanks Mr. McDermott."

"Please, just Blake. It's great to talk to a free American."

"Thanks Blake. . . for saving my life."

He smiled and gave a thumbs up signal, then retired to a cot. Throughout the night, the journalist awoke to Blake's violent coughing; he wondered if the pilot had contracted a disease while imprisoned.

✿ ✿ ✿ ✿ ✿ ✿

He awoke the next day, exhausted. Phantasms of Armstrong, coupled with Blake's incessant coughing, had periodically interrupted sleep. But the pain in the leg had diminished and he felt like getting some fresh air.

The hut was empty. A wood stick was beside his cot. He grabbed it and pushed against the cane to gain some footing, then limped across the dirt floor and out the door of the hut.

The sunlight greeted him fiercely, another muggy day in the Golden Triangle. He limped into a dirt street lined with identical mud huts like Quang's. The small village contained about two dozen huts and a few rickety stalls containing skinny-ribbed cattle and oxen.

Dirty children played out in the street, running up and down the thoroughfare. Kapok trees grew in between the huts with an occasional cane grove.

Stephen noticed groves of poppies in the distance, the staple crop of the village. A tiny Buddhist shrine known as a *wat*, cast a long shadow across the street while its gold plated statute of a cross-legged Buddha reflected the sun's rays in white flares of light.

A pile of dirt caught the reporter's attention. Behind it was a deserted bulldozer—a Caterpillar. The yellow excavating equipment struck an amazing contrast—Western industrial technology against a backdrop of isolated Third World depression.

He remembered the trucks and tractors at Dach Lu in Vietnam. Now rural Thailand. What the hell was going on?

His eyes peered around the corner of the hut and spied Quang's daughter. Mi-Ling was kneeling over a wooden tub washing clothes. She looked up and her eyes met his. He smiled but it was not returned. Her glance was brief as it was expressionless.

She returned to washing by hand. Stephen leaned against the cane, observing each motion as she scrubbed the clothing in the tub water.

The sun's heat was uncomfortable but she seemed unaffected, content upon completing the chore. Sweat beaded around her forehead, running down her nubile neck into the honey-colored coupling of her breasts. She looked up again, the soft, almond-eyes of oval black examining his face, his body.

The golden fingers returned to the clothing, scrubbing, poking and prodding, feeling her way through them. She would stop periodically, wipe her brow, then run fingers gently through the long, dark strands of hair which rolled straight down the small of the back.

She stood for a moment and stretched. The silk dress was stained with perspiration. Stephen could see the outline of her body against the glare of the sun. Her round, puffy lips were dry from the heat but she moistened them with a slow, circular motion of her pink tongue, then rubbed them together until the mouth was smooth, wet.

Again, she pulled her straight, black hair back with the brush of a hand, then slipped off her sandals and bent down on her knees to begin washing another batch of clothing.

Something stirred inside of Stephen, something he had not felt in a long time. He could not explain the attraction which pulled him toward the young woman. Perhaps it was an intrigue, a desire to know her.

She appeared so delicate, so simple, so lonely there washing clothes in the middle of this desolate village. And yet she impressed him as strong, independent, and motivated. He limped toward her but she took no notice and continued washing.

He walked beside the tub. She looked up at him but again, inexplicably, no smile or acknowledgement, as if she did not know an appropriate greeting for a foreigner.

He reached down into the tub and pulled out a cloth, wet with cool water and walked behind Mi Ling. She was not alarmed and continued to work. He watched her from the back, her silk dress dark with sweat, delicate hips moving back and forth in rhythm against the tub as she scrubbed.

He saw the provocative legs, torso and feet exposed. The warm, moist back of the neck, golden from the rays of the sun. He limped up near her. She felt his presence behind her.

Mi Ling stopped washing, looking slowly up toward the sky but without fear. Stephen gazed down into the soft, oval, onyx pools, the red, sensual lips and appealing oriental face.

His hand touched the black hair, running fingers down to her back. Taking the wet cloth in his other hand, he placed it on her moist forehead, wiping the perspiration gently from the brow.

Then he plunged the cloth into the tub again, withdrew it and wiped Mi Ling's entire face, running the dampened cloth down the front of her neck, easing into the front opening of her dress.

Stephen felt her chest rise and fall as her breathing became sporadic. She did not panic nor did she speak. He retracted the cloth from the chest, then dabbed it on her precious lips.

He dropped the cloth and reached for a pan that Mi Ling had placed beside the tub. He lowered the pan into the tub, withdrawing water and gently began pouring the cool liquid over her head. Tiny streams ran down the black hair, moistening her neck. Other streams danced upon her brow, running along the nose, across the lips and meandered down the dress.

She licked her lips, tasting the cool water, and looked up at Stephen. The sloe-eyed orbs spoke her mind, expressing the joy felt from his kindness. He pulled the wet hair back, squeezing out water, caressing the strands with his fingers, absorbing the vitality of her essence.

His fingers groped down her neck, grasping the tender shoulders, rubbing, feeling the smooth skin. Gently, he pulled Mi Ling back against him, her head touching his stomach. The warmth of her body penetrated his clothing, he squeezed the nimble shoulders tighter.

Stephen leaned over the tub and dipped the pan, never moving his eyes from hers, pouring the contents slowly, methodically, once again over Mi-Ling's head. He rubbed her face with his hands, wiping away the excess water. His fingers touched her lips, gently prying the orifice open and extending his index finger inside.

Hot, tender flesh eagerly greeted his appendage, massaging, mesmerizing Stephen. A sea of emotion washed over him, gurgling and churning inside. He withdrew his finger and pressed it against his lips. The aroma of her bodily fluids seized him, almost in a frenzied panic.

Mi Ling nudged the back of her head into his torso. Stephen, standing over the kneeling woman-child, groomed her face and neck with his fingers, prodding and exploring. She closed her eyes, leaning farther back into him.

Her breasts, supple and fertile, moved up and down rhythmically as her breathing became heavier. Fecund thighs shown through the wet dress, warm and inviting. Stephen embraced her round face in his hands, pushing her against him harder. She did not protest but let her arms go limp as if to welcome his intrusion, submissive and docile.

Clasping her face, he leaned down toward the crimson lips, nubile and moist. He came closer to their redness, supple and provocative. Mi Ling's lips trembled but opened to welcome its desired guest.

"Stephen, hey, Stephen!" A voice pierced the silent ceremony of love, breaking the tenderness into a thousand pieces upon the ground. The startled reporter released Mi Ling from his grip, abruptly separating the intertwined bodies. He shook his head and looked around with glazed, unfocused eyes.

Mi Ling lowered her head, edged toward the tub and quickly resumed washing clothes. Stephen saw two figures in the distance walking toward the hut; it was Blake and Quang. He picked up the cane, walked out from behind the figure on knees, and limped toward them.

He glanced back over his shoulder. Mi Ling raised her head and met his eyes but this time, no blank stare greeted him. It was a look of wonder, like a child had awakened inside, puzzled, intrigued and precocious.

Stephen tried to wipe the sense of embarrassment from his face but it was flush with emotion. Blake had disturbed him as if from a dream.

"God, what am I thinking? What am I doing?" he mumbled to himself as he limped toward the pair. Still, the lonely, bare-foot figure leaning over the tub was fresh in his thoughts; the sight, the feel, the smell, infatuated him.

Blake and Quang met him at the entrance. They entered Quang's hut together.

"You're gettin' around soon, making good progress," Blake said with that strange, Eastern accent. "I see ya found the stick I left beside your cot."

"Yeah, thanks."

"Helping Mi Ling with the wash?"

"Pardon?"

"Outside with Mi Ling."

"Oh, yeah. I was helping her...we were helping each other."

"I've never introduced you to Quang."

Blake spoke in broken Thai to him and the elderly oriental man said some unintelligible words to Stephen, then bowed. They shook hands.

"Tell him how much I appreciate his help and generosity."

Blake delivered the message, then translated Quang's response.

"He says any friend of mine is a friend of his. And if Armstrong is your enemy, then you're definitely a good person."

"He knows Armstrong?"

"All the poppy growers know him, in one way or another."

Quang took out a pipe. It was like no other smoking instrument the journalist had ever seen. About two feet long, resembling more a flute, with a metal cup mounted three-quarters from the mouth piece to accommodate the opium.

Quang began cramming opium into the cup, then he took a small tree branch, placed it in the fire, withdrawing a flame which he used to light the flute-pipe.

"Listen Stephen. Quang pulled a few strings and got a jeep. It's parked around the rear of the hut. It's gassed up and ready to go. We'll use it to escape after I kill Armstrong."

"I want to talk to you about that. I've been thinking. Why don't we head back to the United States and forget about Armstrong. We can nail 'em with your testimony. Why risk it. Let's get back home where we'll be safe and we can have him prosecuted. You're a real, live POW for God's Sake. The authorities will listen to you."

"Hell no. I've waited for this damned moment all my stinking, rotten prison life. I'm not gonna let this opportunity slip through my fingers. I'm not leaving Thailand until the bastard is six feet under. He killed my friends, made us work in something we despised. I'll never forget that."

"I'm not asking you to forget. But if you got killed by Armstrong's goons, there'd be no one to represent the American POWs still being held captive. You're their only hope. I want revenge too but we've gotta listen to reason. With your knowledge, we'll get him extradited back to the states and make him face an American court of justice."

"There's no guarantee he'll be extradited or even convicted. Our government left me to rot in that Vietnamese prison. We served our country faithfully. They abandoned us to die. I don't trust the U.S. government. Armstrong is a part of 'em. They'll conspire to get him off like they conspired to keep us hidden away. We gave everything. My life is over. I was abandoned just like thousands of others. And you expect me to take my chances in what you call a court of justice? There ain't no justice, pal. The only justice is a bullet through the head."

"Blake, I understand your feelings. But here in the Golden Triangle, Armstrong's in control. At least in America, we have a fighting chance."

"I saw him kill a POW once, a fellow American mind you, because he didn't think the guy was working hard enough. He kept striking Dwayne and finally, Dwayne had had enough of being treated like an animal. He hit Armstrong in the face, knocked him to the ground. It was great. Do you know what that coward did? He pulled out a gun, shot Dwayne in the back. He was dead before he hit the ground. They wouldn't even let us bury him, just hauled off the body and threw it in one of those mass graves they dig every once in a while for purges. No marker, no eulogy, no nothing. I swore that day I'd kill 'em."

"I want you to think about what I'm saying. It's no good fighting him on his own turf, he's too strong. We won't win and if we get killed, the rest of those POWs will be lost forever to the world. You and I hold the keys to liberating the POWs and Armstrong knows it. You've gotta think about them too."

"I am thinking about 'em. That's why I'm gonna kill the son-of-a-bitch."

"But even if you kill him, the POWs will stay in prison working for someone else. With Armstrong gone, another drug merchant will take his place. The only way to get 'em out is to put pressure on our government and we've got the ammo to do it. Our government will have to demand their release from the Vietnamese government. Their backs will be against the wall once we go public with this. The American people will demand action. But we can't do it by ourselves. It's the only way to save the rest of the men."

Blake sighed and leaned back in the tikiwood chair, running fingers through a greasy mat of gray hair. He coughed a little and crossed his legs. Stephen could tell he had gotten through to him. Those years in prison had not dulled his capacity to think reasonably. He coughed again, then spoke.

"Quang and I worked hard to get that jeep. We also got some guns for the job. I was looking forward to dispatching that asshole."

"Fine. We can use the jeep for travel and guns for protection. Let's get back to Washington, D.C. We'll kick those politicians off their dead asses and finally get some action on POW accounting. We'll get our revenge for Dwayne and Paul, okay?"

"Who's Paul?"

"Paul Mathis. My friend who was killed by Armstrong's goons."

Blake stared at Stephen, perturbed. "I'm not convinced this is the best course of action. But ya have a point. The guys need help. We'll go."

❁ ❁ ❁ ❁ ❁ ❁

The POW and journalist agreed to leave the village in three days for the coast of Thailand in order to obtain transportation by boat. They studied their chosen route to the coast with the assistance of Quang, who was quite familiar with his native land.

They would hop a freighter leaving for the Philippines. Asian boat captains were notorious for accepting bribes for stowaways. They felt ship travel was their best chance of leaving the country without Armstrong's notice.

Once in the Philippines, they would catch another ship heading toward North America. Stephen's leg was improving though sore and tender. Blake too was resting his weary body and eating well thanks to Mi Ling's cooking.

Stephen noticed a change in Mi Ling's personality. She now would smile ever so slightly at him while performing her chores during the day. But she made sure her father did not see. He would never permit such activity from a female.

Stephen would return the smile while the dark almond eyes, crowned with long, black eye lashes, seemed to peer into the depths of his soul.

When Quang would leave for the poppy groves, Stephen would talk to Mi Ling though she did not understand a word of English. It didn't matter, she relished the attention, despite the language barrier, laughing and clapping her hands like a child.

He did not understand what had overtaken him that day at the wash tub nor did he try; it was beyond his comprehension, his grasp. But he did know that a fragile, gentle, peasant girl, whose boundaries of the world were limited to a rural village in Thailand, had been transformed into a Mandarin princess before his imaginative eyes.

Mi Ling faced the fate of all Thai women outside the mainstream of opportunities. She would probably be sold into a marriage by her father to another villager and toil in the poppy fields for the remainder of her days, tired and broken.

But for one brief moment, kneeling at the wash tub, she shared a communion with a man whose kind she had never seen before. A man whose touch, whose feel, unveiled a curtain of darkness from her eyes, revealing her true self: beautiful, enticing, and wanted.

Chapter Seven

Two days passed. They would leave in the morning.

"Blake, I saw the bulldozer outside. Where'd the village get it?"

"A gift of sorts, from Armstrong."

"How?"

"Armstrong's group came to the village, promised agricultural improvements in exchange for a cut in their poppy farming. You know, fertilizer, tractors, herbicides, irrigation, transportation, like at Dach Lu."

"Did they take it?"

"Yeah, at first, it was a great deal. But Kuhn-Sah Duc had negotiated for the village's poppy groves."

"Ahh. Duc, huh."

Quang and the"other village elders decided they shouldn't trust an outsider, especially a Westerner. Felt more comfortable with Duc. Armstrong had already brought the bulldozer to dig a canal to the fields. They told 'em their decision and he went nuts. Brought a squad of assassins and they leveled the village. Tried to terrorize 'em into leaving Duc. The village was twice this size before the attack."

"I never realized."

"Fortunately, Duc intercepted the squad before they tortured everybody. His army pushed 'em back but not until most of the villagers had been killed in the crossfire."

Blake spoke to Quang, who was again indulging himself in opium smoking. The elderly man took the flute from his mouth and babbled, shaking his fist. The POW nodded.

"Quang says a drug war has erupted across Southeast Asia between Armstrong's group and Duc. They're competing for poppy production while villages have been drawn into the middle. Thousands of peasants unwittingly became pawns in their struggle, taking sides, taking up arms and dying in the process. Despite the devastation, Duc and Armstrong remain untouched, above the din of war, lording over their drug fiefdoms."

Quang grimaced at every mention of Armstrong's name, trying to emphasize what Blake had translated though he didn't understand a word of it. Satisfied with his show of defiance, he lifted the flute-like pipe to his lips and inhaled a long draw of opium fumes.

"So the village is loyal to Duc?"

"Well, yeah because he's Laotian but he's just as bad. Armstrong's group has gained a lot because of their ability to provide improvements, very alluring to peasants. It's a choice of the lesser of two evils."

"Who's all in Armstrong's group?"

"Seen some during my years at Dach Lu. Mostly Americans, trained in military, covert techniques."

"Like CIA maybe?"

"Yeah, maybe. You think it's them?"

"I do. Armstrong worked for the CIA before transferring to the state department."

"I'll be damn. Hmm. That reminds me of a story I heard years ago while in Da Nang."

"What?"

"Back in 1965, a French inspection team headed by a Colonel Roger de Tassigny traveled through Laos and Vietnam gathering evidence on an alleged booming narcotics trade that locals claimed was supervised and protected by CIA agents."

"Really. Jim Laramie mentioned something like that."

"Colonel de Tassigny and the team were departing Saigon in a U.S. helicopter when they were killed in a mid-air explosion. The official explanation given for the chopper's explosion was accidental but rumors persisted that CIA sabotaged it. The French inspection team was seen as a threat to its drug network throughout Indochina. But it was only speculation."

"How does Armstrong get the funds for the equipment?"

"I got no idea. We always wondered how he was able to get brand new American made stuff. We're talking millions of dollars worth over many years. The Vietnamese government isn't known for kicking in that kind of dough for anything. It must be the drug cash."

"But he has to launder it to make it legit. That much equipment and money would attract attention unless…wait. You said millions of dollars."

"Yeah. So?"

"Get me the manilla envelope."

"What is it?"

"Just get it."

Blake grabbed it off the table and tossed it to Stephen. The reporter began thumbing through the documents quickly. He stopped and read inquisitively. He popped the page with the back of a hand.

"God, that's it Blake. That's how he's doin' it."

Quang gave the excited journalist a queer look, wishing he could decipher the lingo and participate in the conversation.

"How?"

"The Mack trucks and roads, refineries, the bulldozer. He's funding it from the United Nations Drug Control Program to enhance heroin production. The infrastructure improvements listed on this ledger—canals, transportation, fertilizer, tractors, everything—looks benign on paper but it's been diverted to enhance poppy cultivation, not wean peasants away from it."

"What are you talkin' about? What's the United Nations got to do with this?"

"The UN Drug Control Program was created to finance economic development programs in opium producing countries so peasants would have an incentive to stop growing poppies."

"Uh-huh."

"Armstrong handles the American portion of the UN money for Southeast Asia because of his state department position. I bet he's misappropriating the funds earmarked for the UN Drug Control Program in order to improve his group's hold on poppy cultivation. That's how he's able to afford to build all this infrastructure and make it look legit. It's suppose to be used for stopping poppy growing, not increasing it."

The Vietnam vet's eyes grew bigger as Stephen related the sordid theory, covering his mouth with a hand to deflect occasional coughing seizures.

"So you're saying he uses the U.N. money under the guise of economic development to increase drug trafficking."

"Exactly."

"Well, that explains the fighting between Duc and him," Blake noted. "Armstrong's trying to drive Duc out of the Golden Triangle, using the lure of infrastructure improvements to win over the villages. With this UN money, he probably thinks he's gotta way to purchase the growers' loyalty."

"Yep. He can peddle influence among the poppy growing Asian countries. With American funds from the

UN Drug Control Program at his disposal, he's got financial power to persuade them over to his side."

"Armstrong's goal is to control all the heroin grown and refined in Southeast Asia. I know it. And Duc is the only one standing in his group's way of achieving that."

"I've always heard the only repertoire the CIA knows is to bribe or butcher, whichever works. It seems Armstrong has perfected it. If he can't buy you with U.S. tax dollars, then he'll kill you."

Quang cut in, babbling at Blake, jabbing the acrid smelling pipe in the air, as he spoke.

"Quang says the last time he saw Armstrong was when he brought the bulldozer. Had another American with him, wearing glasses, carrying a big camera."

"Armstrong definitely has good help, right up to the president's National Security Advisor. The NSA ordered the destruction of the POW-MIA files at the embassy here in Bangkok. Now I understand why."

"Yeah, he doesn't want the POWs discovered. We'll blow his cover."

"An aid at the embassy thought the shredding was connected to files stolen from the embassy. Records on a UN program. These have gotta be those records."

Stephen snapped his fingers and pointed at the POW. "Jim Laramie must have been the one who stole the UN files. Discovered what Armstrong was doing somehow. They didn't want anymore secrets coming out so they destroyed the POW-MIA files, fearing Laramie would also try to get 'em."

Quang was quiet again, content to smoke opium in the stark house he had built years ago in his youth, a young man eager to settle down into a simple life with a wife and raise a family.

Stephen watched Mi Ling out of the corner of his eye while conversing with Blake. Her pleasure was evident. When Stephen would become animated, she would watch him closely while cleaning the pots and pans.

The flame from the oil burning lamp on the tikiwood table illuminated her figure, emphasizing the exquisite features of the honey-colored face. The reporter watched the shadows of the flame dance upon her brow, giving her a wicked appearance and yet, tempting, forbidden.

Mi Ling and Quang retired to their cots for the night while Stephen and Blake plotted their escape. The men checked the guns Quang had obtained on the black market, making sure the weapons were mechanically sound, no jams, and had sufficient ammunition. Blake loaded the jeep with provisions generously provided by his host.

Stephen limped to his cot, placed the cane on the dirt floor, and eased his weary body down. Blake extinguished the lamp and fell in the cot, turning on his side.

Periodic coughs disturbed the silent hut followed by unceremonious spits. Stephen was thankful Blake could not see the expression of disgust etched on his face. But the Vietnam vet couldn't help his condition.

The Thai moon floated rings of pale, white light through the open windows. Wild monkeys chattered in the distance, howling under the lunar illumination like a cabal of pagans worshipping their profane deity.

Stephen looked over at Quang and Mi Ling's cots. The cloth curtain was not drawn completely across. He could see Mi Ling peacefully sleeping, oblivious to the world's problems, content with her narrow life. He heard her faint breaths, in and out, and the delicate sounds soothed him. He rolled over, stopping momentarily to adjust the sore leg, and closed his eyes.

A burst of fire scorched the hut, blowing chunks out of the mud wall, propelling the journalist across the dirt floor and ramming him into the table. He shook his head and tried to regain his bearings. The hut was in flames, smoke billowing everywhere.

The thatch roof was on fire with pieces collapsing into the interior of the home. He tried to get up but was shaken from another blast outside the hut. He heard chilling screams while the rattle of automatic gunfire rang out. Pain clinched his leg and he fell back, hitting his head on the table.

He began to cough from smoke inhalation. The flames were more intense. Suddenly, he spied a rain of flaming palm leaves detach from the ceiling and fall toward him. He covered his head, trying to roll out of the way. But the table halted his momentum and the shower of flaming debris fell on top.

He screamed and slapped the burning palms away. He kicked at the hot debris, despite the pain which surged through his leg. The flames began burning into the shirt and pants. He could feel the excruciating agony of the heat lacerating his skin, a kind of pain for which there is no description.

Adrenaline coursed through his veins and the instinct of self–preservation overrode all other feelings. He concentrated his strength and kicked the table away, rolling on the dirt floor.

He grabbed handfuls and frantically spread it on the clothing. The cool dirt smothered the smoldering shirt and pants.

Stephen stumbled to his feet, feeling his way through the smoke-filled hut. He hit a clear patch of air and saw two men standing at the entrance, brandishing guns.

Another figure jumped out from behind the cloth curtain, hit the ground and began firing a gun at them. The men returned fire inside the hut. Stephen leaped across the room to dodge the gunfire as a hail of bullets rearranged the hut's interior. He covered his head as the bullets zinged by within mere inches.

He lay in the fetal position as bullets ripped into the mud walls and floor. He looked up and saw the man on the ground fire again, striking both men several times. They hit the ground, dead.

The figure rose and came toward him, the barrel of the gun still smoking; it was Blake. "Are you alright?"

"Yeah, I think so," he said, trying to catch his breath.

"C'mon, we've gotta go sooner than we wanted. They've come lookin' for us."

He grabbed Stephen's arm and helped him to his feet. He pointed to a huge hole in the wall. The hole was large enough to accommodate a human being; both men fled through it and around back of the hut.

The POW threw some bags into the parked jeep and gave Stephen a firearm. "Here. You'll need it. We're gonna make a break for it. Get ready cause there's still a lot of 'em out there. They'll shoot anything that moves."

The pilot got into the driver's side and turned the jeep's ignition key. The engine turned over several times, then hit and hummed. More explosions rocked the village. The Buddhist shrine collapsed in a ball of fire. Rapid gunfire resonated followed by bloodcurdling screams.

Stephen's head was clearing; he realized they had forgotten something in all the commotion: Mi Ling.

"Mi Ling and Quang!" he screamed to Blake. "We've gotta go back and get 'em."

"You can't! It's too late. They're dead. We've gotta go. They'll be on us in a matter of seconds."

"I'm not leaving her to die in this place!"

Stephen placed an index finger on the gun trigger and dashed back into the gabbing hole in Quang's hut. Flames greeted his entry and he frantically looked around while covering his face from the smoke.

The pain in the leg had disappeared, only thoughts of Mi Ling permeated his mind. He ripped back the burning cloth curtain and saw a limp figure lying across the cot. Two bullets penetrated the abdomen and chest, leaving in its wake only bloody holes the size of dimes. It was Mi Ling.

Stephen tried to revive her. He felt under her nose. Shallow breathing, a dim pulse. He put his arms under her back and legs, lifting the fallen woman, carrying her through the hole to the jeep.

"She's still alive" he yelled to Blake.

"Put her in the back."

Stephen gently placed the fragile cargo into the back end of the jeep. Mi Ling opened her eyes and looked at him. He smiled and spoke her name. He told her it would be okay though she understood nothing but the sound of her name.

She smiled back and lifted her hand toward his face, touching his cheek and lips with her nimble fingers, as if trying to understand him, communicate with him.

Then the golden hand fell by her side. A pall of darkness cast over the round face, and the breathing diminished. The vitality, the life force, in the dark almond eyes waned, then was extinguished.

Stephen cupped her face in both hands and tried to wake her. He grabbed Mi Ling by her shoulders and shook her violently. But the soul was gone, only the shell remained.

"Stephen! Stephen, dammit! She's gone man. We can't save her. We gotta go," Blake yelled, pulling the reporter's arms from Mi Ling.

"It wasn't suppose to work out this way. She was just an innocent bystander. For Christ's Sake, Blake! She died for nothing!"

"I know buddy, but we can't bring her back. Move over. Get in the jeep."

Blake picked Mi Ling up, her body still warm, and placed it on the ground beside the automobile. Stephen crawled into the passenger's side. Blake jumped into the driver's side and geared the jeep into first.

The journalist watched as Mi Ling's body grew smaller and smaller in the distance, just lying there among the burning huts. He remembered another person he left behind in the jungle except he was still alive, barely; his heart sickened, his soul was malignant with hate.

The jeep reached the outskirts of the village when three armed men jumped out of the bush and began firing. They ducked down and the front glass of the jeep shattered.

"We'll have to run 'em over!" Blake yelled as they crouched below the dashboard.

"I'll move the bastards outta the way" Stephen said calmly.

"Hey, wait a minute. What are you...."

Before the POW could finish the sentence, Stephen jumped up in the seat, firing rapidly as the jeep sped toward the assailants. The men returned fire but the journalist was unfazed; he didn't budge.

He kept the trigger depressed while fire and smoke erupted out of the barrel. Spent cartridges spewed out of the machine gun and piled up in the floor board.

Blake sheepishly peered over the dashboard and saw the three men fall one-by-one. He continued to fire the gun.

"Stephen, whoa, hey Stephen! They're dead. You got 'em. It's over. Sit down and relax."

He dropped into the seat and did not say a word, staring at the road with a blank expression, gripping the machine gun. Blake slowed the jeep slightly to anticipate the hump in the road from the dead bodies. The jeep rolled over one of the dead assassins with a mediocre bump.

The POW turned toward Stephen. He was still staring as if oblivious to what just happened. He worried he was going into shock. The pilot took him by the shoulder and gently shook him.

"Yah alright? It's okay. We made it."

"Uh-huh."

He returned his glazed eyes to the road, silent.

❁ ❁ ❁ ❁ ❁ ❁

The two Americans drove into the night, leaving behind the rubble of what had been a Thai village. Armstrong had again vented his wrath upon the village which rebuked him, except this time, he had succeeded in destroying it.

"What about Quang?"

"He ran outside to help defend the village. They had grenade launchers, that's how they blew that hole in the wall beside your cot. I ran out a few minutes later. Quang was in the middle of the street. One of the bastard's launched a grenade at him. Blew up right beside him, killing him instantly. I ran over but there was nothing left."

"I'm sorry Blake."

"He was a good friend, helped me out many times. You get few opportunities to make a genuine friend in this life, especially in a Vietnamese prison. I would have died in Dach Lu if it hadn't been for him. He showed me how to survive."

"You think the attack was planned by Armstrong?"

"Hell, yes. It was his hit squad. They were looking for you and those records. We should've left earlier."

"Wouldn't matter. They'd still have leveled the village and tortured everyone to death trying to find out where I was. How do you think Armstrong knew we were there? Maybe someone in the village snitched on us."

"I dunno that he did. He was probably doing a wide sweep of villages around the perimeter of Bangkok. Gave him an excuse to destroy those villages which had sided with Kuhn-Sah Duc."

Stephen stared out at the white headlights which illuminated the deserted road.

"I'm sorry we couldn't save Mi Ling. I could tell you cared about her, you made her feel special."

"What makes you say that?"

"Quang told me. Peasant girls are condemned to the material advantages of an arranged marriage. For what it's worth, her last few days were happy ones."

"It's funny what you remember about people. I knew her a few days and yet I felt she was as familiar to me as one of my own family. And I think she felt the same way. Tell me, why are you allowed to meet someone you instantly click with just to have that person taken away?"

Blake turned the steering wheel, easing the jeep onto another road.

"I dunno. Tell me why patriotic Americans who put their lives on the line are abandoned by their government to rot in a foreign prison, forever forgotten. Can you answer that?"

He looked over at the pilot, shook his head, then looked up at the stars hanging low in the night sky. The celestial bodies dotted the twilight canopy as far as the eye could see.

At least Mi Ling had been spared the rigors and hardships of life in the poppy groves, he thought, but perhaps that was wishful thinking, more to soothe his guilty feelings than express grief over her loss.

"Stephen?"

"Yes."

"Enough is enough. He killed Quang and Mi Ling. I can't leave without squaring things up. We can have our day in court anytime, but we'll never have this chance like we do now. Before we hop a freighter into the Gulf of Siam, I'm gonna finish this one way or the other. It's been going on for 25 years unresolved. No more murders. No more prisoners. No more drugs.

"I know you're not with me," Blake continued. "You can wait at the harbor. If I don't come back, hop a ship and get the hell out. You've got the records. It won't matter if I don't return. As far as the world is concerned, I died 25 years ago anyway. Don't try to talk me out of it. I've made up my mind and..."

"I won't," he interrupted. "I've made up my mind too."

"Huh?"

"You're right. We can have our day in court but getting justice is another matter. We both owe Armstrong. We owe him a lot. I can't leave Thailand in good conscience without settling this mess. Not now. It'd haunt me the rest of my life if I walked away without fighting. Let's pay him a visit."

"Listen, this is my decision. You don't have to go because of me: my life is over, yours isn't. Someone has to get the records back to the states and blow the cover on this CIA drug ring."

"We'll blow the cover but first, let's cut the head off the snake which runs the drug ring. I'll show ya the way to the U.S. Embassy."

Blake pulled the jeep off the dirt road and opened one of the bags in the back. He grabbed a change of clothes for him and Stephen; some traditional peasant clothing Quang had given him, so they would look inconspicuous in Bangkok. Blake shed the gray prison uniform, leaving it on the side of the road.

❀ ❀ ❀ ❀ ❀ ❀

At daybreak, the jeep entered the congested streets of Bangkok. Smog hovered over the urban landscape, compliments of Thailand's growing industrial base spurred by international investment. Bicycles and rickshaws crowded the streets. It took nearly two hours to find the harbor.

Blake stopped the dusty jeep on a dock and told Stephen to watch it. He put a pistol in his belt and stuffed some bhats—Thailand's currency—into his pocket and left to visit a sea captain Quang had recommended.

They parked along the banks of the Chao Phraya, dotted with numerous small boats and rafts, utilized by harbor laborers as dwellings. Siamese women huddled under paper parasols displaying foods in an open air market.

In the distance he could see the Wat Arun Buddhist temple, one of Bangkok's most famous religious shrines. The "Venice of the East" was dissected by numerous waterways throughout the metropolis.

Stephen watched the longshoremen load cargo into the freighters, keeping his finger on the trigger of the gun he had used to dispatch the three gunmen in the road.

He observed women working side-by-side with their husbands, loading sacks off a fork lift onto a wooden pallet, which was lifted by a crane and deposited into the bowel of a cargo ship.

He spied rice, tin, teak, rubber, salt, fish, tobacco, bird nests and animal hides being loaded into various freighters for export.

Blake returned and seemed to express an air of satisfaction.

"So what happened?"

"We hop the freighter tonight. I bribed the ship's captain. We set sail in the morning for the Philippines. We should arrive in Manilla Bay in about three days."

"Where'd ya get the money to bribe him?"

"Quang gave me the bhats. The captain will sneak us on board tonight under the nose of the port authorities."

"Maybe things are finally going our way."

"Well, there is one little thing."

"I'm listening."

"The ship runs on steam. We'll have to stay below the entire trip and shovel coal into the burners for fuel."

"What? We pay this guy and he's gonna use us as free labor shoveling coal and we can't go above during those three days."

"Understand, we're stowaways. That's illegal. We've really got no choice if we want out of this damn place. It won't be so bad, it's only three days."

"Man, I can't believe this shit. I hate this country. We pay him for the privilege to ride on the boat and he puts us to work."

"Like the captain said, we've gotta stay below deck so we're not seen. By working below in the boiler room, few people of any consequence will see us. This is a backwards country Stephen and people take advantage of you. In three days, we'll be in Manilla and almost home free."

"I won't feel safe until we touch American soil."

The two men arrived at the gray stucco, two-story building which housed the U.S. Embassy, parking the jeep just out of view of the front entrance.

"We need a plan. I don't know if Armstrong will have some of his goons in there or not. When Paul and I were here, there was only one person on staff."

"Here, take this pistol. You walk into the front entrance. I'll take the AK-47, go around back and see if I can get in."

Stephen casually walked to the front entrance, past the bronze plate which read "United States Embassy." He took a deep breath, steadied his nerves, and placed his hand on the pistol butt sticking inside the pants. The gun was there, loaded; everything was in place.

A trickle of sweat beaded on his forehead and rolled down his cheek. He wiped it away and grasped the knob of the door. His heart was pounding and he could actually feel it thumping against his chest. He turned the knob slowly and pushed the door opened.

❀ ❀ ❀ ❀ ❀ ❀

He walked into the foyer, trying desperately to stay calm. He saw Felix Berger at the front desk. He approached. Berger looked up from the papers scattered across the desk.

"You!"

Stephen withdrew the pistol, pointing it in the embassy employee's face.

"Don't say a word. If you even so much as breathe hard, I'll blow your brains out. Understand?"

Berger nodded quickly and held his hands up. Stephen motioned with the pistol to walk into a back room while he followed behind.

"Get down on your knees."

Berger dropped to his knees and put his hands behind his head. Stephen struck him behind the head with the butt of the firearm. He slumped down face first on the floor.

He quietly made his way down the hall toward Armstrong's office. At the end of the hall stood two double doors displaying a plate that declared the deputy secretary of state's name and title.

He ran toward the doors, leaping into the air and kicking the right door off its hinges. The door collapsed and fell inside the office.

Stephen landed on his feet like a cat and sprinted into the spacious suite holding the pistol in both hands. Armstrong was sitting behind his desk, like a snake curled up in his lair, caught off guard by the reporter's intrusion.

The deputy secretary of state was holding a cigarette in one hand while punching in numbers on a fax machine with the other. The surprise vanished from his face as he stared at Stephen. Then a smile crept across the lined face.

"Well, well. Isn't this a twist. The pigeon has come to the fox. I've been looking all over Thailand for you and here you come to me. You've saved me a lot of work Mr. Decatur. I appreciate your kindness."

"Shut up asshole. We thought a little visit would catch you by surprise."

"We? Is that mystery gunman who killed Wong and saved your ass here too?"

"Don't worry about it."

Armstrong dropped his right arm by his side. Stephen's sight was partially deflected because of the desk. Sitting in the chair, he eased his hand beside the small holster around his ankle, pulling out a snub-nosed revolver. He held it in his right hand just below the desk.

"Who is he? Tell me."

"He's an escaped POW who's gonna blow the lid off your operation here in Southeast Asia."

"Ahhh. A POW. He must be from Dach Lu. Where is he?"

Stephen did not answer but shifted nervously back and forth, keeping the pistol stiffly pointed at the deputy secretary of state.

Armstrong crushed out the cigarette, rose from the chair and began walking around the desk, still concealing the revolver by his side.

"Hold it goddammit or I'll shoot!"

Armstrong continued around the desk.

Stephen squeezed the trigger. At that very moment, the deputy secretary of state extended his right arm with the agility of a leopard, revealing the revolver. The reporter's shot missed, striking the back wall.

Armstrong returned a shot at the startled journalist, who reactively flung his body to the floor the moment he saw the gun. The bullet grazed his shoulder; he hit the floor and began to roll, firing. Bullets struck the desk.

Armstrong fled toward the double doors, jumping over the broken down one. Stephen fired, striking the door but the ex-CIA agent was gone. He felt a burning sensation in his shoulder. He put his hand inside his shirt collar and withdrew blood.

He got up and ran toward the broken door, peering out into the hall, the pistol extended in front of him. Nothing. Cautiously, he hopped over the fallen door, walking beside the entrance of each room off the hall, ducking in quickly, searching it, keeping the firearm in front of him everywhere he went.

He walked out into the foyer where Berger's desk was located. He saw nothing. He kept low and scrambled behind the desk. Where was he hiding? What had happened to Blake?

He decided to go upstairs. He groped to the staircase and peered up to the top; then took a deep breath, pistol extended, and quietly began climbing each step one-by-one.

Gunfire erupted. He immediately fell to the staircase. The exchange was coming from the second floor. He ran up the steps, reached the top and stopped; the gunfire ceased. He looked around, holding the pistol in trembling hands. Then, some kind of commotion. It was coming from the next room over.

He entered the room. Blake was on the floor, lying up against the wall. Armstrong was standing over him with the revolver, about to pull the trigger. Furniture and filing cabinets were overturned and spilled. Both men were cut and bleeding.

"Hold it Armstrong!" Stephen yelled.

The deputy secretary of state slowly turned toward the journalist, the revolver still in his hand. A red line of blood trickled from the corner of his nose.

"I want those records, Decatur."

Blake dived at Armstrong, tackling him in the legs. Both men fell to the floor.

Stephen couldn't shoot, the figures were too closely intertwined on the floor. Armstrong struck first, hitting the POW in the face with the revolver.

He got to his feet and pointed the gun at the fallen Vietnam vet. A shot rang out. Armstrong dropped his gun, stumbled, then turned around.

Stephen was standing behind him, white smoke rising from his pistol barrel. He staggered but kept his eyes on the journalist. He reached out a hand and stumbled toward him.

Stephen squeezed the trigger again. Another discharge pierced Armstrong's chest, blood spattering across his suit. He staggered backwards, then fell, hitting the floor, motionless.

"Are you all right?"

"Yeah, I'm okay." Blake wiped the blood from his mouth and coughed violently.

"I didn't see you come in. I thought something had happened."

"I couldn't find a way into the rear of the building so I ran around the front and entered. That's when I saw Armstrong running upstairs." Blake coughed again. "I followed him. He jumped me and we fought. He knocked me over the head with a chair. That's when you walked in. He was about to kill me. I guess we're even now."

"Even?"

"I saved you from Armstrong, now you returned the favor."

They heard a creak in the floor just outside the door of the room. A trembling, pasty-white hand appeared, clasping the inside of the door from the outside. The door began to open slowly.

Stephen raised the pistol. The door opened completely, revealing the owner of the pasty-white hand. It was Felix Berger. He was conscious. He saw the gun and froze, the whites of his eyes becoming large. He threw his hands in the air.

Stephen exhaled a breath of relief. Blake rolled his eyes. But the reporter noticed something caught Berger's eye. He seemed to look right through the two men and across the room, focusing on some object.

Stephen saw a figure stirring out of the corner of his eye. He turned and spied Armstrong. The deputy secretary of state had somehow crawled to his revolver and picked it up.

"Blake, look out!" he screamed.

The Vietnam vet instinctively hit the floor as Armstrong squeezed off a shot. The bullet missed Blake and struck Berger in the shoulder. The embassy employee fell back into the hallway.

Stephen grabbed Blake by the arm and pulled him behind a filing cabinet. Armstrong stumbled out of the room. The ex-CIA agent ran past the wounded Berger and made his way to the stairs. The journalist and POW pursued. Stephen reached him as he was about to descend the staircase.

"Armstrong!" he screamed.

The deputy secretary of state spun around at the top of the stairs, aiming the revolver back at the pursuing reporter. But he was poised and fired before Armstrong could pull the trigger. The bullet struck him in the forehead, just above the left eye.

He instantly dropped the gun and fell back, his body tumbling down the entire flight of stairs. The pair ran to the top of the staircase and peered down. Armstrong was at the bottom, dead.

❁ ❁ ❁ ❁ ❁ ❁

The men, now political fugitives, fled the U.S. Embassy and made their way to the Bangkok harbor. Neither looked back, only ahead to the journey that awaited them.

The pair grabbed their gear and found the sea captain on the dock beside the freighter, dressed in a dark turtle neck shirt and white skipper's cap.

He sneaked them aboard the cargo ship without notice. It seemed everyone in Thailand in any position of authority operated on a system of graft and bribery.

The men descended into the bowels of the vessel, level through level, until they reached the boiler room, a musty inferno of coal air and hot iron.

"I see why they call it the boiler room," Stephen said, a look of disgust etched on his face. "It's hotter than four hells down here."

The captain barked some orders to Blake and threw down two shovels, pointing to the heaps of coal he wanted thrown into the furnaces to fuel the ship.

"This ain't no pleasure cruise. I get the feeling if we don't do as he says, Captain Bligh there will make us walk the plank."

"You can bet your ass we'll be lost at sea if we don't do as he orders," Blake replied, thrusting a shovel blade into the coal pile. "They could care less about human life over here, he'd just as soon dump us overboard. I don't want to end up shark bait after getting this far. It's not all bad. He promised to bring two meals a day in exchange for the jeep."

"Wow, great deal. Our task master is going to feed his galley slaves. Are you sure we can trust 'em?"

"No. But we don't have much choice. Anywhere is better than here."

"True. We can't stay in Thailand or Southeast Asia for that matter."

"Right. So let's be thankful we're getting the hell out. Shoveling coal for me isn't much different from picking poppies."

The sea captain returned to the dock, meeting with a dim figure behind a fork lift. They spoke for several minutes and money was exchanged. Satisfied, the captain returned to the ship.

The men worked one furnace while several native laborers stoked an entire line of furnaces, yelling and gibbering back and forth to each other, oblivious of the two Americans. The hellish furnaces belched flaming debris while the smoke and heat rose up the pipes, generating precious steam.

"I wonder what's gonna happen when American authorities discover Armstrong?" Stephen asked, wiping his blackened face with a sweat stained shirttail.

"Who cares."

"Felix Berger can put the finger on us. We walked out of the embassy and forgot about him. He may be alive."

"I don't think it'll matter. Certain levels of the American government don't want something like that to go public. All the drug ring stuff and POWs would come out. Those involved in the Golden Triangle don't want his death investigated."

"Yeah. Armstrong's renegade CIA buddies will probably think it's a drug hit by Kuhn-Sah Duc or something like that. Maybe write it off as just another casualty in the drug war and go on."

"Let's hope so," the pilot replied, shoveling a pile of coal into the furnace. "Nobody else knows about those records of yours, do they?"

"I don't think so. The people I was aware of who knew are dead: Laramie, Paul and now Armstrong."

Drenched in sweat, the two Americans continued to shovel loads of the black rock into the iron monstrosity for hours. Stephen's eyebrows felt scorched; his skin singed from the boiler. He rested periodically due to the stinging shoulder, a stark reminder of what he left behind in Bangkok.

Echoes of anchors being hoisted rumbled off the iron hull, penetrating the bowel. The metallic hulk began to shutter, then slowly ease out of the Bangkok harbor, carrying its booty of rubber, teak and tin along with assorted contraband toward the Philippines.

Rumbles of waves swirling off the hull emanated within the boiler room. Finally, they were sea born, heading away from Thailand, into the Gulf of Siam and toward the murky waters of the South China Sea.

Hours passed in the sweat shop; Blake was slowing down. Stephen feared he might collapse from heat exhaustion. Suddenly, the POW dropped the shovel, bent down, placing his hands on knees, trying to catch his breath.

"Hey, take it easy. Sit over there and rest. C'mon man, rest. The captain's above, he won't see you."

"Yeah, okay," he whispered through puffs of breath. He collapsed on the black metal floor, lying flat on his back and coughing.

"Just relax. I'll do the work, no problem."

The Americans took turns in shifts stoking the boilers of the steam ship along with eight laborers. They slept on dirty cots located along the inside hatch of the coal room.

The excessive heat made slumber almost impossible, except for periodic exits into sleep for short intervals of time. Stephen performed the brunt of the work. He worried Blake would take ill if subjected to anymore harsh conditions.

But the unbearable temperatures and contaminated air forced him to surface; he decided to go up top and see the ocean. He would take the POW along; the ocean air would be good for him, he figured.

Stephen decided to prow above during nightfall, when their shift ended, under the cover of darkness. Blake protested but his cough worsened due to the foul air. He realized the reporter was right, ocean air might help clear his lungs.

The sea captain was good to his word regarding the two meals a day though the selection was questionable. Each day at noon and evening a first mate would bring some kind of gruel for them to eat. It was a grainy slop, composed of leftovers from the ship's galley.

The other laborers gave harsh looks of jealousy, forced to bring along their own crappy food for the trip.

"Hold you nose. Here comes the ship's household garbage," Stephen said as the captain's first mate plunked down two bowls of slop at their feet. He gave them a look of contempt, disgusted at the thought of providing food to foreigners.

"This stuff's as bad as prison food."

"Have you still got the guns hidden?" the journalist asked, between mouthfuls of gruel.

"Yeah, under the cots where you put the records."

"We gotta be prepared when we disembark. Armstrong's buddies could be waiting in Manilla. Hell, they may have the same set up in the Philippines using United Nations money to peddle drugs.

"We'll be ready. I've still got enough ammunition to last us for a good while."

"What are we gonna do when we get to the Philippines. Do you want to try and hop another freighter?"

"Nope. I've gotta better idea."

❀ ❀ ❀ ❀ ❀ ❀

"What?"

"I know a few of the air strips around Manilla since I was there at the U.S. base for a while during the war. I got familiar with the air transportation. Hopefully, it hasn't changed much. We'll get a plane, much faster than going by boat."

"Yeah. We could hire someone to fly us."

"Nah. The bhats Quang gave me are almost gone. Not enough left for that."

"So how are we gonna fly?"

"I'm gonna fly. Remember, I'm a Air Force pilot."

"Do you remember how? I mean, it's been 25 years."

Blake placed the bowl of gruel down.

"Of course. It's like riding a bike, you never forget. I could do it in my sleep."

"Yeah but since we got no money, how are we gonna get a plane for Christ's Sake? It's great you can fly but it doesn't mean diddly-squat without wings. We'll have to sneak on another freighter."

"We'll steal a plane."

"Mmm. I dunno. We've already killed a prominent U.S. government official in Thailand. I obtained sensitive records in Vietnam which could expose a conspiracy in the American government. Now you want us to steal a plane from the Philippines. The entire world will be after our ass."

"Relax. It's easy. Thefts go on like that all the time. I can hot wire a plane and we'll be up in the air before the air traffic controllers know what happened."

"Can you navigate and tell what direction we need to go? There's a lot of damn Pacific Ocean to cross."

"I can do it. I was trained for that. I know the islands and can estimate our fuel supply and coordinate it with the available air strips across the Pacific."

Stephen put down his bowl and got to his feet. He motioned Blake upstairs. "C'mon, let's go up top."

"If we get caught...."

"Chill partner. It'll be good for both of us."

Stephen looked around. Several of the laborers were asleep in cots. Three others were stoking the furnaces. They slipped out of the boiler room into another area through the hatch. They climbed up a metal stairwell into another level.

They saw no one. Stephen preceded up the next stairwell with Blake bringing up the rear. The POW stopped, placing his hand over his mouth and coughed.

"Shhh," Stephen warned.

"Sorry."

They continued climbing up the stairwell. The journalist could hear the wind and ocean clearly now; they were close.

They entered the top deck and Stephen slowly opened a hatch, turning the iron wheel to release the doorway. He pushed and the door popped; fresh air seeped into the cracked opening.

He pushed the metal hunk back and stepped out, into the open air while Blake followed. The wind rushed across his face and through his hair, invigorating and life-giving. The pilot stepped up to the metal railing harnessed along the side of the ship, gulping in the fresh sea air.

The shimmering ocean was barely perceptible under the dull moonlight. They heard the crash of water split by the freighter's hull as it propelled forward while sea spray lightly powdered their faces. It was as if they had come up for air, lungs bursting, after being submerged for an eternity.

The fresh air filled Stephen's nostrils as he peered down into the murky depths below. The fog horn of the ship blared out into the night, startling the two sight seers. The face of the moon was partially covered by a cloud bank; the yellow orb would appear, then disappear, as the misty smoke traveled across it.

They could periodically perceive the vast expanse of the South China Sea when the hazy lunar illumination broke through the clouds. The musty smell of the salty sea spoke of teeming fish and other marine life.

Both leaned against the railing, drinking in the sights and smells like newborn babes exploring their environment for the first time. Even Blake's coughing seemed to diminish as the salt air purified his corrupted lungs.

They did not speak for several minutes but quietly enjoyed the pleasure of the ocean under the blanket of twilight. The Thai freighter moved on, cutting through the South China Sea like a hot knife through butter.

Stephen held the railing, watching the myriad of moonbeams dance upon the ocean waves. The wind howled, the waves roared. The mixture of sea and air relaxed them, triggering memories, invoking areas to reminiscence. The freelance journalist spoke to his companion.

"Where ya from?"

"Iowa. Once, a long time ago, I called it home. I had a life there. You?"

"Georgia. Do you have a wife and kids?"

"No. Only my parents back home in Ames. If they're still alive."

"You must be pretty cynical about the government, what with being abandoned and dealing with Armstrong."

Blake gave a sarcastic laugh. "I was cynical before I got captured and left behind. Secretary of Defense Robert McNamara had passed down the word not to make any long range plans. The war would be over by June 1966, five years before I got shot down. What a joke."

The POW rested his chin in his hand, leaning against the railing, staring out over the body of water known as the South China Sea.

"How does the American public remember the war?"

The reporter shook his head. "Not good, a war we lost. Lotta opposition and protests against it."

"I remember. Even before I went MIA, I knew victory was impossible. This war wasn't like our others. Funny thing is we had some spectacular battles like the battle of Hue. Our men fought with courage and bravery same as in World War II. But Vietnam wasn't Europe. It wouldn't be honored like World War II. Nor would the soldiers who fought in it."

It was amazing, Colonel Blake McDermott—locked away 25 years—predicted the legacy of the Vietnam War without historical perspective, without hesitation. He just knew, deep down in his guts.

"Yeah. Washington, D.C. will make ya damn cynical," Stephen said, watching the Asian moon. "I came out of journalism school on a crusade, wanted to work in the big time—a national newspaper. Shine the light on corruption. Well, I got it. But it wasn't what I thought. The mainstream media I so worshipped is nothing more than the fourth branch of government."

"What'd ya mean fourth branch?"

"We publish PR releases from the federal government, rewrite 'em and pop on our bylines. No in-depth analysis, no investigative journalism, just endorse government policies and programs. I tell ya how mainstream the media is. The major media outlets present the same perspective, same slant, they never disagree among themselves. That means the same puppet master is pulling their strings."

"The government."

"Yep."

"I was like you. I became disillusioned too. I lost my idealism, my youth. All I have left is my hate. That's the only thing that keeps me alive Stephen. My hate keeps me goin'."

He stared at the POW. There was no hostility in his voice, only a matter-of-fact tone.

Suddenly, a light pierced the darkness and shown on the two men. It was a flashlight glaring in their faces. They heard a foreign voice. It was the captain. He had discovered them.

Blake responded in the captain's native language but judging from the noise level and tone of the conversation, Stephen perceived he was losing the argument. The captain pushed Blake toward the hatch.

"Hey, wait a damn minute," Stephen yelled. He grabbed the captain by the arm.

"It's okay Stephen, it's okay. Leave him alone. Let's get back to the boiler room."

"Are you sure? This bastard is pushing you around."

"He's just mad at us for breaking the rules. C'mon, let's go."

The captain pushed the reporter, yelling at him in that funny foreign tongue. The journalist looked at him with blood in his eyes and raised back a fist. Blake caught his hand.

"No! It'll ruin everything. They'll throw us overboard. This is our only chance of getting back. One more day. We'll be in Manilla tomorrow."

Stephen took his eyes away from the antagonizing captain and focused them on the POW. Blake nodded. He lowered his fist and turned toward the hatch.

They descended into the boiler room while the captain followed, yelling and waving the flashlight about.

❀ ❀ ❀ ❀ ❀ ❀

As the freighter sailed into Manilla Bay its massive horn blared the arrival of its cargo to the island country known as the Philippines. The men stopped their shoveling and listened intently. The horn heralded the completion of their journey; they had reached their destination.

Smiles cracked across their dirty faces. It felt strange to smile; a queer but welcomed feeling. The iron hulk docked in the bay's harbor with the aid of anchors and gigantic ropes tied to the docking rails.

The captain's first mate entered the boiler room, set up a table and began distributing wages to the Thai laborers. Blake shook his head at the minimal currency, telling Stephen the men were ripped off for the amount of work they performed.

Each laborer left one by one, intent upon catching another ship destined for Thailand, to shovel coal again for a pitiful few pieces of coin while dreaming of home. After the blackened workers departed, Blake spoke to the first mate about leaving.

He nodded and swept his hands at them, indicating he wanted them to leave immediately. They looked at each other and again, smiles broke out across their black faces; then abruptly, ran to the cots and gathered their belongings.

A blur of figures climbed the stairwells, ascending each level until they penetrated the deck; a flash of powerful sunlight struck their eyes and blinded them momentarily. Spots appeared, then dissipated after adjusting to the new environment.

Stephen spied the busy hum of commerce along the harbor; ships coming and going, being unloaded, goods transported by fork lift, goods being removed from one ship, placed in another. Filipino workers scurried along the dock, loading and unloading freight.

Blake elbowed him. "C'mon. I think I know where a small airstrip is." The men descended the ship's platform onto the dock and waved good-bye to their iron prison of three days.

A dark figure stirred near them, in the shadows of a large warehouse located centrally on the dock, used to temporarily store cargo from incoming ships.

Longshoremen walked in and out of the warehouse while forklifts carrying an assortment of Asian goods hummed back and forth inside the structure.

But the shadowy figure stood inside the warehouse, on the left side of its entrance, hidden in the shade, peering at the two gaunt figures as they discussed their travel plans in the noonday sun.

He watched as Blake pointed down the harbor at something. The journalist nodded. Both men began walking in that direction. The figure disappeared into the warehouse.

The last of the bhats were spent acquiring a taxi. Thankfully Filipino drivers accepted the foreign coin with relish. The bombed-out Renault—an obvious reject from a French assembly line—drove over the potholes in Manilla, around the bay and toward the airstrip Blake had described to the taxi driver.

The young man seemed to know it and readily accepted the cash offer to take them there. Loud, obnoxious rock music blared from the car radio, some kind of Filipino version of Billy Idol. The kid wore an earring and sported greased-back hair. His dark, oily head bounced to and fro to the beat of the song.

Trash and debris littered the vehicle. An abundant crop could be grown in the fine top soil that had accumulated in the floor boards. The doors and arm rests were dark with sweat and dirt. Stephen noticed stains from soft drinks and God knows what else on the seats and dashboard.

They left Manilla and drove into a mango grove. Just beyond the grove, a dirt strip could be seen with an accompanying building and hangar. Red wind socks flopped in the air.

The taxi driver pointed and rapidly fired off Filipino words which left Stephen clueless. Blake nodded in approval, saying something which seemed to please him. Mission accomplished, the driver had not screwed up the destination.

He pulled the Renault around to the building, a pathetic excuse for an air tower. It was a block building, painted white but no tower overhead; simple paneless windows open to the dirt strip—a modest 5,000 feet in length, plenty to get a small aircraft into the air. Blake said so.

The POW paid the greasy-headed punk rocker, who smiled, revealing a row of gray teeth. He drove off in a cloud of dust, leaving the two men looking at the white building. No one seemed to be around.

Blake spotted a mechanic working on a small single engine wreck. They walked around the white building and cautiously peered into the open windows. Nothing. Not a stir.

"This is good," Blake whispered. "Not many here. We can get away with a minimum of observation or resistance." Spoken like a true soldier, Stephen thought.

Another vehicle quietly pulled up beyond the white block building. A passenger got out. He walked to the front of the vehicle and placed his right foot on the bumper, raising a pant leg. Carefully, he placed an object along his lily white calf and released the pant leg.

He put his foot down and motioned the driver. The car slowly backed out. The man crept toward the white block building.

"I don't see any good planes except that junk there by the strip." Stephen seemed displeased. "And a mechanic is working on it. There's nothing here we can go up in."

Blake pointed to the silvery metal hangar. They crept toward the rear of it, out of the sight of the Filipino mechanic. Blake looked around the corner of the building. The mechanic was now under the plane, twisting a wrench around something.

He waved forward and both men, staying low, ran around the front of the hangar and entered. They were startled to find a young boy staring them down, face-to-face. Stephen looked at Blake. Blake looked at Stephen. The Filipino kid looked at them.

Suddenly, the youth let out a yell but was caught in mid-sentence by the POW's quick hand, which cupped around the brat's mouth. Stephen grabbed his legs. They carried the squirming kid to the back of the hangar, where they tied him up with wire and gagged his mouth with a greasy rag. Stephen tossed him in a tool locker.

He wiped his hands, satisfied and turned around to Blake.

"So much for that."

But Blake wasn't there. He looked around the hangar, sudden panic gripping him.

❁ ❁ ❁ ❁ ❁ ❁

"Blake? Blake?"

No answer.

He walked around the wreckage of a twin-engine Gulfstream. Still nothing. Then he saw an airplane door open and a head inside the cockpit. It was Blake. He climbed into the plane.

"What the hell is wrong with you? Leaving me like that."

But he wasn't listening. He just stared at panels and fondled switches.

Stephen looked at the plane's instrument board. To the novice eye, it resembled high-tech machinery out of a science fiction movie. He looked at Blake. His face displayed a dreamy look, like having been reunited with a long, lost lover.

"Did you hear me?"

Finally, he turned and acknowledged him. "What? I'm sorry. I wasn't listening. Never mind. It doesn't matter. Would you look at this. Just look at it."

He waved his hands over the instrument board like a magician with a wand.

"Yeah, so?"

"So? Stephen, this is our ticket out. It's perfect! An amphibian with a full tank of gas. I took a look at the engine while you were stashing the kid. It's beautiful, just beautiful. This baby's in excellent shape and its going to take us home."

The journalist smiled and looked at the instrument board again. Now he understood. Yes, this was a long, lost lover. He fondled the dashboard too.

"What is it?"

"Grumman G21 Goose. It's gotta cruising speed of about 190 miles per hour."

"It can land on water or land?"

"Yep. It's the oldest model of Grumman's amphibians but it'll do the trick. Got a wingspan of about 49 feet, length of around 38 feet. If I remember right, the Goose was built in the late 30s to late 40s. It's such as old design that many of the characteristics on this plane have changed. Look, the cockpit and fuselage windows have been altered. The old radials replaced by turboprops. I noticed it has retractable floats that fold up and become part of the wing surface in flight, that wasn't on the originals."

"How do you know so much about this Goose plane?"

"I use to fly one similar to this. I'd recognize the Grumman G21 Goose anywhere despite the modifications. The angle-out engine position is what gives it away. I still see the Grumman origins, its old-fashioned boat lines. Fully rounded tail planes and fin. Twin engines that angle out from the centerline of the aircraft. It can hold about six passengers."

"So it'll be easy for you to fly this thing then?"

Blake panned an insulted expression as if asked to recite the alphabet.

"Of course. This is turning out better than I thought. Damn, does this bring back memories. Grumman use to make the Navy's A-6 Intruders and EA-6 Prowlers. That was the Navy's basic all night, all-weather bomber, used since 1960. Kinda like our newer Air Force 111s we used for night precision bombing."

Blake ducked under the instrument board without a word. After about 20 minutes of fiddling with screws and wires, he emerged and began flipping switches. Lights on the panel lit up and the Goose G21 starting powering up.

He had not lost his touch, the hot wire was complete. Now if only he could still fly. There was thousands of miles of water between them and the United States. Stephen said a prayer under his breath, then his jaw dropped.

A figure was standing at the entrance of the hangar, smiling, like a ghost from the past.

"Who the hell is that? Shit, we've been discovered."

Blake looked at Stephen, then back at the man. The figure walked toward the plane but Stephen did not make a move. He seemed paralyzed as if he didn't believe his eyes.

"What's wrong? Do you know him?"

"It's a friend," he mumbled, leaving the cockpit.

Paul Mathis climbed inside the plane and looked at his old friend with a sly smile. Stephen stared, shook his head and looked again. The same picture.

He rubbed his eyes but Paul didn't disappear in a puff of smoke, it was no mirage. He was standing right in front of him, eyeball to eyeball. The ghost even spoke.

"Well, are you gonna say anything? Like you're glad to see me."

"My God. Paul, it's really you. I thought you were dead. How . . . . How did you find me? Where have you been?" Questions clouded the journalist's mind.

Blake stepped out of the cockpit. Paul gave him a funny look. Blake stopped beside Stephen, not saying a word. He watched the video journalist quietly.

Stephen grabbed his friend, hugging his neck.

"I'll be damn, you got away from 'em. I thought they killed you. Paul, I'm sorry I didn't get you outta the car. I tried, you've gotta believe me, I tried. I felt miserable. The Bangkok police picked me up in the alley and threw me in jail."

Paul swatted his shoulder. "It's okay. They didn't hurt me. I know you tried. It was impossible to save me."

Blake continued to stare at the resurrected video journalist as if struggling to pass judgement upon something. Paul's eyes darted toward Blake and then back to Stephen.

"How'd you escape?"

Paul's eyes continued to move toward the gaunt POW, then return to Stephen. Blake stepped forward, pointing an index finger at Paul. "It's you. I know you, don't I?"

"What?" Stephen looked at Blake. "You're imagining things. This is my friend Paul Mathis I told you about. You know, the one I thought had been killed by Armstrong's goons. He was with me when they nabbed us in the motel in Bangkok. I got away but Paul was captured."

But the American POW was adamant. He shook his finger at Paul. "No! I do know you. I saw you at Dach Lu."

Paul remained silent, his eyes shot back to a perplexed Stephen.

"What the hell are you talking about? Blake, no offense but you were at Dach Lu a long time. Maybe prison affected your memory. This is Paul Mathis, my friend and colleague."

"I know who he is!" Blake was animated, his eyes got big, the expression manic, as if recognition was complete. "It's you! I can't believe it. You sorry son-of-a-bitch, I'm gonna kill ya!"

He stepped toward Paul, then suddenly stopped and whipped around to Stephen. His expression rapidly changed to dismay.

"You're in on this, aren't you? This has all been a damn trap, hasn't it? You're nothing but a plant for the drug ring."

"You've lost your mind. I don't know what you're talking about. This is a mistake. You've got Paul mixed up with someone else. Knock it off, you're scaring me."

"When I shot Armstrong's goon and saved you at the mango grove, it was all a setup, wasn't it? You been playing me like a violin. You're part of Armstrong's traffickers."

"Blake, I killed Armstrong. You saw me do it. How can you say I'm a part of the CIA drug ring?"

"To take his place. Goddamn! How could I be so stupid? You used me to get to Armstrong. I know how it works, each drug kingpin knocking off the competition like all those poppy wars between Armstrong and Kuhn-Sah Duc.

"Sure, you pulled the trigger but you've got the perfect cover. A deranged POW attacks a deputy secretary of state because he thinks he was left behind by his government and then tries to escape to the Philippines. I'm gonna take the rap for his murder after you kill me."

Stephen was speechless. Blake walked toward him, hatred boiling up in his face, but stopped as shiny blue steel took center stage. Paul had reached down and taken a pistol from an ankle holster.

"What are you doing?" Stephen asked, totally muddled.

"Stephen, I want Laramie's records."

The journalist gave his friend a bizarre look. Paul did not react, no facial expression, no nothing, just the cold stare of a pistol greeted him. He slowly walked into the cockpit and returned with the envelope.

"Careful. Be very careful."

Stephen slid the envelope over to him.

"Walk slowly outta the plane. If you make one wrong move, I'll fill ya full of air. Now move."

The POW did not budge. Paul aimed the pistol at Blake's head.

"Paul, I don't understand any of this." Stephen stepped closer to his friend but he turned the pistol away from Blake and toward him.

"That's right Stephen. You don't understand. You never did. Now raise your hands where I can see 'em and step out of the plane slowly, v-e-r-y slowly."

They stepped down from the Goose G21 and out into the hangar. A cool breeze blew into the metal structure. The sun cast a bright haze through its open entrance. They stopped, knelt on the floor and put their hands behind their heads as instructed.

"Why Paul, why?"

"Heroin controlled me. Being a junkie is the lowest form of life. But I got saved, shown a better way. Now I control it and heroin's made me rich beyond my wildest dreams. We're all addicts Steve in one form or the other. From the tobacco companies to the pharmaceutical industry to the caffeine in your coffee. Pick your poison."

"All these years, lying to me, carrying on a charade of being a reformed addict. You damned hypocrite."

"Me a hypocrite? Hardly. Heroin is illegal because it competes against pharmaceutical and alcohol companies for chemical dependents. Those industries have access to Congress because of their money. Therefore, they make the laws. One drug is called legal, another illegal.

"I deal to the street junkie," he continued. "A doctor prescribes Prozac to a ten-year-old kid, and gets him hooked. He can't get through the day without it. The analogy's the same. The farmer in Southeast Asia grows opium poppies. The American farmer grows tobacco. It's their livelihoods. Both addict and hurt. So what? It has nothing to do with right or wrong. It's just business. Because I chose to traffick narcotics doesn't make me a bad person."

"You're pathetic, Paul."

"And you're ignorant, Stephen. More people die of misprescribed drugs from licensed physicians than illicit ones. This 'war on drugs' is a hoax. It's the same as the Prohibition frenzy of the 1920s and 30s. The government is protecting its tax take on alcohol, tobacco and pharmaceuticals while using property forfeiture statutes to seize assets. It's got nothing to do with protecting the public. Far from it."

"It still doesn't excuse you."

Paul looked at his colleague, impatient and uneasy, then stared off into the distance. He seemed reluctant to speak anymore, at least to Stephen. Anyone but him, he would never accept it.

He groped for a response but an increasing sense of humiliation, of being exposed and laid open to an intimate friend, angered him. The real Paul Mathis was now naked in the sunlight while years of fraud and deceit melted away in the Pacific humidity.

"You're too damned naive for yer own good. Perfect for the media but not business. This is more than drugs or murder or misappropriation of funds. It's about power, leverage, having what you want now instead of talking about it."

The journalist and POW were quiet.

"You and McDermott are full of surprises. We never thought you two would get as far as you have. We certainly never thought you'd kill Richard."

"He use to visit Dach Lu with Armstrong," Blake said calmly. "He's as much involved as Armstrong."

Stephen returned the glare to the man holding the pistol, wondering if he really ever knew him; the revelation began taking hold: this friend and co-worker was a complete stranger, years of friendship, down the tubes, living a lie. Paul Mathis had perpetuated a false identity, hid his true self from everyone, no small accomplishment.

"I wish I could have remained dead Stephen. It would have been better for everyone."

"All these years we worked together at the newspaper. I never knew you. We were friends, colleagues. But all that time you were working undercover for this CIA drug ring in Southeast Asia."

"Working in the media was the perfect cover, useful too. The CIA employs numerous contract players in the national news media to help its image and perpetuate propaganda beneficial to the agency. My work involved covering the tracks of the POWs and making sure the image of the Golden Triangle remained a gook-run business, with no hint of American involvement."

"And I suppose soften up the American public to accept the elimination of the trade embargo."

"We educate the public, set the media agenda, create the issues and public opinion. We've worked hard on the select committee hearings to close the book on Vietnam POWs. It's important to our interests. Your little escapade would have screwed all that up. But it's a done deal now. Senator Bainbridge and Simpson have fixed things."

"What about Bainbridge? Is the committee chairman purchased too?"

"We pumped a lot of money into his campaigns. He would've been nothing but a peon bank vice president had it not been for us. We bankrolled his political career."

"Who's Simpson?"

"Ahh. He'll clinch the deal for us. The trade embargo may already be lifted thanks to him."

"Why in the hell get me involved in the first place?" Stephen asked.

"You were key in our plan for getting close to Jim Laramie. You see, we knew he had the records from Kuhn-Sah Duc. I needed you to help me infiltrate his group without suspicion. He'd been around Southeast Asia for years causing us headaches. You played the part of the crusading journalist brilliantly, helped me gain his confidence."

"You had plenty of opportunities to kill Laramie yourself."

"I didn't know what Laramie had done with the records. I was at the end of my rope. When he went down to break out the POWs, I thought I'd never find out. But it worked out."

"So you tipped Armstrong about the attack on Dach Lu."

"Of course. Unfortunately, McDermott escaped in the battle. Laramie always did give a great fight. But no other POWs got away except him. We shot several before they reached the Po Tong."

Stephen dropped his head and rubbed his temples. The extent of the conspiracy overwhelmed him. The world as he knew it evaporated. His point of reference was shattered.

He had tortured himself over the death of a colleague, only to learn the beloved friend was alive and well. And the enemy.

It was quick. Stephen never saw the flash of the barrel. He was so disoriented, he didn't even hear the Filipino kid burst out of the tool locker, pulling the rag from his mouth and yelling.

Paul was momentarily startled, his attention distracted long enough for Blake to reach into his shirt and withdraw the gun.

Stephen heard a loud groan; he looked up and saw Paul stagger backwards, his hand across his chest. His other hand still grasping the pistol. He reactively squeezed the trigger but the lowered gun only struck the hangar's dirt floor. The video journalist dropped the gun, envelope and slumped to the ground.

"C'mon, let's go!"

Blake grabbed the envelope. Stephen glanced at the crumpled body, the cracked eye glasses lying beside it.

"That damn kid went to get the mechanic. We've got no time!"

The POW cranked the plane and taxied out the hangar, down the runway. Out the side window, Stephen saw the mechanic running after them, waving his hands. The aircraft inclined, climbing faster and faster, gaining altitude. They were airborne. Blake began to breath easier.

"Sorry I questioned you. When I saw him, I went crazy and thought you had lied to me. That guy you call Paul visited Dach Lu many times. I'm sorry about accusing you. I should have known better."

"Forget it. I should have known better. I don't know anything anymore. It's all one big lie."

Chapter Eight

Two weary travelers, unshaven, unkept and emitting a body odor worthy of a herd of buffalo, dozed in and out of fitful sleep as the taxi pulled up to the apartment building in Alexandria, Virginia, a suburb of Washington, D.C.

The taxi driver stopped at the street address given by Stephen and looked back at the withered pair lying in the back seat.

"Hey buddy, yo buddy. Wake up. We're here. It looks like you got'cha a welcome back party."

The journalist opened his eyes and scratched his scalp. He raised his head from the seat and peered through the window. Dozens of reporters and cameramen were gathered at the front steps of his apartment building, waiting for something, but what?

"Hey Mac. Thirty-six bucks."

"Huh, what?"

"The fare is thirty-six bucks."

"Yeah, right. Blake, hey Blake. Wake up. The man wants his money."

Blake stirred, rubbing his eyes. The taxi driver was becoming increasingly annoyed.

"What is it?" the POW asked.

"Pay the driver, okay."

"Me. What about you? I'm. . . "

"I got no time to talk," Stephen interrupted. "Something's goin' on out here." He opened the door and exited the yellow automobile.

Blake stared at the unhappy driver. The man, clenching a chewed up cigar in the few teeth left in his mouth, carried the five o'clock shadow of a baboon. His nose was flat and heavy scar tissue decorated his eye sockets; obviously a former prize fighter. Blake decided to pay him, albeit reluctantly.

He gave the burly driver the last of the money Stephen had picked up from an ATM in D.C. and quickly got out. The taxi spun out with a squeal of tires.

"Lousy, stinkin' bums," muttered the driver as he left. "Homeless people need to be introduced to soap and water."

Before Stephen made it to the steps, the crowd of reporters met him like a pack of wolves pouncing on a rabbit.

Throngs of media representatives jabbed microphones in his face, screaming questions in his ear, hoping to get that sacred three-second sound byte for the eleven o'clock news.

Caught off guard, he pushed his way through the hoard, thinking only of a shower and warm bed that awaited inside his apartment. The questions hurled at him were confusing and scary.

He decided a tight lip was the best course of action until he found out why he had become a media event. A reporter from the *Washington Post* elbowed his way through the pulsating mass and confronted him in the lobby, blocking his entrance to the stairs.

"Mr. Decatur, is it true you were involved in the killing of an American government official in Thailand?" he asked, poking a micro-cassette recorder in his face.

"I dunno what you're talking about. Who are you?"

"Ted Mitchell with the *Post.* A Deputy Secretary of State named Richard Armstrong was killed at the U.S. Embassy in Bangkok. I understand you know what happened."

"No way buddy. Now get outta my way."

"What about allegations you're involved in drug trafficking for the Golden Triangle. Is that true sir?"

"No, it isn't. You're way out in left field. Now I want to go to my apartment. Please get out of my way." Stephen was becoming irritated. Blake caught up and tapped him on the shoulder.

"Are you Blake McDermott, the prisoner of war?" asked the pugnacious reporter.

"Uh, yeah. How'd you know that?"

"I understand you know what happened regarding the murder of Deputy Secretary of State Richard Armstrong in Bangkok. Can you tell me about it?"

"Where are you getting this information?"

Mitchell ignored the inquiry and plowed forward, undaunted. "What about allegations you ran drugs for Asian drug lords in the Golden Triangle. I understand you were a drug pilot while in the U.S. Air Force during the Vietnam War and flew hundreds of missions transporting heroin. Is that true?"

"You're crazy man."

"Don't answer any more of this shit Blake," Stephen interjected. "Look Mitchell, you're way out of line with these ridiculous, inflammatory questions. Now get outta our way!"

Stephen slapped the micro-casette recorder out of the reporter's hand. It flew across the lobby, hit the floor, breaking in several pieces. He grabbed Mitchell by the shoulder and shoved him away from the staircase. They climbed up the steps.

"How did that reporter know my name?" Blake asked.

"I don't know."

"How did he know about Armstrong and the Golden Triangle?"

"I dunno Blake." Stephen stuck the key into his apartment door and unlocked it. They entered.

"Jesus Christ, we just got into town. We haven't said a word to anyone. How in the hell does the news media already know about this?"

"Like I said Blake, I dunno but something is definitely going on, something rotten. I'm gonna find out and I know who can tell me."

❁ ❁ ❁ ❁ ❁ ❁

The elevator door opened and Stephen Decatur entered the fourth floor of the *Washington Post*, the premier daily of the nation's capital.

He was greeted by rows of small desks crammed together while the iridescent blue of word processor terminals illuminated the faces of eager reporters, hungry to make a name for themselves in the narcissistic world of journalistic news.

Each wore a headset similar to that used by a telephone operator—much easier than a telephone—talking to potential interview candidates while typing in quotes on row after row of PCs.

The fax machines and wire services hummed, spitting out important bulletins. The fourth floor was divided into sections. It was remarkably huge and seemed to cover acres of heated space. The *Post* operation was mind-boggling, covering an entire city block.

He walked to the south end of the floor where the metro news section was located. His friend, Malcolm Whitaker, had been metro editor for three years. Their friendship was kindled when Stephen worked for the *Post* seven years ago.

Whitaker, 45, thrice married with four children, had been a loyal trooper to Katherine Graham, spending his entire career at the *Post* since leaving Summa Cum Laude from the University of Missouri's School of Journalism 23 years ago.

Finally promoted to the metro editorship after a long and tortuous work schedule marked by numerous peaks and valleys, Malcolm figured he had reached his pinnacle for career advancement at Madam Graham's sweat shop. No more climb on the corporate ladder for him, he was tapped out. Metro editor would have to fulfill his life ambitions.

But he held no grudge nor bitterness for the years of hard work and 60-hour work weeks. In that way, Malcolm was practical and down right philosophical about the situation. No anger, just a cynical world weariness, a begrudging acceptance of his lowly position in society.

Embracing defeat wasn't so bad, he rationalized, if you can make the rent and child support. The hopes and dreams of Pulitzer Prizes were left back in Columbia but ambition dashed under a mountain of paper work wasn't terminal.

At least there was a shred of security and dignity derived from the little cubicle of an office he maintained on the south end of the fourth floor.

"Steve, you've created quite a hum within the beltway. We thought the POW case was closed after the shooting in Hanoi. Our editors figured the La Mai document would be history and Congress would wash their hands of it. Who would have thought one of our own brethren would be part of the most fantastic news story of the 20th Century."

Malcolm, a chain smoker, pulled out a Vantage 100 and lit it, blowing a ring of smoke above his head. "But not all the Washington press corp fraternity is happy."

"Oh? Like who?"

"Don't know but there's talk. Someone is out to smear you, destroy your credibility. Someone wants this POW and records you brought back to disappear. I'm talking a major character assassination here."

"Yeah, the press hit me like a hoard of vultures the minute I arrived at my apartment. I saw the story in the *Post* relating my activities in Southeast Asia to that deputy secretary of state's death and Golden Triangle drug cartel. The same son-of-a-bitch who wrote that story was there at my apartment asking me all kinds of absurd questions.

"What I want to know is how he knew so much about what happened back there," Stephen continued. "I had just arrived in Washington with Blake McDermott. Yet he seemed to be supplied with a lot of information before I even publicly spoke of our experience in Vietnam and Thailand."

"He's gotta inside source."

"This reporter wrote a story on Blake indicating that he had been busted down in rank because of a fight he had in a bar with a superior officer that happened years ago. Now how in the hell does a grunt reporter get personal military records on a pilot who's suppose to have been missing in action for 25 years? Someone is leaking classified information to him in an effort to discredit us. Yet no one is questioning this reporter's intentions."

"He's a snitch. His name is Ted Mitchell and believe me, he's one sorry bastard. The guy would sell his grandmother to the Arabs to make a good byline for himself. All he's interested in is digging up dirt on people, making a name for himself and he's got you in his sights. The whore should go down to Lantana, Florida and get a job at the *National Enquirer.* Of course the *Post's* journalism is beginning to reflect a supermarket tabloid mentality too. But everyone here at the paper hates him. Yet for some reason, management tolerates him."

"Why?"

"Frankly, I think the little worm does hatchet jobs on people that the *Post* management doesn't like. But that's just my lowly opinion and it's strictly on the QT. What do I know? He was here in metro but I had him moved. He's a real muckraker. I dunno where he's getting his info but I can tell you this, it's coming from the highest echelons of government. Mitchell wants to become famous at anyone's expense. He's a hired gun and somebody's got him on your trail."

Malcolm took a deep draw on the cancer stick and exhaled.

"I can't see it, touch it or taste it but I can feel it. There's definitely pressure being exerted from higher up to squash those announced congressional hearings scheduled with you and that McDermott fellow. And Mitchell is the pimp that has been hired to help do it in the pages of the *Post*. I've tried to find out who is calling the shots in management but it's a dead end. Whoever it is, they've been very careful to conceal their identity which is incredible considering the leaks we have around this place. But don't ya know Mitchell?"

"No. I've never seen him before in my life. Why would you ask that?"

"I thought Mitchell was a friend of Paul Mathis. You and Paul were good friends, weren't you?"

"Yeah."

"Are you sure you didn't hear anything over there about that deputy secretary of state's murder in Bangkok?"

"No. Why?"

"Ah, it's nothing but rumors. It seems this guy had a checkered past. You know, allegations of CIA involvement and drug trafficking. Mitchell wants to link his murder to you and that POW. But for the life of me, I can't figure why except to discourage you from testifying before Congress. But why would he want to do that? I mean, what evidence does the jerk have? It's ridiculous."

❁ ❁ ❁ ❁ ❁ ❁

"What about Professor Wallace's alleged suicide? I haven't heard anything since I left for Vietnam."

"Strange. His autopsy hasn't been released."

"Good God Malcolm. How long ago did they find him dead?"

"A month ago. Supposedly shot himself in the mouth while in his car. I'm working on it. I'll let ya know if I find out anything."

"Sounds fishy."

"Like a mackerel in the moonlight, it shines and stinks at the same time."

Malcolm moved the cigarette from his hand to his mouth. He raised his head and his eyes darted toward the entrance of the cubicle office, scanning for spies. Then he leaned low, placing elbows on the desk and whispering gently.

"You might be interested in this. I gotta friend at CNN's Washington bureau who was part of a television crew which interviewed a Vietnamese-American businessman in Florida. This man claimed the Secretary of Commerce had made an arrangement with an Asian front company to use his influence to lift the trade embargo in return for a percentage of profits from American businesses which located in Vietnam following the embargo's elimination."

"Really? When did it air? Do you have a copy?"

"It never aired. It was pulled and as far as my friend knows, it's locked away in their tape vaults never to see daylight. It was killed by CNN superiors in Atlanta. The interview with him took place a while back. I dunno if the piece will ever run. Probably not."

"Do you know the name of this businessman and where he lives?"

Malcolm frowned and drew a long breath.

"Malcolm. This is important. I can't explain but it could mean my life, literally. Please, if you know, tell me."

"Oh shit! Do you know what kind of position you're putting me in? Do you have any realization?"

"Malcolm!"

"Alright dammit! His name is Uyen Minh. He lives in the Miami area. If I remember right, my friend said he was involved someway in the petroleum industry or something like that. Seemed to think this guy was pretty credible and on the up-and-up."

"And you say this Minh fellow says the Secretary of Commerce is taking payoffs to lift the embargo."

"No, I didn't say it. My friend at CNN said Minh said it. Make sure you get it straight."

"Right, of course."

"Yeah, he claims Simpson is compromised."

"Who?"

"Collin Simpson. You know, President LaFleur's Secretary of Commerce. Don't tell me after covering D.C. for years you haven't heard of him, a member of the president's cabinet. C'mon Steve, get into reality."

He stared at Malcolm and the wheels in his brain began to turn; pieces of the puzzle were falling into place. "Can you tell me anything about his background?"

"A lawyer but who isn't one in the LaFleur administration. Became a big-time executive for an multi-national corporation called Equity International, headed up their American subsidiary. The company's diversified—real estate, banking, insurance, construction and so forth. I'm surprised you don't know about him."

"Yeah, I know of him. A friend told me about him before checking out. What can you tell me about Marlin Kwolski?"

"Veteran CIA operative, got his ass kicked trying to get the directorship so LaFleur threw him a bone, gave 'em the National Security Advisor position."

"Okay, I remember."

"Let's see. Oh yeah. He also served as a consultant for the United Nations concerning financing and implementation of economic development programs for Third World drug producing countries. You know, give the peasants some seeds and a shovel and they'll quit making cocaine and heroin. Real Pollyanna bullshit, wasting taxpayer money. But like I said, what do I know? I'm just a peon desk editor."

"Interesting."

"Speaking of lawyers, you know what sperm and lawyers have in common?"

"What?"

"One outta every hundred-thousand becomes a human being. What'd ya think of that?"

Stephen wasn't laughing. He managed a smile which lasted a split second. Malcolm caught his drift and realized he was in no mood for comedy.

He leaned back in the black leather swivel chair and flicked cigarette ash into the waste basket. "Steve, this is serious, very serious. If I was you, I would stay low for a while. Get outta town, take a few weeks off. Someone wants to silence you badly."

"Can't do it Malcolm. Remember, I've got the hearings coming up."

"If Congress decides to have 'em."

"Why do you say that?"

The *Post* editor raised his hands and shrugged his shoulders. "All I'm saying is powerful forces are at work here and I get the creepy feeling it goes all the way to the White House."

"I think so too."

"We heard back here through the grapevine that you were fired by Reuters, that you disappeared for a while in Southeast Asia. No one could find you. What happened? What happened to Paul? Is he really dead?"

"I'm afraid so Malcolm. Paul was very confused. But I really can't go into it. It's a long story, too long to recount. You'll hear all about it at the hearings."

"Steve, remember, we didn't have this conversation. I got four kids to feed and three ex-wives to pamper. It's not worth going against the Washington establishment. I tried that when I was a young reporter but I've no longer got the stomach for it. They wore me down. I realized the *Post* is just a part of it. We have no objective, independent view of the federal government. We are the government. Now, all I'm interested in is putting in my time, get my retirement and watching Star Search every night on the boob tube from the recliner. Know what I mean?"

Stephen smiled and got up from the chair. "I know what you mean."

❀ ❀ ❀ ❀ ❀ ❀

The flight into Miami was tense and disturbing; not because of wind shear or air turbulence but because of Stephen's state of mind. He was concerned about the upcoming congressional hearings. He was concerned for his life and Blake's. He was worried about the ignominious records bestowed upon him by Laramie, a dangerous responsibility.

Perhaps Uyen Minh could support their case, corroborate their allegations and possibly testify at the congressional hearings.

He got up and walked to the lavatory. Yep, the blond-headed man wearing the dark Ray-bans was sitting in the back of the 707. The journalist had noticed him hanging around Dulles Airport just before boarding the plane.

He read the paper, talked on the pay phone, basically tried to look inconspicuous but the reporter's powers of observation detected a subtle eye watching him. It gave him the creeps; the hair on the back of his neck was standing straight up.

America's southern mecca for drug commerce was sunny and hot as emerald green water beat against the shores of Biscayne Bay. Dark, Latin women in revealing thongs bounded up and down the white sands of the sun-kissed beach. Uyen Minh lived in an affluent section of Miami.

The taxi driver drove up into the entrance of Minh's house; iron-wrought gates greeted him, announcing the letter M on each. Stephen identified himself to the guard posted at the front gate and the taxi entered the tropical estate. The entire layout covered several acres of finely manicured Bermuda grass and lush palm trees.

A Peruvian maid, dressed in the traditional black and white garb, greeted him at the front door, led him through the spacious mansion and out onto a patio of marble. There a man sat in a lounge chair beside a large swimming pool. At the bottom of the pool was painted the gigantic M while a stone fountain, in the form of a naked female, continuously poured water from her pail, replenishing the dark blue chlorine water.

Uyen Minh was a short man, about five feet five, early forties, with a dark, bushy mustache, well groomed, immaculately dressed in a Tommy Hilfiger outfit. He displayed a nervous facial tick which demanded attention despite the efforts of the best mannered guest.

Each man made cordial, bland introductions but Minh seemed perturbed when Stephen identified himself as a free lance journalist. He spoke fluent English without a trace of an accent. Stephen was impressed with his intelligence and the way he presented himself; very dignified, gentlemanly.

"Mr. Decatur, I've talked to reporters about my situation until I'm blue in the face. No one has bothered to print my story in the newspapers or air it on television because it's too controversial. You're wasting your time. Whatever media you represent, they'll never allow you to print what I say."

"I don't think you understand Mr. Minh. I want to hear your story for my own information. I don't know if you've heard but I'm the journalist who is going to testify before Congress along with the American prisoner of war. We're going to present evidence of government officials involved in drug trafficking in Southeast Asia and the misappropriation of taxpayer funds to aid the drug trade as well as the existence of Vietnam War POWs."

His expression instantly changed and the Vietnamese-American businessman became receptive, almost anxious to talk to the journalist as if no one else except Stephen understood him.

"Yes, yes. I read about you and that POW."

"Right. I want to compare my notes to yours so to speak. Perhaps you can help us in our case before Congress and we can help you."

"I'll try. What do you want?"

"Simply tell me your story. I want to hear everything from beginning to end. Don't leave out any detail, no matter how insignificant. I need every shred of information I can get."

"Are you really sure you want to know? The people I was dealing with are potentially dangerous."

Stephen raised the hem of a pant leg and pointed to a deep flesh scar. "I believe the same people you dealt with did this to me. Believe me Mr. Minh, if anyone knows how dangerous they are, it's me."

Minh seemed convinced. He leaned back in the patio chair and began to recount the bizarre story.

"Okay. Last year, I was introduced to Trang Van Ho by a business associate. Ho was a deputy prime minister of the former Republic of South Vietnam. He has connections, especially oil connections, so I was interested. I'm a petroleum engineer. Ho asked me to join him in establishing the Southeast Asian Economic Development Council Incorporated. I would serve as vice-president of the EDC as we called it since I was familiar with many American corporations because of my ties to the oil and gas industry. Plus I spoke fluent English in addition to Vietnamese. I would facilitate deals between the EDC and American business.

"Ho served as chairman of the corporation. The EDC would establish economic links between the Vietnam government and United States companies in the event the American trade embargo was eliminated, which, according to Ho, would happen soon. Ho sent a Federal Express package to the Secretary of Commerce—Collin Simpson—describing the Southeast Asian Economic Development Council and outlining mine and Ho's credentials. You must understand Mr. Decatur, I did not realize the EDC was merely a front group for Hanoi until later."

Stephen tried not to look directly at the quivering mouth and cheek but instead focus on his expressive hands. He noticed the tattoo of an exotic dragon on his left forearm.

"Collin Simpson met Ho here in Florida about a month later. They struck an agreement that Secretary Simpson would have exclusive lobbying rights for the Vietnamese government while Ho would be the exclusive agent through which American business contacts between Simpson and Vietnam would be arranged. Ho said Simpson offered an agenda of what he could line up as soon as Vo Van Kiet, Prime Minister of Vietnam, gave him his lobbying contract as requested of the prime minister by Ho. Ho knows Vo Van Kiet well from his days as a deputy prime minister."

"What kind of agenda are you talking about?" Stephen inquired.

"Ho told me Secretary Simpson outlined five major investment vehicles for Vietnam once the trade embargo was lifted. They were oil and gas, telecommunications, housing and real estate, banking, and tourism which included restaurant and hotel development. Naturally, I was interested in the oil and gas category because of my profession."

"Did he mention any specific companies?"

"I don't remember. But under banking, Ho did tell me that $50 million was scheduled to come from a Swiss bank account maintained by the United Nations as arranged by Simpson. The funds would be used by the EDC to open a private bank in Vietnam to conduct financing for the business deals that would result after the trade embargo was lifted. The bank would be owned by stockholders of the EDC."

❁ ❁ ❁ ❁ ❁ ❁

"Explain this money from the United Nations."

"Ho wasn't clear. We never got into the fine details of the bank financing since I bailed out later and blew the whistle. All I remember is he said Simpson could get his hands on American taxpayer money allocated to the United Nations, under some drug eradication program maintained by the UN."

"Sounds familiar. Please continue."

"Ho wanted me to move to Washington, D.C. right away. He had arranged with Simpson for me to move into an office maintained by the secretary's former employer, Equity USA. I would manage the business contacts generated by Secretary Simpson in order to smooth the transition process of investing in Vietnam. I would coordinate contacts while Ho would handle negotiations with the Vietnam government.

"In December of last year, Ho, myself and two associates he recruited for the EDC flew to Hanoi and met with Vo Van Kiet. We discussed Simpson's fee and arranged to place $800,000 in an offshore account plus oil concessions and shares of the business profit from companies that locate in Vietnam. In return, Ho told me Simpson pledged to use his influence to lift the embargo and lobby for most favored nation trading status within the LaFleur administration and Congress."

"Yeah, go ahead."

"After returning from Vietnam, I became concerned about our involvement with Simpson and this plan to siphon money from the United Nations. I confronted Ho and questioned him extensively about the ethical implications of the arrangement. He tried to reassure me, he said Simpson wanted him to manage all the business the commerce secretary would deliver. In fact, Ho said there would be representatives of about 100 U.S. companies accompanying us to Vietnam on the next trip.

"This of course was after the Bush administration agreed to allow U.S. companies to set up offices in Vietnam in preparation of doing business in the future when the embargo was lifted. Well, in January of this year, Ho told me he had received a Fed Ex letter from Simpson to give to Prime Minister Kiet. It finalized their agreement. Ho left for Vietnam to deliver the letter. While he was gone, I decided to bail out of the EDC. I'm a businessman and I've worked hard to achieve all that I have."

"Yes, I can see that."

"I won't allow my reputation to be ruined. I refuse to knowingly participate in anything illegal or criminal. So when Ho returned, $800,000 was deposited in a French bank in Singapore for Simpson. In addition, hundreds of thousands of dollars was forthcoming from Prime Minister Kiet to cover EDC expenses while I would be compensated with equity shares and cash. He showed me confirmation that the money had been transferred to Simpson's account at the French bank. Ho also told me another account was opened at this bank to deposit the $50 million from the United Nations."

Minh got up and walked into the house. He returned shortly with a briefcase. He placed the briefcase on top of the patio table and opened it. He withdrew some papers and handed them to Stephen.

"Here's my affidavit about the whole thing."

"An affidavit? Did you give it to the government?"

"I gave it to the FBI."

"They're aware of this?"

"Yes."

"Are they bringing charges?"

"That's a good question. I don't know. But let me finish my story."

"Go ahead."

"Tension between Ho and myself began to mount. I told him I was leaving the EDC and did. He threatened to use Simpson's influence to hurt me. At one point, he threatened to have the Vietnamese government send agents over here to kill me. I contacted the FBI office in North Miami who initiated an investigation. A special agent who speaks fluent Vietnamese was called in from FBI headquarters in Washington. If you look through those papers, you'll find copies of the agent's business cards I made. They even gave me a special code name and beeper to keep in touch with them."

"So basically, Commerce Secretary Simpson entered into a deal with the Vietnamese government to use his influence to lobby for lifting sanctions against the communist country in exchange for compensation," Stephen explained. "And it involves millions of dollars in payoffs by the Vietnamese government and American companies in addition to embezzling United Nation's funds."

"Exactly. The Southeast Asian Economic Development Council was set up by Ho at the request of Hanoi to make arrangements with the LaFleur administration in order to lift the embargo and further economic links between the two countries. Simple as that. Secretary Simpson was to be the exclusive lobbyist."

"So what about the FBI probe?"

"I think they've received pressure from the top. They've taken back the beeper and I haven't heard from them in months. Officially, the FBI will neither confirm nor deny it's conducting an investigation."

"What about Ho and the EDC?"

"We opened an office for the corporation on Wall Street in New York City in order to establish direct links between Simpson and Prime Minister Kiet. I understand the office is now closed. I believe Ho returned to Vietnam after I contacted the FBI. CNN sent a crew to interview me. One of them seemed very interested in my story. But it never aired."

"Did this journalist wear glasses, in his 50s."

"Yes."

"Was his name Paul Mathis?"

"I believe it was. Do you know him?"

"Once, a long time ago. I guess it's useless to contact the FBI office here in Miami."

Minh fiddled with some dark stubble on his chin. Then he took a gold cigarette case, encrusted with the initials UM, from his pocket and withdrew a slim fag. He lit the cigarette with what appeared to be a gold-plated butane lighter.

"That special agent sent from D.C. seemed very concerned about my plight. He called several times to inform me of the progress of the probe. He was helpful, seemed frustrated at the bureaucratic stifling from Washington. He told me the FBI director was personally calling the shots on my case. He seemed to be independent, not tied to the cult of secrecy like other agents. In my years of business, I've become a pretty good judge of character. I think he's a good guy. It's just a chance but you might talk to him. He could open up with a little assertiveness. You never know."

"Mr. Minh, do you feel like someone is watching your every move?"

"Yes, I do."

"Me too. Do you think it's Ho or the FBI?"

"Both."

"Will you testify at our hearings? You have information that will corroborate our claims. Please, this is of upmost importance."

Minh crushed out the cigarette and looked straight into Stephen's eyes. "Yes. I want these people stopped."

He smiled. Finally, an ally. "Okay, let me tell you my story."

Chapter Nine

The Miami headquarters of the Federal Bureau of Investigation was located in a small brick building behind the office of the Florida State Patrol at the intersection of Interstates 95 and 595 near the Fort Lauderdale-Hollywood International Airport, just above North Miami.

The red brick structure wasn't much for the country's top law enforcement agency but Stephen figured public servants should work in austere conditions; he had already seen one government employee take more than his fair share from the public hog trough.

FBI Agent Brad Richardson was pouring steaming coffee from a glass pot into a white styrofoam cup. He was just as Minh had described him: early 30s, tall, about six foot three, slim build, with brown hair and hazel eyes.

He wore a long sleeve white Oxford shirt, tie and black slacks. His gold badge hung on the front of his pant waist while a shoulder holster held a 9 millimeter semi-automatic pistol.

Stephen introduced himself, briefly explained his experience in Southeast Asia and told Richardson that

Minh had recommended he speak with him. Interest percolated underneath the agent's calm, cool exterior.

"Yes sir, I've heard about you Mr. Decatur," he said matter-of-factly.

It seemed everyone had heard of him. He was becoming a national phenomenon, albeit a strange one. It was an uncomfortable feeling to be scrutinized by the American media. All these years he used the press to pry into people's lives, now he was on the receiving end.

It was not a pleasant feeling. Only four days home and anyone who read a newspaper or watched television had heard of the malcontent reporter Stephen Decatur and renegade POW Blake McDermott as they were so aptly described in the mainstream media.

Richardson sipped his coffee and studied the reporter's face. He felt awkward as the FBI agent looked him over from head to toe.

"Would you like some coffee?"

"No thanks. I would like to hear what you've got in the Minh investigation. It would be held in the strictest confidence of course. I have a plane to catch back to Washington this afternoon. You understand."

"Mr. Decatur, I can't officially comment one way or the other about any investigation being conducted by the FBI. Any information collected in a federal investigation is classified and not for public consumption. You understand."

"Right. I've heard that classified song-and-dance stuff before from a CIA agent. If my memory serves me correct, this agent got away with breaking the law under the guise of national security. I found out the hard way that protecting our country's interests certainly gets in the way of finding out the truth. It makes me wonder whose interests we're protecting."

Stephen was in no mood for more cover–ups. He felt he was wasting his time with another government stiff when Richardson changed his tune.

"Come with me."

He led the journalist down a long hallway, illuminated by florescent lights, into a corner office. He closed the door, offered Stephen a seat, then sat behind a broken-down wood desk. He opened a panel on the wall behind the desk and flipped some switches. A green light appeared on the panel. He slammed the panel door shut.

"This scrambles the audio in the room. It's bugged you know. Everything we deal with is bugged. As I said out there, officially I cannot comment. But in here, unofficially, I can. We know about you and your friend Blake McDermott."

"You do?"

"Sure. We collect dossiers on every citizen. We knew you two were on your way to the states when you stopped and refueled at Wake Island in the Pacific. We've been following you since you landed in Hawaii."

"I've had the feeling people are following me. Someone followed me down here to Miami. Is that your guys or others I should know about?"

"We've kept a watch but as far as others, I can't say. There's always the possibility."

"Tell me the truth Agent Richardson. If the Feds are following us, you must know we're probably being tailed by the same guys who tried to kill us in Southeast Asia. If you know anything, please tell me. Our lives are in danger."

"I'll tell what I can of the investigation into the allegations of Mr. Minh. I like you. I believe your telling the truth. I know Blake McDermott is telling the truth. My father was a Vietnam vet; lost both legs when he stepped on a land mine back in '67. Now his life is confined to a wheelchair. He told me American servicemen were left behind. My old man is good friends with Jim Laramie. I think you might have met him."

"Maybe."

"He supported many of Jim's trips into Southeast Asia to find evidence of POWs. Helped raise money for the expeditions after government financing dried up. That's why I would like to see you succeed at the congressional hearings and expose the bad guys. I know you need information. I can't provide much but I'll tell want I can under the circumstances."

Richardson propped up his long legs across the desk and looked out the window.

"I'm sure Uyen Minh mentioned Trang Van Ho to you."

"Yes."

"Ho has a long history of cooperation with the current regime in Vietnam. In 1974 Ho became deputy prime minister in charge of industry for the Republic of South Vietnam. He was the only high official of the South Vietnamese government to remain in Vietnam after the fall of Saigon to North Vietnamese communist forces in 1975. Ho joined them and endeared himself by acts of loyalty which in reality were acts of treason against his own country. When communist forces seized Saigon and entered the presidential palace, Ho was the only high ranking South Vietnamese leader there to greet them.

❁ ❁ ❁ ❁ ❁ ❁

"Officials of the communist Military Management Committee, which had taken over the city, asked Ho if he would advise 'em on economic affairs," Richardson continued. "He accepted, advanced through the ranks of communist hierarchy and became close friends with Vo Van Kiet, now prime minister of the united Vietnam. Ho was allowed to leave Vietnam in 1992. He settled in Chile for a while. It was prearranged that Ho would make his way to America to pursue Hanoi's efforts to get the U.S.

government to drop its trade embargo, which has strangled their economy since the war."

"Uh-huh."

"I'm sure you're aware the embargo has been in place since 1975, when the war ended with the North Vietnamese violating the Paris Peace Accords by, among other things, not totally accounting for thousands of American POWs and MIAs in Southeast Asia in addition to invading South Vietnam."

"Yep. And dropping the embargo will destroy America's last vestige of muscle to force Hanoi to account for the missing American servicemen."

"Correct. Upon reaching Chile, Ho was told by officials of the U.S. Embassy in Santiago that he was determined to be an undesirable and would not be allowed to enter the United States because of his connection to the Hanoi regime."

"So U.S. officials were already aware that Ho cooperated with Hanoi before he entered the U.S.?"

"Yes. Ho met Collin Simpson in Chile, who at the time was a business executive before becoming Secretary of Commerce. Ho remained in Chile until 1994 when he was able to slip into the United States as a resident alien and settled in the Miami, Florida area. From there he launched the Southeast Asian Economic Development Council Inc., financed by Hanoi, to attract American business to Vietnam once the embargo was lifted."

Stephen decided to send up a trial balloon and measure the agent's reaction. "You mean lifted by Simpson and those CIA operatives involved in using American POW labor in the Golden Triangle heroin trade."

Richardson shrugged but did not say anything.

"So American law enforcement has been tracking this guy for years?"

"That's right. Sources in the State Department told us Ho's plan was much more elaborate than just creating the

EDC as detailed by Mr. Minh. He along with Prime Minister Kiet and Vietnamese Communist Party Chairman Du Muoi worked out a strategy to change the name of the Vietnamese Communist Party to a less provocative identity, establish a smaller opposition party to compete against the communist party in a general election and thereby encourage reestablishment of diplomatic relations with the United States.

"Ho planned to head the new opposition party in order to show the United States and the rest of the international community that Vietnam was instituting democratic reforms. It was planned that Prime Minister Kiet and Chairman Muoi would retire while Ho would be groomed to lead a new supposedly democratic Vietnam into the 21st Century. It was planned to portray Ho as a pragmatic, enlightened leader but from the old South Vietnamese government in order to attract overseas Vietnamese who left the country after the fall of Saigon."

"I see. Kiet and Muoi would allow Ho to emerge as a so-called progressive, democratic leader who reestablished diplomatic ties between Vietnam and America, thereby healing the wounds between the two nations, so to speak," Stephen interjected. "He would be hailed a hero in his country and by the Washington establishment and this fraud would encourage the United States to lift the trade embargo."

"Right. We believe Ho, Kiet, Muoi and others in the Vietnamese Communist Party have accrued massive fortunes through drug trafficking in the Golden Triangle. From what I've heard, you and Mr. McDermott are sort of experts in that field."

"Yeah, we gotta crash course while over there. Blake had to stay a little longer than I did."

Richardson smiled. "We've followed their flow of drug cash here and in offshore accounts. The FBI may not say much but we aren't naive Mr. Decatur. We know high-ranking American officials are involved."

"Listen Agent Richardson, I appreciate your candor."

"Don't thank me. It's the least I can do for you, McDermott and my father. If you tell anyone I told ya, I'll just deny it, standard bureau procedure. See no evil, hear no evil."

"I've got one more question. Is the bureau gonna help us at the congressional hearings? Will the agency turn over the evidence it's discovered during the Minh investigation? We need all the help we can get. You obviously know the forces we're up against."

"You have no idea of the forces you're up against. You and McDermott only scratched the surface. As far as the agency is concerned, well, it's a political animal vulnerable to the whims of the current administration. I can't say."

"Thanks anyway. You've been very helpful. I've gotta plane to catch." Stephen got up to leave.

"By the way, Mr. Decatur, did you ever meet a deputy secretary of state, Richard Armstrong, at the U.S. Embassy in Bangkok?"

"Uh, yes, why?"

"I guess you heard he met an untimely demise. Seems two gaunt white men barged into the embassy and shot him dead in a gunfight. Some people are saying the two assassins shredded all the embassy documents regarding sightings and evidence of American POWs and MIAs in Southeast Asia. Seems someone wants to cover up this POW issue bad, so bad they'll murder to accomplish it. I understand some of the records you turned over to the Justice Department came from the embassy. I just wondered if you knew any clues into Armstrong's death or the shredded documents or maybe both?"

Stephen steadied himself. Richardson seemed to have a twinkle in his eye as if he already knew the answer to the question. Stephen did not betray his emotions.

"As I said, I met him once, an unpleasant fellow. I don't know anything about his death or the POW files—officially."

"Touche," Richardson replied.

The weary reporter had not even had a chance to put the luggage away in his dingy apartment when he punched the telephone answering machine and heard three alarming messages.

"Uh, Mister Decatur, this is Doctor Patel at Washington Memorial Hospital. Mister Blake McDermott asked me to call you. He's been admitted to the hospital with some serious injuries but we think he'll be alright with the proper convalesce. If you could come down to the hospital as soon as possible, we would appreciate it."

Jesus, he thought, now what's happened? Next message: "Steve, it's Malcolm. I don't know if you heard but somebody tried to dust off your friend McDermott with a bomb. He's at Washington Memorial. Listen, I've got some interesting information you might want to hear. It's important. Call me."

Then a shrill voice pierced the quiet sanctity of the one-bedroom flat on the third message: "Stephen, Stephen, if you're there, pick up the damn phone. . . I've been trying to get in touch with you for days. Why in the hell haven't you returned my calls? This relationship is pathetic! You never share anything with me. You stay in your own little world, writing those stupid stories nobody wants to read. Do you hear me? Are ya there? You go off half-cocked to Vietnam for a week and instead, you're gone a month."

It continued. "Then I hear you've been fired and nobody can find you. Then I read about you and some crazy POW in the papers. So you're back but you haven't even called me. What the hell's goin' on? You're so irresponsible and inconsiderate. You never gave a damn about me. Don't bother calling me back. I just called to tell you it's finished, over, kaput. I'm goin' out with that gynecologist I met at the bistro. He's responsible, got a Porsche and a house in Reston. Enjoy your life!" Click.

Stephen ran a hand through his hair. They had fought the night before he left for Vietnam. Damn! He forgot about Michelle. Jesus, how could he do that? But he seemed to have forgot about her a lot during their stormy three-year relationship.

Thoughts of Mi Ling permeated his mind. Perhaps it was a sign. Maybe Michelle had done him a favor. Well, at least now she'll benefit from her new relationship; free medical check-ups, he thought, that will please the hell out of her.

So much for getting back to normal. His apartment would have to remain a stranger. His temples throbbed, his head ached down to the shoulders from the jet lag. A note had been left on the coffee table by his landlord saying he was two months behind in the rent. The hell with the old bag. Stephen threw the luggage down, grabbed the car keys off the kitchen table and left.

Blake wore a hospital gown and a white bandage across his forehead; black rings encircled his eyes. The antiseptic smell of the hospital was nauseating.

Stephen was filled with fearful anticipation as he entered the POW's room; he looked bad, what with all the cuts across the face but at least he was alive.

"Jesus Blake, what happened?"

"This afternoon, I was getting into a taxi near the Pentagon to go home to your apartment. I had just gotten outta nine hours of interrogation with the Defense Department. A guy on a bicycle came riding by. One window of the taxi was partially rolled down and he tossed a bomb through it. I saw it. As I was getting out, it exploded. That's the last I remember. When I awoke, some FBI agents had taken me to the hospital. They apparently pulled me out of the wreckage. The taxi driver was killed."

"Did you get a look at the fellow on the bike?"

"Just briefly. But I know he's Vietnamese."

"How can you be sure?"

"He was Asian. I'd bet the farm he was a Vietnamese national."

"What happened to these FBI agents?"

"We're right here, Mister Decatur," a voice answered behind him. Stephen turned around. In the doorway, stood Brad Richardson, groomed to perfection, and a blond headed man, looking suspiciously like the suit he saw on the flight to Miami, except without the Ray-bans.

"Sorry to disturb you but we wanted to talk for a minute."

"You certainly got to Washington in a hurry. You must've left Miami the same time I did."

"Can we speak outside for a moment?"

"Blake, I'll be back in a minute."

"Sure."

Stephen stepped out of the room and accompanied the two FBI agents down to the hospital lounge.

"Blake says you pulled him out of the car?"

"Yes. We observed the assailant toss a bomb into the taxi."

"So you have been following us. Dammit Richardson, we need protection, federal protection. The evidence we're presenting to Congress is gonna get us killed. Why in the hell don't you guys do your job and protect us? We're gonna help the bureau indict some high government officials. Why doesn't the bureau cooperate with us? Investigate our claims and Uyen Minh's claims. We're telling the truth; what Minh is saying corroborates our story."

"Hold up Mister Decatur. We have agents staked out at your apartment. We have for some time. But as of now, all we have are accusations, from you and Minh. We can't act on mere allegations and innuendos. We need proof."

"Proof! There's a damn American prisoner of war sitting back there in that hospital bed. What else do you need? The Justice Department must have shared the UN records with the FBI if you're watching us. C'mon man, give me a break."

"Mister Decatur, please, take it easy. I know you've had a rough time. Don't worry. We have it covered."

"Do you know who tried to kill Blake?"

"Not yet. We're working on it."

"He was Vietnamese."

"We know."

Suddenly, Stephen felt a hand on his shoulder. He jumped and turned abruptly.

"Whoa, Stevie, it's me. Calm down." It was Malcolm Whitaker.

"Oh. Sorry Malcolm. It's my nerves. I'm a little bit jumpy these days."

"Hey, I understand. You have a right to be. I thought you might be at the hospital visiting your friend."

"Agents will be posted outside of Mister McDermott's door," Richardson said. "Don't worry about him. He'll be fine. We've gotta go."

"Hey, wait a minute."

"I'll be in touch. Good-bye." Richardson and the blond agent exited the lounge.

"Shit, I hate dealing with government."

"I know what you mean," Malcolm answered. "Who are the two suits?"

"It's a long story."

"I've been trying to getta hold of you for two days."

"I know. I've been out of town. I got your message. Listen, wait here in the lounge. I'm going to see Blake for a minute. Then we'll talk."

"Okay."

Stephen went back into Blake's room. A cute nurse was giving him a painkiller. He was joking with the young woman, patting her on the rear end. She giggled but became straightfaced when the journalist stepped in. She quickly took his pulse, then left.

"Damn you've got lousy timing."

"I see being locked up 25 years didn't diminish your libido any."

"Diminish it? Are you kidding. It's made it worse. Can you imagine goin' that long without female companionship. Talk about torture. I'm about to go blind as it is. If the doctors really want my health to improve, they ought to let me have a night with that nurse. Shit, forget the night. All I need is two minutes and I'll be good as new. Asian women are alright but you can't beat American femininity."

"I've got one named Michelle you can have."

"Who's that?"

"Never mind. Tell me more about your meeting with the Pentagon. How'd it go?"

"Well...they finally decided I'm who I said I was after checking dental records and taking my fingerprints," Blake said disdainfully. "Bastards didn't believe me."

"And?"

"Gettin' a discharge. They don't wanna promote me during my years of captivity since I'm a political hot potato. I'm suppose to getta lump sum settlement. But they're waiting until after the congressional hearings.

What I say may effect my military compensation. No...it will effect it."

"The POWs?"

"I dunno." He threw up his hands. "I told 'em the whole sorry story including what I thought of 'em. It's hard to read 'em. These two generals talked to me while their military liaison took notes. They recorded everything. I demanded they re-expatriate the missing servicemen back. I told 'em I would personally lead 'em to where the POWs are imprisoned. I demanded they give an ultimatum to Vietnam. But they just looked at me with blank stares. Their questions indicated they're more interested in Vietnam's military capacity than how many American servicemen are still being held.

"I don't know any Vietnamese military secrets, only that they worked the hell out of us in the poppy fields during the day and beat us at night. A psychiatrist came in and gave me some kind of damn mental test. They think I'm crazy from all those years over there. You know, imagining things. I told the shrink to shove the test up her ass and get the generals back. When they came back in, I told them I wasn't crazy and that they'd abandoned the men, left 'em behind to die after they served their country in a no-win war. I guess I came on a little too strong."

"Perhaps. The Defense Department isn't use to demands."

"The lousy bastards made me tell about my imprisonment, the other POWs, and our escape over and over again, about twelve damn times. They transcribed every offhand remark I made, like they didn't believe my story. I felt like I was on a witness stand being grilled by a prosecutor. I told 'em we ought to nuke those lying gooks with a hydrogen bomb. I was really angry. Then something weird happened."

"What?"

"As I looked into their faces, I realized Hanoi wasn't the only one to blame. Our government is also an accomplice. Then I thought, 'Whose the real enemy anymore?' It's hard to tell. They're no more bad guys in the jungle wearing black pajamas. They all wear suits or military uniforms and speak self-serving diplomatic babble."

His voice trailed off. He looked depressed. He held his hand to his mouth and coughed.

"Is Jane Fonda still around, ya know, alive?"

"Yep."

"We use to get mad as hell at Hanoi Jane. She was used by the North Vietnamese communists for propaganda purposes. But looking back, I think the American military was used too. We were pawns in a deadly struggle. Maybe she knew she was being used and didn't care. Funny thing is, we weren't even aware of it. Took 25 years in prison for me to realize it."

"When do the doctors think you'll be out?"

"They're telling me a couple of days. They say I need rest and recuperation because I have the body of a 80-year-old due to the neglect. The doc tells me my body functions really deteriorated while imprisoned. Who knows? The Pentagon boys already visited me an hour ago. I just want to get outta here. But enough about me, how did the trip to Miami go?"

"Great. Uyen Minh is coming up to present his story and testify along with us."

"So his story kinda jives with ours?"

"Yes, it does and he revealed a lot more. You remember Simpson, the name Paul dropped before you dropped him."

"Yeah, I remember."

"Well, Minh says that Secretary of Commerce Collin S-I-M-P-S-O-N has arranged a deal with Hanoi to lobby for discontinuing the trade embargo in exchange for $800,000 and a share of the profits generated from American business that invests in the country."

"Holy shit! Paul said Simpson was gonna take care of everything. That's gotta be him."

"Yep. And that FBI Agent Brad Richardson told me that most of the high ranking communist officials in the Hanoi regime are involved in the Golden Triangle drug trafficking. Minh will fly into Washington later to help us prepare for the hearings. He contacted the FBI but seems to think the feds are backing out of the investigation because of heat from the top."

"Did he say anything else?"

"That's the main stuff. I'll fill you in on the details later. You get some rest. You need it. This'll give the doctors a chance to look ya over."

"Do the FBI agents know who tried to kill me?"

"They know he's Vietnamese like you said but that's all they're telling me. But you can bet he was hired by Marlin Kwolski or Collin Simpson."

"Both," Blake replied.

"Uh-huh. I think the FBI followed me down to Miami and back here to Washington. But I'm getting this queasy feeling that Simpson and Kwolski are watching every move we make too."

"Listen Stephen, I was able to sneak two of the handguns off the Goose before the FBI seized it. I took one of the guns and taped it under the toilet in the bathroom of your apartment. Get it and carry it with you. This place is just as dangerous as Southeast Asia, maybe more. I wouldn't trust the FBI any sooner than Simpson and Kwolski."

"Shit, this is getting too crazy. I'm so sick of the bloodshed." Stephen collapsed in a chair beside the hospital bed and rubbed his eyes. "I'm sick of looking over my shoulder all the time. I'm tired of distrusting everyone, suspecting everybody's motives. Blake, my world's falling apart. I unknowingly get involved in drug trafficking, POW slave labor and misappropriation of global funds, and then some crazy government official tries to kill me. I get locked up in some hell-hole jail, then my long-time friend rises from the dead and tries to kill me.

"I've got no job, no girlfriend and except for Malcolm hardly any friends since our story hit the papers. I thought I left all that behind in Southeast Asia. I thought we left those goons across the Pacific but they're here in the nation's capital, setting up shop."

"Stephen, we can only trust each other. We've gotta stick together and see this through. We're so close to testifying, we can't let 'em scare us away now, after all we've been through. Besides, those GIs over in Vietnam are counting on us. We can't think of ourselves even though I know this has been sheer misery. We gotta think of them and concentrate on that.

"Just a little longer man." Blake turned and coughed. "We'll testify and get the ball rolling. I know your life is in ruins, so is mine. But this is something bigger than ourselves. The entire integrity of our country is riding on it. Like they told us at the Tet offensive, this is not for us but for our country. I didn't believe 'em then but I believe in us now. We're fighting a real war now."

"How, of all people, can you be so optimistic after all you've endured? I mean, none of this is your fault. You got the shaft."

"I'm too scared not to be optimistic. Besides, we do have a few more friends than you think."

"Yeah, like who?"

"Take a look." Blake pointed to the wall beside his bed. One large mail bag were leaning up against it, crammed full of letters and cards.

"What's this?"

"People from around the country have been sending you and me letters of support. Even sent money to help during the hearings. Can you believe that? It seems some of the negative press we've received has backfired on those prostitutes like Ted Mitchell. People aren't buying the media's white-washing of our affair. They know if we're being criticized by the press, there must be something truthful we're saying, something the government doesn't want out. Remember, the fourth branch of government?"

"I remember."

Blake reached into the drawer of the nightstand beside the bed and pulled out a pile of cash and checks. "This is just some of the money I pulled out. Besides individuals, we also got money from several veterans organizations and POW-MIA family groups who pledged their support. Take a look."

Stephen browsed through the checks. He scanned names like the American Legion, Veterans of Foreign Wars, Amvets, Vietnam Veterans of America, Disabled American Veterans, American Ex-POWs and the Retired Officers Association.

He continued looking. Cards expressing support, admiration and commitments to attend and provide assistance at the congressional hearings flooded his vision from such sources as the National Alliance of Families for the Return of America's Missing Servicemen and the National League of Families of Prisoners and Missing in Southeast Asia.

Suddenly, his heart began racing. Someone did care. Others felt the same way he and Blake did. Someone else in those 50 states wanted an accounting of American POWs and MIAs from Hanoi and Washington, D.C.

Americans were smart enough to see through the smoke and mirrors. Some did care about the truth. He felt his courage return, his resolve invigorated.

"This is fantastic. We'll go through all this tomorrow. Malcolm is waiting for me outside. I'll be back to see you. FBI agents are stationed outside the door for protection. So you'll be alright, okay?"

Blake smiled and felt under his pillow. He revealed a pistol and shook it in the air. "I don't trust 'em. I've got my own protection. This is the other gun I took off the plane. The FBI missed this baby. Snuck it through under the doc's nose."

❀ ❀ ❀ ❀ ❀ ❀

Brad Richardson walked down the hall of the J. Edgar Hoover Building, national headquarters of the FBI, toward the suite of FBI Director William LaCross, after completing numerous security clearances including a palm and retina scan in addition to audio and visual confirmation.

The agent entered the spacious office without uttering a word. The paneled walls were littered with plagues, citations and one large, gaudy picture of Hoover himself. The 40-year FBI director's little, squirrely eyes seemed to follow Richardson's every move as he eased toward the bulky desk located at the west end of the suite.

The swivel chair behind the desk turned and Director LaCross stared at him. He was on the phone, the special one equipped with the scrambler.

LaCross cupped the phone receiver in his hand and motioned Richardson to take a seat. He held up one finger to indicate the phone conversation was coming to an end.

"Yes, General Smith. I will General. We'll have this situation resolved soon. I have one of my agents here right now to brief me on the current status. Don't worry. Stephen Decatur and Blake McDermott are under our protection. That bombing won't happen again. We're monitoring them closely. Yes, I know the Pentagon debriefed McDermott. Right. That's what I understood.

"The records Decatur submitted to the Justice Department have corroborated what we suspected and gave us information we've been needing to tie up loose ends. Yes, those are copies. Decatur is very paranoid and he won't reveal where the original records are located. He's hidden 'em. Okay. I'll be in touch."

LaCross hung up the telephone, cupped his hands behind the back of his head and leaned back in the chair.

"What have you got for me Richardson?"

"We've located the bomber. He's Vietnamese, carries several aliases, living in New York City's Asian community on the west side."

"You're definite about this?"

"Absolutely. He immigrated here two years ago but has kept contacts with the Golden Triangle. He pushes heroin on the streets but sometimes does free lance hit jobs, which we believe is the case with Blake McDermott. We've been in contact with the woman he lives with in an apartment there. We struck a deal and she's set him up. All we need is your approval."

"Go to the judge and get the warrant immediately. I want him apprehended. He could be our link to Uyen Minh and the Golden Triangle."

"Yes, sir."

"What about Minh?"

"He left the country. Minh told Decatur the same thing about Secretary Simpson and the EDC as he told us. We recorded their entire conversation through the surveillance monitors. Nothing provocative. The story he told Decatur was exactly the same. But he's getting nervous. He told Decatur the investigation was being stalled from the top. He told him to visit me at the Miami station. He wants to use Decatur to push us along with our probe into Simpson's deals with Hanoi. He also promised him he would testify at the congressional hearings and present his allegations about Simpson."

"What did you tell Decatur?"

"I gave him the background information on Trang Van Ho. It got him real excited."

"You didn't say anything about Minh though, did you?"

"Of course not, sir. Just Ho. Decatur left satisfied."

"You say Minh has left the country?"

"Yes, sir. The Miami boys called me this morning, recorded a phone conversation he had with the airlines thanks to the clipper telephone surveillance chip they installed. He boarded an American Airlines flight today headed for Ho Chi Minh City. He plans to visit Bangkok. We think he may rendezvous with his superiors but it's too early to tell."

"If he is meeting with 'em, you know what that means. Have you notified the Pacific Asian division?"

"They're on alert. They'll be waiting for him at the airport when he touches down. Our intelligence officers will maintain constant surveillance. We've also got agents waiting in Bangkok."

"Good. I understand the problem with some of the CIA agents over there has been eliminated."

"Yes sir, for right now. Our friends at Langley think the bad guys are temporarily clear. Richard Armstrong, as you know, was spearheading the CIA drug cartel but with his death, the mercenary faction has fallen into fighting among themselves for the poppy territory."

"Our intelligence reports indicate Kuhn-Sah Duc is making strides to recapture some of his lost territory in the Golden Triangle countries."

"Yes, sir. There now exists a power vacuum created by Armstrong's death that has divided the renegade CIA faction. Duc hopes to exploit their dissension and retake a majority of the heroin production before they regroup. But I don't know how long the internecine fighting will last."

"It won't last long if Simpson and Kwolski finalize the deal with Hanoi and are successful in lobbying to lift the trade embargo."

"Yes, sir. With access to the money from the United Nations Drug Control Program, the cartel still wields influence over much of the heroin production among the poppy producing countries of Southeast Asia. And with the promise to lift the embargo, they think their power over the heroin trade will be without challenge and Kuhn-Sah Duc will be forced out entirely. Kwolski is moving fast to fill that void left by his accomplice Armstrong."

Richardson stopped, pleased with the timing and tone of his elaborate briefing delivered to the director. A picture of Director LaCross shaking hands with President LaFleur hung on the back wall of the suite. The director paused for a moment, looking at J. Edgar's weasel eyes, then spoke.

"The deputy secretary of state's assailants were positively identified. There's no doubt, Decatur and McDermott killed him. Found their fingerprints all over the embassy. I got the ballistic report back from the crime lab. The bullets from the firearm we seized from their plane matched perfectly those found in Armstrong's body."

"So what do you want me to do?"

"Nothing. It worked out fine. They did us a favor. At least the CIA or us don't have to dirty our hands as usual."

"No investigation? No charges?"

"I don't think so. It seems self-defense but who knows for sure. The only witness to it was committed to a mental institution." The director shuffled through some papers on the mahogany desk.

"Let's see, here it is—Felix Berger, an aid to the deputy secretary of state, was there when the shooting occurred. He went nuts, can't remember any shooters. But it doesn't matter. We have enough evidence to hold it over their heads like the sword of Damocles. We'll just keep it to ourselves for now. The information could come in handy later. They seem to exhibit a strong sense of independence and disdain for authority. We could use the information to motivate them to do as we say, understand?"

"Understood. I guess the Attorney General is pleased with the records Decatur provided."

"It's a mixed bag. Some things should not go public. Other areas are definitely out of our jurisdiction."

"Sir?"

"As for Kwolski and Kuhn-Sah Duc," LaCross smiled slyly and tapped his fingers on the desk, "they must be squirming."

"Any news on Senator Bainbridge?"

I'm glad you mentioned that. We have statements from the senator's Seattle bank. The National Security Agency finally unscrambled the bank's computer software and broke into the electronic mail. It looks like money laundering. There's a paper trail leading back to Southeast Asia. His committee chairmanship may be compromised. Now, I've gotta brief the president. Is there anything else?"

"No, sir."

"Remember, apprehend that bomber, whatever you do. We need him. Report to me daily on Uyen Minh's itinerary over there. I want to know his every move, who he meets with, who he dines with, who he sleeps with, when he goes to the toilet, everything. McDermott and Decatur's lives depend on it."

Chapter Ten

Planet Hollywood was crowded and loud rock music blared, vibrating the movie memorabilia that hung on the walls. The restaurant chain—started by several movie stars as sort of a Tinsel Town version of the Hard Rock Cafe—was not well lit but Arnold Swartzneggar's Terminator body double clearly glared at patrons as they passed the illuminated figure in a glass container.

The starlit night scene on the ceiling caught Stephen's attention; it was nice but Planet Hollywood wasn't his choice for a night out. He would have preferred a quiet, casual setting to calm his nerves. Pressure from behind his eyes ricochetted against throbbing temples, caused by the nagging jet lag of the Pacific trip, compounded by the Miami excursion.

This yuppie–wannebe haven was much too dark and loud for his taste but Malcolm, for some odd reason, liked the atmosphere, despite his advancing age and the strain of three failed marriages; something to do with the young waitresses in their tight Planet Hollywood t-shirts. The *Post* editor may have reluctantly settled for stagnation in his job but his personal life still resembled that of an 18–year–old in heat.

They were led by one of Malcolm's favorite waitresses to the smoking section, despite Stephen's protests. They took a seat and Malcolm grinned at the teeny bopper, who looked young enough to sport a training bra; but then everyone was looking younger and younger to him. She left to get two Rolling Rock beers.

"Okay, what's so important," Stephen yelled over the squawking of Madonna.

alcolm took out aMigarette and leaned across the table so his words would be heard better. "I found something in the *Post* index, an article we ran about a *New York Times* journalist. Very interesting." He popped the cancer stick in his mouth and lit it from a book of matches; then took the fuming toxic dump in his left hand.

"Shit Malcolm, cool it with the cigarettes. Yah know they make me sick."

"Sorry, sorry." He lowered the left hand below the table and fanned the smoke away.

"So tell me about this guy. You said he worked for the *Times* ?"

"That's right and he ended up dead under very suspicious circumstances."

The nubile waitress returned with a Vanna White smile on her face and plopped down two green bottles of Rolling Rock. Malcolm patted her hand and expressed a syrupy "thank you." Stephen was beginning to lose his appetite. Child molestation came to mind.

"So what's this gotta do with me. C'mon, I'm tired and want to go to bed. I'm not staying up here at Planet Dollywood....."

"Hollywood."

"Yeah, right, Planet Hollywood all night giving out tootsie rolls to pick up jail bait."

"Stephen, I'm shocked. You think I come here to pick up little girls off the playground? How could you?"

He didn't say a word but gave the metro editor a harsh look. A sheepish grin broke out across his face.

"Okay, okay. So I'm not perfect but who is? Don't hold it against me. I know your vices too. We use to be a pretty good team."

"I don't hold it against you. I want you to tell me the info so I can split. You can stay here, just leave me out of the babysitting. I'm not staying here with you to run women. Forget it. We're not a tag-team anymore. If you want to go to jail for statutory rape, that's fine but leave me out."

"I think you're going to extremes here, making me out to be Ted Bundy or something. There's nothing wrong with having a little fun. That's all it is. I just look, never touch the merchandise. It's harmless, for Christ's Sake. Lighten up, will yah?"

"I'm sorry. I'm just not in a fun mood these days, especially today. And Planet Dollywood's clientele doesn't help."

"Hollywood dammit. What clientele?"

Stephen pointed to a booth across the room shared by a couple. The pair were all over each other, hugging and kissing, as though they needed a motel room instead of a restaurant.

"God! Isn't that Michelle?"

"Uh-huh."

"Who's that with her?"

"Well, according to her phone message, it's a doctor, a gynecologist she met."

Malcolm smiled and was about to make an off-colored remark but Stephen saw it coming.

"Don't even say it. I'm not in the mood."

"Hey, I'm sorry. I didn't know you two had broken up."

"Me either. But enough about that. I'm depressed as it is. Michelle is old news. Give me some new news."

"Well, you're in the right place to forget about Michelle. The babes here. . ."

"Malcolm, I mean it."

The *Post* editor shrugged and folded his arms. Their 18-year-old Vanna White returned, all 32 teeth exposed, white and polished, and presented them with the standard chicken finger plate and french fries.

Thank God for the Rolling Rock, Stephen thought. Is there any restaurant in the United States that doesn't serve chicken fingers, nachos or buffalo wings? But on the other hand, it sure as hell beat Thailand mystery meat.

Malcolm crushed out the fag and stabbed a chicken finger with a fork. "So, you want to hear it?"

"I've been wanting to hear it for the last 20 minutes."

"Some friends of mine at the *Times* knew this kid. His name was Ben Corbett, a regional correspondent. He wrote a series of articles on the Central Intelligence Agency, including alleged involvement in drug trafficking in Southeast Asia. He quoted some high-ranking government officials in Thailand, Burma, Laos and Vietnam who accused renegade CIA agents stationed in their countries of heroin trafficking. What's really strange is one of the so-called officials he quoted."

"Yeah, who?"

"According to my friends, he quoted extensively a Laotian man named Kuhn-Sah Duc. Apparently, this Duc guy is the largest drug kingpin in the Golden Triangle. Now why would this fellow risk public exposure, especially in America, by accusing CIA agents of the very thing he does? It doesn't make sense. What also doesn't make sense is how Corbett got in contact with him and then got'em to talk. It's weird, man."

"Very weird. Perhaps Duc felt he had nothing to lose by talking to the American press. Maybe in Southeast

Asia but not way over here in the USA. Probably wanted to use the press to put domestic pressure on the CIA to move out of the drug business in the Golden Triangle by creating a public awareness in this country."

"I guess it's a possibility. He certainly seemed comfortable enough with Corbett to talk a lot about American intelligence officers. That in itself is odd."

"Yes, very odd, as though they were working together, maybe."

"Corbett and that Asian drug lord? Nah."

"Are you sure your friends told you Kuhn-Sah Duc?"

"Absolutely. That's who they named. Your claims about the CIA and the Golden Triangle triggered my memory about Corbett. That's when I reviewed the *Post* index and called my friends."

Stephen popped a crispy fried finger in his mouth. "So go on."

"From what I understand, Ben Corbett first wrote an in-depth story of CIA covert operations in Asia. He followed that up with an expose of CIA agents stationed in Southeast Asia who became involved in drug trafficking, all the way back to the 1960s."

"Did he mention any names?"

"Uh-huh. My friends say he fingered that deputy secretary of state, Richard Armstrong, who was recently killed in Bangkok. Corbett claimed Armstrong was a CIA agent before he transferred to the state department. His transfer, according to Corbett's story, was because of heat from the White House. They decided to hide him out in the state department because his drug activities with the CIA had become public knowledge for some unknown reason. If that's true, I bet his murder in Bangkok was drug–related, don't you think?"

"Uh, yeah. It could have been drug-related."

"Well, another article concerned banks used for drug cash laundering by this alleged drug ring."

"Did he mention any banks in the article?"

"Yeah, he did. He named the Seattle National Bank as one and also a French-owned bank in Singapore. I don't know if you know but Senator Walter Bainbridge is a large stockholder in the Seattle National Bank."

"Do you have copies of these stories from the *Times* ?"

"That's a funny thing. My friends can't locate any of Corbett's stories in the index or on the microfilm. It's as if they've disappeared from the editions they appeared in."

"No, that isn't funny."

"Well, let me finish. It gets more bizarre. My friends say Corbett had a mole at CIA headquarters in Langley. This mole was feeding him the information that he was using in his stories. The night he died, he was supposed to meet with his mole. Police found his body a day later in some seedy hotel on the east side of Manhattan. The autopsy said he died of a heroin overdose."

"Heroin overdose?"

"Yeah, creepy huh? He's writing about the corrupt heroin trade and then suddenly, he decides to sample it. It doesn't sound right. My friends say Corbett was a straight arrow, never took drugs."

Malcolm took a sip from the green longneck of Rolling Rock.

"The FBI investigated his death. You would think it was a case for the local authorities but the feds were there too. I understand the coroner's report is suspect. It seems as though he rushed through the autopsy and concluded drug overdose without checking other things. Corbett's parents wanted the body exhumed but got the shock of their life. He was cremated without their permission. No one knows who did it. The police blame the coroner, the coroner blames the police. So the evidence went up in flames so to speak."

Stephen grimaced as Guns-N-Roses gave him a "welcome to the jungle" that made his eardrums ache.

"I've heard from sources that heroin was found in Professor Wallace's car and traces in his bloodstream. The FBI also investigated his death. My friends told me Robert Wallace talked to Corbett."

"Really. What did they talk about?"

"Apparently Wallace was interested in his stories on the alleged CIA drug trafficking. Why, I don't know."

"Any news on his autopsy?"

"Get this. The cops said he placed a gun in his mouth and pulled the trigger. But one of the medical examiners, who wished to remain anonymous, said there was no thick residue of gunpowder around or inside the wound nor on the tongue. No damaged or broken teeth. No blood found on the barrel of the gun. In fact, only a small trickle of blood was found from the corner of his mouth. I know because he showed me the scene photos."

"What about the bullet?"

"It's never been released."

"You mean they did find it?"

"Stephen, there wasn't an exit wound. The bullet was in Wallace's skull the entire time. That autopsy is trumped up like Ben Corbett's. It'll never be released to the public."

"So he was murdered and it was staged to look like a suicide."

"One more thing, a Visa to Laos was found on him. He had recently returned from there on a POW fact–finding mission at the behest of the National Security Advisor. Believe it or not, Wallace met with Kuhn-Sah Duc and some reps from an Asian company called Equity, uh, Equity something. . ."

"Pacific Equity."

"Exactly. Kwolski made it big news in the press here. He wanted the professor's trip publicized big-time. The intelligence community never wants publicity. Why President LaFleur let his NSA spout off in the press about Robert Wallace's supposedly secret trip is beyond me. This whole situation is bizarre."

Malcolm's eyes got big. "Uh-oh. Michelle is coming over here."

At age 32, Michelle Johnson was striking with brown hair and blue eyes. She was an upwardly mobile yuppie looking to climb up that next rung of the socio–economic ladder. Her career as an attorney with the Food and Drug Administration was profitable.

She enjoyed the position of a beltway lawyer, proud of her achievements. She wore her resume and credentials on her sleeve and would show it to anyone, anytime, even without an invitation.

Cellular phones, fax machines, E–mail and BMWs were instruments of power in her life—her ambition, her way. Reading the *New York Times* was a fashion statement according to her logic; acquiring information from such organs delegated to the masses.

She would settle for no less than a fat bank account, bulging IRA, American Express Gold card, annual vacations to the Caribbean and a mansion in the hills.

Michelle became embarrassed at Stephen's profession as her's advanced in the FDA. The salary and prestige of a journalist, no, make that a reporter as she termed him, was inadequate for her needs and desires. His trip to Vietnam was used as an excuse to drop kick him out of her pre-arranged life.

Anyone that became an obstacle on her way to advancement—or useless in furthering her career—was immediately decreed banished from her life forever. Stephen had just received such an honor. No wonder they did not agree. Her values and his mixed like oil and water. He braced for the oncoming verbal assault.

"Well, I see that you're indeed alive. Finally decided to rejoin society did we? Or did you just emerge for a meal before going undercover again to expose some big conspiracy?"

"Hi, Michelle."

"That POW and you are appearing in the newspapers everyday now. You're really getting those headlines you always wanted. Except you're not on the byline but in the story. Hi, Malcolm."

"Hello, Michelle."

"Stephen, I don't understand. The press is making you out to be some kind of lunatic. What happened over there in Vietnam? Have you gone mad? It's humiliating. My friends at the office ask me questions. They want to know what's going on with you. The media is constantly calling me. Ted Mitchell calls me all the time at my office and home wanting personal information about you."

"You didn't tell him anything, did you?"

"Of course not. I'm a lawyer. I know my rights. But if this media barrage continues, I may be forced to take other action."

"What are you talking about?" Michelle's self–centered ways were beginning to get under his skin, as usual. She was seeking cover.

"My career in the federal government is important to me. If these media allegations are substantiated and you're indicted, heaven forbid, I must tell the authorities what I know about you."

"All bullshit Michelle. You don't know anything incriminating about me. I've never broken the law or done anything illegal during our relationship. I'm not on trial here. I haven't even been called in front of a grand jury. All you know is that I snore in my sleep and pick my toes."

"Cute Steve, cute. You call this a relationship. It was nothing but a fiasco because you were never serious about anything. I mean it. These stories in the press are hurting my position at the FDA. They know I dated you."

"Oh, so you're guilty by association, right? Presuming I'm guilty without the benefit of a trial. The press has decided to be the judge, jury and executioner."

"Well, it's your profession, not mine. Don't blame me. It seems you're getting what's coming to you. You always blamed attorneys for all the problems in the world. Well, see what your profession is doing to one of its own. And you dare to talk about my job. Your industry is nothing but cannibals, feeding off one another."

"Michelle, please. Knock off the courtroom theatrics. We don't need the melodrama. If Ted Mitchell continues to harass you, call me. I'll take care of it. But don't say anything. He's looking for any scrap of personal information to use against me. He will do anything, honest or dishonest, to discredit me and stop the congressional hearings before they begin. Those things printed and on TV are nothing but bold-faced lies, presented as inuendo and claims from unknown sources. So getta grip."

"There you go again talking about conspiracies and cover-ups. Stephen, you're so paranoid and unstable, so immature. I'm glad I called it off with you. You did get my message?"

"I got it." He took a long gulp of the Rolling Rock. Malcolm fidgeted with his chicken fingers and watched the waitress.

An older gentleman, dressed in an Armani suit, walked up beside Michelle and placed a mink coat around her shoulder. "Oh, Stephen. This is my friend, Dr. Benjamin Oppenheimer. You remember him from the bistro, don't you? He's a specialist here in the D.C. area."

"Yeah, I remember. Nice to meet 'cha."

The doctor tipped his head in a small gesture of acknowledgement, then returned his eyes to Michelle. Great, Stephen thought, she's got a valet that moonlights as a gynecologist. How convenient.

She stroked the fur coat. "Do you like it?"

"Uh, sure, I guess. I'm not much into Siamese."

"Cute. It's not a Siamese cat. It's mink. Benji gave it to me."

"Well, that's awfully sweet of old Benji. But I'd be careful. Those rabid animal rights activists may strip it off your back. I mean, of all people Michelle, you, being a lawyer, ought to be sensitive to the rights of animals."

"You're impossible Stephen. Good–bye." She stormed off with her gynecologist following quickly behind.

"Well, I don't think you scored any points," Malcolm interjected. "You really agitated her. She may talk."

"It doesn't matter. She's gonna talk anyway. The press is turning up the heat and she'll want to distance herself from me. There's no better way than to say some nasty things, whether it's true or not. Her career is the most important thing in her life, not me, not Benji."

The nymph waitress reappeared after Michelle's grandstanding and Malcolm was delighted. She plopped down two more Rolling Rocks and Stephen finished off the finger plate.

"One other interesting tidbit about Corbett."

"Yeah?"

"He was a journalism major but after college, he went to work as a congressional staffer for one of his home state's senators. Later, he joined the *Times*. Do you know who that senator was?"

"Who?"

"Walter Bainbridge."

"Hmm. That may explain his knowledge of Seattle National Bank."

"Here's a copy of the *Post* story about his death."

"Thanks."

"One more thing. Corbett discovered that a large chunk of the stock in Seattle National Bank was owned by some French national conglomerate. I guess he found out during his stint with Bainbridge. It's headquartered in Versailles and has companies throughout Europe, America and Asia. This European corporation also owns that French bank in Singapore that Corbett wrote about. That's what my friends told me."

"Interesting. The French bank in Singapore is basically owned by the same stockholders who own Seattle National Bank. That makes sense."

"Does it?"

Yep. Anything else you found out?"

"Yeah. I did confirm that Ted Mitchell was good friends with Paul Mathis. They hung out together a lot. I just can't understand how you never knew of him since you and Paul were friends."

"I can't either but Paul never said anything about him."

"Stephen, I know some traumatic things happened to you and McDermott over there. Are you sure you don't know what happened to Paul? The wire services said his body is being shipped back to the states this week. He died of two gunshot wounds at some airport outside of Manilla in the Philippines. You were shot. You were in the Philippines. What the hell went on over there?"

"Malcolm, all of it will come out at the hearings. Is that about it?"

"Yeah."

"Thanks. The info is a big help. If there is anything I can do for you, just ask."

"Mind if I smoke?"

"Well, maybe just this one time."

❀ ❀ ❀ ❀ ❀ ❀

The black sedan entered the alley, killed its headlights and quietly coasted beside the building of chipped red brick.

Located in the Asian community of New York City, the apartment building was a seedy, dilapidated structure, dark from years of constant pollution belched out of the Big, Rotten Apple.

The seven-story hazard resembled more of a bombed-out building from World War II than a habitable residence for human beings.

Three FBI agents stepped out of the sedan. Brad Richardson signaled the other two to climb the fire escape while he entered the front of the building. Slowly, Richardson climbed the grimy stairs, one by one, as brown gunk caked on the soles of his shoes.

He heard yelling of tenant couples and cries of babies emanating from behind closed doors. Only a small lightbulb hanging from a chain attached to the ceiling offered scant light as the agent gently ascended the squeaky wooden steps.

The overwhelming smell of garbage and raw sewage almost made him choke while angry Asian tongue—mostly illegals brought in to work in the sweat shops—could be heard arguing, echoing down the stairwell. Methodically he climbed, gun drawn, head raised, until he reached the grungy sixth floor.

Richardson eased quietly to the paint chipped door with the number 606. He placed his ear against it and listened. Nothing. Then, a crash of glass, yelling, and gunfire.

He stepped back and kicked the door in. A small Vietnamese man, in boxer shorts and a tank-top shirt, came running toward him, screaming and brandishing a gun.

The agent quelled his instinct to pull the trigger and kicked the man in the stomach. He fell back but popped up again. Richardson kicked the gun out of his hand and hit him across the face with the ball of a fist.

The Vietnamese man went crashing into a table. Again, he got to his feet, pulling out a switch blade from the back of his shorts. He twirled the blade at Richardson and attempted to stab him. They circled each other cautiously, waiting for the other to make a wrong move, then strike.

Another agent, blood streaming down his forehead, entered the room, gun drawn.

"No!" shouted Richardson, pointing at the agent. "I told you I want him alive. Stay back!"

The Vietnamese man continued shouting at Richardson, thrusting the switch blade in his face. The agent shouted something back to the assailant in his native tongue. He leaped at him but Richardson—lightening quick reflexes—grabbed the wrist with both hands, twisted the arm, until the blade dropped, and pulled the arm over his shoulder, breaking the man's elbow joint with a quick yank.

He screamed in agony, dropped to his knees before the agent met him in the face with the sole of his shoe. He fell on his back, blood running profusely from a flattened nose.

"Where's Olsen?" Richardson asked the other agent between gasps of air.

The agent pointed to the back room where they had entered a window from the fire escape. "He's back there. He's dead Brad. Shot. The guy had a gun under his pillow."

"God–dammit Lee. Can't you do anything right? Jesus, what will I tell LaCross? We lost another agent in the line of duty or some bullshit like that. You know how damn important this mission is. What are we gonna tell Olsen's family or the press? Our orders are to conduct this investigation in complete anonymity. We can't have casualties."

"Yes, sir. I know. I'm sorry."

"You don't know shit. Two FBI agents can't take some two-bit drug pusher. If I hadn't met him at the door, he would've been long gone buddy–boy."

"Brad, look!"

The Vietnamese man regained consciousness, placing his hand over his mouth. Richardson ran to the fallen foe and kicked the hand away, then kneeled beside him and forced his fingers into his mouth.

Gurgling sounds came from Vietnamese man. Richardson was choking him as he pried his fingers into his throat. He withdrew his hand and emerged with a tablet.

"Cuff the son-of-a-bitch and search him. Then get Olsen."

"What is it? Poison?"

"Yep." Richardson held the pill up to his eyes, turning it in his fingers. "Cyanide. He doesn't want to tell us anything. He'd rather die. But he wasn't quick enough." He withdrew a plastic bag from his coat pocket and placed the tablet inside.

"If he tried to kill himself, he may not talk," said the other agent.

"Oh, he'll talk. I'll make sure of that. He had his chance but he blew it. Now it's our turn."

The agents searched the apartment before leaving with the cuffed suspect and the body of the dead FBI agent. They placed the suspect and body in the back seat of the sedan and left the depressed neighborhood.

The suspect gibbered in Vietnamese. Richardson looked back at him in the rear view mirror and barked something. The suspect became quiet instantly.

"We're goin' to the FBI headquarters in Manhattan and question him ourselves," Richardson told the other agent as he drove.

"Don't ya think we had better get'm to a hospital. You screwed up his arm pretty bad."

"Time is short and we need answers. LaCross is on my butt. Lives and a lot more are riding on this one. His arm can wait. Besides, the injury might just give 'em a loose tongue."

"Yes, sir."

Chapter Eleven

Bobby Lockett looked about 50 years of age. Puffs of gray hair poked out underneath the Stetson, running along the sides of his balding head. He wore Levis, Tony Lama cowboy boots and a pair of prescription glasses with dark tint.

He reminded Stephen of the Marlboro Man. Tan, leathery face, pockmarked and wrinkled from sun damage. Defined crow's feet splashed from corners of the eyes. Lines etched his face as if cut by the pallet knife of a sculptor. Those lines spoke a lot about the man; years of acquired knowledge and wisdom.

Lockett accompanied Mrs. Doris Wilson to Stephen's apartment. Wilson was past president of the National League of Families of Prisoners and Missing in Southeast Asia, a volunteer organization dedicated to definitively resolving the American POW–MIA issue.

Lockett, an ex-Marine, was an activist in the Vietnam Veterans of America organization despite the fact he had been convicted of collaborating with the enemy while a prisoner of war in Vietnam.

Cordial but brief introductions, spiced with some small talk, began their meeting. Blake and Lockett hit if off immediately; nothing like the common thread of war can make absolute strangers intimate friends.

"Mr. Decatur, Mr. McDermott," Mrs. Wilson said, "I'll be frank. The reason we requested this meeting was because we heard your story in the news media. I must say we were skeptical at first about your claims. They seem far-fetched at best. But I talked with Bobby and the more we talked, the more it bothered us. We came to the conclusion that any help, no matter how ridiculed, was needed. We've fought our government over the POW-MIA issue for years and been stalled at every turn. Perhaps it's time for a different approach.

"Maybe you two gentlemen have that approach. We just need help, any help. The National League only wants the Vietnamese government to make a full accounting of MIAs and POWs, that's all. If my son is dead, so be it. But I have to know one way or the other. It's hard to go on like this not knowing anything. Families are suffering because we can't get an answer, any answer, either from Vietnam or our government."

"I understand," Blake replied.

"My son John was an Army infantryman. He was captured in 1970 and officially listed as dead. However, a retired Air Force colonel and former POW reviewed Johnny's file for me. His folder contained reports he was sighted in 1975 and as late as the 1980s. I was totally shocked. Make that devastated. Why would this type of information continue to flow into his file if Johnny is dead?

"The pain and suffering is in not knowing," she continued. "If I found out Johnny was dead, I could live with that. At least I would have some peace of mind. I've lived without him now for over 25 years but I have to know. . . you understand. . .I must have some peace of mind."

She began to tear up and Bobby put his arm around her shoulder. Stephen looked at Blake. The war had been over for decades but its effects were still alive as if the Gulf of Tonkin incident happened yesterday. Bobby reached into his back pocket and gave her a handkerchief.

"This is a sensitive subject to many POW-MIA families across the country," Lockett said. "That's why the VVA and Doris' group would like to help you prepare your testimony for the congressional hearings. We've dealt in particular with the Senate Select Committee on POW-MIA Affairs and know the personalities you'll encounter.

"Our organizations collectively accumulated a lot of data over the years and we want to share it to help support your claims. We've been stymied many times while trying to give the select committee this info. I understand you'll have a national televised forum when you go in front of 'em. This is an opportunity to bring our information to the public on a mass basis. I think you'll find it'll supplement your testimony."

Lockett looked at the sobbing woman, pushed the Stetson back on his head and frowned.

"Right now, we're so desperate, we'll do anything. Everyday that passes, another POW could be dying. Everyday, another family member is suffering, not knowing. It's gotta stop. It's been years since the war ended and still we have no definite answer. I got this gut feeling that you guys have some real ammunition to bring this issue to a head. Your claims are outrageous but Blake here is a real in-the-flesh POW, no doubt about that. He alone, without the claims, is enough evidence for the Senate Select Committee to realize American POWs do exist in Vietnamese prisons."

"By the way Mr. McDermott," Mrs. Wilson interjected, wiping her eyes with the handkerchief. "Did you get our cards and money at the hospital?"

"Yes, I did. Thank you very much. I appreciate the generosity. I can tell the veterans' organizations are committed to resolving this POW issue. I'm glad to know someone cares and wants to help us."

"We know how you feel," she said. "We're behind you, both of you. We've organized all the groups on your behalf. We'll provide any assistance you need."

"Thank you, Mrs. Wilson," Stephen replied.

"Well, I guess you know about the La Mai document and all that stuff," Lockett noted.

"Right. I covered it for Reuters when the story broke about Professor Wallace discovering it in Moscow. That's why I was assigned to cover the hearings in Hanoi and got caught up in this mess."

"There is one senator on the select committee who is sympathetic with the plight of POWs and their families, Mel Jones of Nebraska. He's been instrumental in getting us access to government documents through the Freedom of Information Act. He lobbied for those hearings in Hanoi after the La Mai document became public. Unfortunately, the lunatic who shot the place up ruined a golden opportunity. Now you guys may be our only chance."

"That loose gun is another story," Stephen said. "But go on, please."

"Senator Jones requested the Attorney General conduct a criminal investigation into his accusations that top U.S. Defense and State Department officials committed perjury to cover up a high-level government conspiracy to abandon American POWs and MIAs from the war, like you Blake. He wrote the Attorney General a letter and requested the probe, accusing eight high-level current and former employees of the State and Defense Departments. He still believes they're involved in a conspiracy to cover-up the government's abandonment of POWs and MIAs. Here's a copy of his letter he provided us."

Lockett handed Stephen a Xerox copy. The journalist read for a moment, then handed the letter to Blake.

"As you can see, he indicated his willingness to provide documentation of this criminal conspiracy uncovered in investigations by the committee. There's a list of officials Jones accused of attempting to cover-up their failure to follow leads on sightings of live POWs in Southeast Asia after the war and also of perjuring themselves in testimony during hearings with the committee. Several of those accused worked in the Special Office for POW-MIA Affairs in the Defense Intelligence Agency or DIA, an arm of the defense department, and the U.S. Military Joint Task Force-Full Accounting."

Blake nudged Stephen and pointed a finger to a name on the list of those accused in Jones' letter. It read "Richard Armstrong, director of the Office for Vietnam, Laos, Thailand, Burma and Cambodia Affairs of the State Department." Stephen nodded but did not say anything.

❁ ❁ ❁ ❁ ❁ ❁

"If you read the entire letter," Mrs. Wilson said, wiping her eyes, "you'll see he lists several specific instances of false statements given to the committee under oath. Senator Jones charged that the DIA conducted a sub-standard investigation into POW sightings, used inappropriate prejudice to discount information that POWs remain in captivity, and deliberately lied about the location of at least two POW camps utilized by the Vietnamese after the war ended. He wanted to work with the Justice Department in an investigation of the perjured testimony."

"You'll also notice," Lockett interjected, "that regarding the eight accused, the senator refers to efforts by these individuals to quash the La Mai document discovered by the professor in the archives of the Soviet Communist Party in Moscow. The individuals in question, according to Jones' letter, made attempts to discredit the La Mai document. When Wallace emerged with it, those officials scrambled around trying to bury the issue and find some quick answers since they had always insisted POWs didn't exist in Southeast Asia.

"The best they could come up with was—under oath in front of the committee—that the discrepancy between the POW numbers released by the Vietnamese government in Operation Homecoming and General La Mai's figures could have been that La Mai included South Vietnamese captured by the North."

"Hmm. I hadn't thought about that."

"But Professor Wallace specifically stated to the committee under oath before his death that General La Mai used the term 'American' prisoners of war throughout the report."

"Did you actually see the La Mai document?" Stephen asked.

"Of course not. It was immediately classified by President LaFleur. But it didn't matter. Most of the text was translated into English and published in the newspapers. That's one instance where the national media helped our cause."

"Yeah, I remember. The State Department was hot about it leaking out to the press."

"Professor Wallace traveled to Laos to meet with officials as part of the select committee's investigation," Wilson added. "He was found dead in his car right after he returned. He never was able to give 'em a report."

"I heard the National Security Advisor asked him to go," Stephen said. "What part did the committee play in this?"

"I don't really know for sure. I do know Senator Jones was interested in a series of articles written by a *New York Times* correspondent on the CIA, especially a Laotian drug lord who was quoted in some of the stories. He had a strange name. I can't remember it."

"Has the Attorney General's investigation turned up any leads?" Blake asked.

"There hasn't been an investigation," Lockett replied. "Despite Senator Jones' request, the remainder of the committee has stymied investigation efforts. Senator Bainbridge, the committee chairman, even went so far as to tell the Attorney General to ignore his request, according to our sources on the Hill. The Justice Department did a weak probe into Jones' allegations and said no evidence exists to substantiate his claims, so Bainbridge got Jones off his back, if you know what I mean. Bainbridge has never been a friend to us. He's tried his best to push us outta the spotlight."

"Was the media ever apprised of Jones' request for a criminal investigation? I never heard anything about it."

"Nooo Mr. Decatur," swooned Mrs. Wilson. "The committee and Attorney General kept the episode quiet, air-tight. The committee requested Senator Jones not make a public statement until the investigation was complete. Of course, the investigation turned up nothing so Jones had no real statement to make. We aggravated both the committee and Justice Department about the progress of the probe but they kept hiding behind the word 'national security,' telling us they couldn't comment."

"You were a POW, weren't you?" Stephen asked Lockett.

"Yeah. I accompanied Senator Jones on an extensive fact–finding mission to Vietnam two years ago and showed him the existence of camps and areas where I saw Americans being held before I was returned to the United States in 1979. I saw Americans at Dong Ly and at a prison located at Anh Phu, both in Northern Vietnam. I took the senator there where we found concrete foundations of former prisons and other evidence like shackles used to confine prisoners. Listen, the DIA supposedly investigated Anh Phu and reported that no prison ever existed. I took Jones there and pointed the prison building out right to 'em."

"Candidly speaking Mr Lockett, why should we believe you. Weren't you convicted of collaboration with the enemy when you returned to the states?"

"Yes, I was. I've always been up front about that. I don't lie about it. I have no excuse. The years of torture and brainwashing finally broke me down. I did anything I could to get back home. I wasn't strong like Blake here. I let the Hanoi Marxists use me for their communist propaganda. Senator Bainbridge has always discounted my testimony as not credible because of my conviction.

"The media portrayed me as a traitor. I understand it, I'm not asking for sympathy. But Senator Jones tested me. He took me on that fact–finding mission to Vietnam against the advice of the other committee members. I didn't let 'em down. I took him right to those prisons where I saw Americans. He couldn't believe it. The prisons weren't suppose to exist according to the DIA. He thought I was a fraud too. But I showed 'em. I showed 'em all. When he saw those shackles, his eyes almost popped outta his head."

"Mr. Decatur, we've worked with Bobby for many years now. He's provided us and the committee with valuable and credible information on POW sightings in Vietnam," Mrs. Wilson explained. "Yes, he was convicted as a traitor but his circumstances are unusual."

"We'll look this letter over and maybe talk to Senator Jones," Blake confided. "We need someone on our side when we testify. Anything else?"

"The POW situation is a old issue," Mrs. Wilson told the men. "Red China has never accounted for over 8,000 American POWs from the Korean War. That war ended in 1953."

"No. Really?" Stephen asked, surprised.

"Uh-huh but nobody knows about it. It was argued in the 1970s by U.S. officials that normalizing relations with China would lead to its assistance in determining the fates of those missing servicemen, the same argument and logic the bureaucrats are using today to lift the trade embargo against Vietnam. But since the normalization with China by the Nixon White House, Beijing has failed to account for any Korean War POWs or MIAs."

"President LaFleur has praised Vietnamese cooperation as being responsible for the return since last July of the remains of 39 American servicemen," Lockett noted. "But most of the remains have proven to be Asians, probably South Vietnamese. My trip with Senator Jones was unannounced. Usually Hanoi is informed in advance before a live sighting investigation is initiated. Most, if not all, accessible crash and grave sites excavated by the U.S. Military Joint Task Force-Full Accounting were already excavated by Hanoi prior to the arrival of Task Force personnel."

"Vietnam's landscape is dotted with mass graves from the war," Blake said.

"Not only that," Lockett chimed in, "we believe China played a significant role in concealing American POWs from U.S. forces during the Vietnam War. I have some friends who work at the Pentagon. They told me they've seen classified military documents from the early '70s indicating that Red China held hundreds of American Vietnam War POWs for the Hanoi communists and to this day they've never been accounted for. If that's hard to swallow, take a look at this."

Lockett reached into a pocket and withdrew a copy of a newspaper article from the *New York Times*. He handed it to the journalist. The article was buried on the back page of "All the news that's fit to print."

It detailed information obtained from China and released by the U.S. State Department confirming the deaths of two U.S. Navy airmen, who were shot down by the Chinese in 1967 after mistakenly flying into Chinese airspace during the Vietnam War. The Chinese turned over to U.S. officials photos of the bodies taken at the time of their deaths and released the airmen's identity cards.

Stephen popped the copy with a snap of a finger and pointed to a paragraph in the article. Blake leaned over and read it. The article credited a Deputy Secretary of State Richard Armstrong with retrieving the data from Beijing.

The *Times* quoted him as saying "the Chinese initiative reflects a new era of cooperation between our countries in accounting for missing American servicemen." Stephen clenched his teeth; he could feel the heat rising in his face.

"If you'll notice, the article gave no indication of the location of the Americans' remains nor why the Chinese didn't provide evidence of their deaths years earlier," Lockett explained. "I mean Jesus, they were shot down in '67 but China just now accounted for 'em. That's evidence right there they concealed information from the Defense Department. It burns me up. I don't get it. They've never accounted for American POWs yet our government continues to grant China 'Most Favored Nation' trading status and allows 'em to run up a billion dollar trade surplus with us."

Chapter Twelve

WQXE Channel 13 was a local television station within the beltway, located several blocks from the Smithsonian Institute. Besides serving the surrounding vicinities with local news coverage, the station also housed a cable access show, *The Daily Business Channel.*

Similar to C-Span but offering a financial menu, the channel broadcast 24 hours of business trends and forecasts, investor advice and daily activity of stock exchanges.

Gordon Osato developed an illustrious career which quickly turned sour. He worked as an investment broker for the Wall Street firms of Goldman Sachs and Drexell-Burnham Lambert before landing a job as a commodities advisor on the fledgling cable show.

Stephen was introduced to him by a mutual friend who served as a reporter for WQXE. He decided Osato might be able to fill him in on the hysteria generated in the press about the benefits of potential American business investment in Vietnam.

National media pressure was mounting, calling for President LaFleur to lift the trade embargo so American corporations could begin their business of opening shop in the Southeast Asian regime.

"Man, you'd think the trade embargo was the most evil policy ever conceived by the U.S. government," Blake complained as he read the ed–op page of the *Post.* "These corporations don't need the money. I mean, it's the principle of the embargo that's important. POW lives are at stake. That's more important than making a few more bucks, isn't it?"

"I don't know, is it? It depends on one's point of view," Stephen said as he drove to the TV station. "To Richard Armstrong and Paul, it wasn't as important as making a few more bucks."

Blake was quiet for a moment, contemplating his words. He threw the newspaper down into the floorboard of the car. "Did you get the gun I told you about?"

"Yep. Pulled it out from under the toilet. That was pretty ingenious. How 'bout you? Did you sneak yours out of the hospital?"

"I sure did," he said proudly. "If I'd stayed one more day, I would've gone crazy. Those damn Defense Department people visiting everyday, asking me questions over and over again. They actually placed me in quarantine from the rest of the hospital. Police waking me up all through the night, searching my room. Drove me crazy. I didn't get one night's sleep. God, I can't wait until these hearings are over."

"How do you feel?"

"Okay. I'll feel better when we tell those pompous bastards that POWs have been sitting under their noses for the last 25 years."

Gordon Osato was a Japanese-American and carried all the credentials necessary for an ivory tower existence in the shadow of Wall Street—educated at Harvard, Rhodes Scholar, Beta Sigma Phi, Hoover Institute fellowship to name just a few of his scholarly accomplishments.

He had lived the high life in the 1980s, rubbed elbows with junk bond king Michael Milken and finally fell into disgrace when the junk bond frenzy collapsed under its own clay legs of debt. He was glad to have the job at *The Daily Business Channel.* Gone was the fleet of Lamberginis and New York penthouse but his pride was beginning to return.

Blake and Stephen took a seat in Osato's office, having been led there by his secretary. His office looked like a television control room with several TV monitors built into the back wall. On one screen, C–Span was broadcasting the House debate on agricultural subsidies.

On another screen, multitudes of people rushed back and forth like rats scurrying to the next meal, wielding pieces of paper like a sword and screaming figures at each other as if conducting an auction. It reminded Stephen of a Chinese fire drill. The stock exchange never made any sense to him but it was the lifeblood of American capitalism.

Another screen monitored the rise and fall of stocks and bonds every second of the day so investors—stockholders, IRA owners, mutual fund managers, commodities dealers and investment brokers—could keep abreast of the ever fluctuating paper asset value of industry and business.

"Stephen, it's been a while." Gordon Osato entered the room. "Your name has become famous around this town or should I say infamous."

"Hello, Gordy. It's been a long time. Don't believe everything you read."

"I don't. Remember, you taught me that."

"This is my friend, Blake McDermott."

"Yes, nice to meet 'cha. I've heard of you."

"Well, I hope we can still be friends," Blake joked.

Gordon shook hands with both men and took a seat behind his desk. He still looked like the Wall Street manipulator Stephen remembered, impeccably dressed, not a black hair in his head out of place. Beautiful like a colorful snake, but deadly.

"So what brings you to *The Daily Business Channel.* Need some investment advice? Want some stock options? I've gotta great deal on a no–load mutual fund that's provided an annual return of 19 percent the last five years. It's called the Intercontinental Family of Funds. Got a growth fund, income fund, money market, municipal bond, custom made to any financial need you have."

"We're not here. . ."

"You put away a couple of thousand a year and you'll have a nice little nest egg when you retire at age 65. Or you can make the fund an IRA and accrue interest tax free until you begin to draw on it. If, of course, you don't go over the annual deposit limit."

"Listen Gordy." Stephen raised his hand. "The advice I need from you is not that complicated. I just want you to answer a simple question for me."

"Shoot."

"Please don't use that word," Blake interjected.

"Why?"

"Brings back memories."

"Never mind." Stephen glared at Blake. "Can you tell me about the planned investment into Vietnam by U.S. corporations. I want any information you've got on it."

"Vietnam is playing a significant role in your life these days. How come you want to know about American companies?"

"I just want to see if I can pick up any leads. The press has been playing it up big these days. If anyone would know, I figure it'd be you Gordy."

"Well, now that you mention it, I had an interesting little tidbit come across my desk recently. Stock in a French based company has been rising dramatically since it's American partner announced plans to build some infrastructure in 'Nam."

"What is it?"

"A real estate, insurance, and banking conglomerate, called Equity International. A deal was struck by the company's American partner to build a port in Vietnam. Equity has 180 offices throughout North America, Europe and the Pacific Rim. It generates more than $500 million in revenues annually. It's a rising star on the stock market. Equity assisted in brokering a $200 million deal to develop a deep-sea port about 50 miles south of Ho Chi Minh. The company's American outfit, Equity USA, struck a deal with its Asian partner, Pacific Equity, to put together a plan to build the port which would allow heavy transport ships to dock."

"You said Pacific Equity?"

"Right. The port will be built primarily by a Japanese engineering and construction firm. According to a interview I read in the *Wall Street Journal,* Equity's CEO said it will take four years to complete and is the largest foreign investment in Vietnam to date. Because of this deal, their stock has been hot property. You oughtta look into getting some for yourself Steve. It's got long term potential. I think it'll pay in spades."

"No thanks. Their stock is quickly losing value with me. But go on. Tell me more."

"Well, Equity International secured a license to conduct banking services in Vietnam, or I should say their foreign partner Pacific Equity did that for the parent company. A large number of industrial giants like Kodak, Boeing and Du Pont have already opened offices in Vietnam in anticipation of the embargo being lifted. Mobil Corporation announced it's part of a consortium that has been awarded offshore drilling rights by Vietnam. I guess you're aware the U.S. government has in place a trade embargo against Vietnam."

"Painfully aware of it. How can they do that when domestic investment in Vietnam is illegal according to the embargo?"

"The operative word is direct investment. The Equity International deal is legal under embargo rules because it was done through its foreign partner, Pacific Equity, though its American branch was instrumental in putting together the deal. U.S. headquartered multi-national corporations have offices and global partnerships throughout the world. So they can skirt around the Vietnam embargo and exploit the direct investment loophole. They just use one of their foreign subsidiaries to broker the deal. It's simple."

"So these companies are technically not violating the trade embargo, just the spirit of it."

"Um, yeah, that's a cynical way to put it. It's the age old quest for the all mighty dollar. Nothing new. Where there's a will, there's a way, especially when there's a buck to be made."

"Do you know what companies are actively involved in lobbying the LaFleur administration to lift the embargo?"

"That's all I know. But there is an interesting situation developing between Vietnam and the president."

"What?" Blake asked.

Gordon adjusted his tie, then placed his elbows on the desk and spoke in a hushed tone.

"Listen. This stuff is insider information. Very sensitive. Steve, you remember I got into trouble in the 80's with the junk bond scams."

"I remember Gordy."

"I had to turn state's evidence on my partners to a grand jury to escape prosecution. It was a bad scene, ruined my career. I don't want to repeat that mistake. Wall Street blackballed me but I've gotten back into the good graces of some of my former colleagues. I don't want to screw that up. Understand? I like you but. . ."

"Gordy, you can trust us. We won't say a word. I've never let you down. Remember all that free publicity I gave you years ago."

"I remember. You helped me out. But I let a lotta my friends down. Well, I guess it won't hurt to tell ya. The president is expected to make a public announcement any day now anyhow. I don't see where it'll matter this late in the game."

"What announcement?"

"President LaFleur is expected to make a decision regarding Japan's and France's efforts to provide loans to Vietnam through the International Monetary Fund. Member countries contribute to the IMF which in turn lends out that money to fledgling countries in need of economic development. The U.S. has historically opposed IMF loans to Vietnam since U.S. taxpayers contribute a large portion of the money used for lending by this global bank. However, I understand through reliable sources that LaFleur may suspend opposition to the loans favored by Japan and France."

"I haven't heard anything about this in the press."

"Nope. Not a word. I told you it was insider information. The White House wants it quiet until an announcement is made so that no fervent opposition can't be mounted in time."

"Are you sure about this?" Blake inquired.

"Absolutely. LaFleur's cabinet favors it." Gordon grinned slyly, pleased that his guests were surprised at his intimate knowledge. "I understand Commerce Secretary Simpson has endorsed the IMF loans to Vietnam. In fact, he left for Hanoi yesterday. I'd bet money he went there to officially tell them that the president will not oppose Japan's and France's efforts."

Blake pointed to one of the television screens. "There he is now."

Gordon turned in his chair and faced the monitor. He grabbed the remote control off the desk and turned up the volume. President LaFleur was addressing the Washington press corps in the White House Rose Garden.

"I am ending U.S. opposition to International Monetary Fund loans to Vietnam." LaFleur spoke into a microphone while standing behind a wooden podium that carried the seal of the president. "Allowing IMF loans will offer the best hope of providing America's POW-MIA families the answers and peace of mind they deserve. We must heal the wounds of the Vietnam War, look toward a new era of cooperation and focus our energies on domestic issues. Our own country has been neglected too long, our infrastructure decaying. The national deficit, health care reform, and job creation must be our number one priority."

Gordon turned the volume off. In the background of the Rose Garden stood National Security Advisor Marlin Kwolski.

"Same old shit. Sounds like a broken record," Gordon cracked. "You'd think LaFleur never won the election. He's still campaigning. Well, there it is boys, right on schedule. What'd I tell ya. You can bank on my advice. I bet the Dow Jones Industrial is going crazy this very minute. Equity's stock will skyrocket because Vietnam will use those IMF loans to finance the deep-water port deal.

"Look at the players, Senator Bainbridge is a strong advocate of lifting the embargo and he has clout as chairman of the Senate Select Committee. Commerce Secretary Simpson has publicly stated he favors it. Besides, companies are lobbying the president hard to lift the ban. They have a lotta money riding on the president's decision and he has a lot of wealthy campaign contributors to answer to and you guys know who they are, big business. The fix is in. His announcement on the IMF loan proves that. Lifting the embargo is a sure bet."

❀ ❀ ❀ ❀ ❀ ❀

Blake was quiet as they drove home, mulling over Gordon's comments. Stephen fiddled with the radio, trying to find some suitable music to soothe his nerves, shaken from his friend's stark prediction. He turned to national public radio and caught commentary on President LaFleur's announcement to halt efforts to suspend IMF loans to Vietnam.

Following the broadcast of the president's speech and question-answer session with the press, public radio began airing points of view on the president's decision from veteran's organizations and the president's own administration.

One representative of Vietnam Veterans of America spoke in an angered tone to public radio commentators.

"We oppose trade concessions or loans to Vietnam under any circumstances until the POW-MIA issue is fully resolved by the communist regime. As far as we're concerned, by granting IMF funding, President LaFleur is putting a bullet in the brain of each of the American prisoners of war Vietnam holds. I mean this literally. Vietnam is now well on its way to having the advantages diplomatic recognition bestows.

"Therefore, keeping prisoners will be a liability while releasing them would only ensure IMF funding was denied," continued the VVA representative. "Killing the POWs will solve Vietnam's problem and the American government's political problem posed by them. The president's actions today is an outright betrayal of America's POW-MIA families."

"Amen," Blake gently whispered under his breath.

Following the VVA representative's commentary, public radio broadcast an interview conducted with National Security Advisor Kwolski. He expressed sympathy for the POW-MIA families and emphatically insisted that LaFleur respected their views but defended the president's actions.

"Believe me, IMF loans to Vietnam ensure the security of our nation and offer the best hope for POW–MIA families in resolving the U.S. POW issue," Kwolski stated. "If the administration can reestablish diplomatic relations with Vietnam, and IMF loans is one way to accomplish that objective, then the communist regime of Hanoi will no longer be a threat to our vital security in the volatile region of the Pacific Rim. Vietnam will be more inclined to provide us with additional information on American POWs and MIAs, if such data does indeed exist."

"Right. Buy your way into their hearts," Blake smirked. "They think money will soften the heart of a communist. Why do we have to bribe them to give us our POWs when they should have done that according to the peace treaty. It's their responsibility. Shit, first our government wanted to blow the place up, now it's decided to buy Hanoi's loyalty. That's the mentality of the federal government, either kill people or purchase their friendship. In either case, it doesn't work."

"Gordon's right. The fix is in. President LaFleur is gonna lift the embargo. As he said, the IMF loan proves that. It's just a matter of time. We've gotta move fast. The hearings begin in three days, thank God. I hope we're not too late."

"The Justice Department has your records. They must have shared them with President LaFleur. Obviously, he knows about me."

"Yeah, but remember his national security advisor is Kwolski. He's probably running interference while filtering the information obtained from the records. Also Simpson must be pressuring LaFleur. The president is living in a vacuum, surrounded by advisors who are insulating him from the truth. That French company, Equity International, Gordon mentioned must be the same one Malcolm told me owned stock in Seattle National and the Singapore bank."

"Well, that was nice that your friend took a chance and told us about the IMF loans."

"He didn't take a chance. If there's one thing I know about Gordon Osato, he never risks his neck. He always covers his butt. He just shared that info to impress us, that's all."

"Really?"

"Oh yeah. He likes to show off and he owes me like I told 'em. He's sly but he keeps an ear to the ground."

"Do you see that car following us in the rear view mirror?"

"Yeah. He's been following us all day."

"Is it FBI?"

Stephen shrugged. "Who knows? Richardson won't tell me shit. He says agents are watching us but this guy could be working for Simpson and Kwolski as far as we know. As long as he doesn't get too close, we're alright for now."

"What about Minh?"

"I called his home in Miami. His maid said he left the country. She didn't know when he'd return."

"Great. You're telling me Minh has tucked tail and left the country?"

"I dunno Blake. It doesn't look good. Perhaps he got scared. He said Trang Van Ho had threatened to use Simpson's influence against him or get Hanoi agents to knock him off. He told me the FBI was dragging its feet on his case. Maybe he decided it wasn't worth it, felt like he should hide out. Hell, it's anyone's guess."

"So he's not gonna testify with us like he promised."

"It certainly looks that way."

❀ ❀ ❀ ❀ ❀ ❀

Brad Richardson entered Director LaCross's spacious office after passing through the elaborate security clearances required of all bureau employees. The FBI Director was speaking with two other special agents.

LaCross pointed to a vacant seat for Richardson to occupy and continued talking. The agent's attention was diverted for a moment to the portrait of J. Edgar Hoover hanging on the wall. Again, those weird, frog-like features of the fabled FBI Director disturbed him.

The eerie stare of the beady eyes seemed to penetrate, like a laser beam. Hoover must have been an incredible spook, Richardson thought, maintaining confidential files on politicians and anyone else who threatened his supreme rule of the nation's top law enforcement agency.

Let's face it, he mused, the man kept his homosexuality and penchant for dressing like a woman in the closet his entire illustrious career—the perfect spy. Secrecy and spying was Hoover's main forte. And that grand tradition in the FBI was ably perpetrated by a new generation of agents.

"Have ya got good news for me?" LaCross asked, breaking Richardson's train of thought, as the two other agents departed the suite.

"Uh, yes, sir. We apprehended the bomber in New York City. His real name is Chang. He checked out as a small time heroin dealer and occasional assassin as I told you. INS informed us Chang is here illegally."

"What about a connection to Uyen Minh?"

"He confirmed what we suspected. He confessed to throwing the bomb in the taxi to kill Blake McDermott and also said he was hired to eliminate Stephen Decatur. We've got him cold. He coughed up the entire story and fingered Minh as the main instigator."

"Good. I understand one of our agents was killed trying to apprehend him."

Richardson lowered his head. "Yes, sir. Olsen. Chang shot him as he entered through the window with Agent Lee. I'm sorry Director LaCross."

"We're all sorry Richardson. We can't have sloppy work, no breaches of security what so ever. No public knowledge of our investigation. Our nation's safety is at stake here. I assigned you the job because of your Vietnamese background. Plus I thought you were capable of handling it. You're one of our top agents. I didn't make a mistake, did I?"

"No, sir. Olsen's death was an accident. It's been taken care of. His family has been notified and given an artificial account of his death. All the messy details will be cleaned up. The New York Police Department is cooperating with us so no press will catch wind of Chang's arrest or the shooting."

"Make sure of that. This is of the upmost importance. I understand this Chang tried to kill himself."

"Yes, sir. I got the cyanide tablet out of his mouth before he could swallow it."

"They're desperate to keep this under complete anonymity. They don't want Decatur and McDermott's murders traced back to the Golden Triangle. What about Minh?"

"No word as of today. Our operatives informed me just two hours ago that he's been visiting some dignitaries in Vietnam. But nothing unusual so far."

"Watch him closely. He's gonna make a move. Since Chang was unsuccessful, that will change plans drastically. Things are gonna speed up fast. Monitor Decatur and McDermott closely."

"Yes, sir. We're following them everywhere they go. They met with some veteran's organizations and recently visited WQXE television station and talked to a business commentator. Nothing out of the ordinary. I'll let you know immediately when Minh makes a move."

"It'll be soon. Maybe today. We got word. The $50 million from the United Nations Drug Control Program was wired to the French bank in Singapore. We also finally identified the $800,000 fee paid to Commerce Secretary Simpson for his services. It was transferred to the French bank too. Hanoi opened the account for him in another name but the National Security Agency finally obtained positive ID after copying bank records. Simpson's payment came from the Seattle National Bank."

"From Seattle National? I thought the funds were coming directly from Hanoi."

"They are. Hanoi is one of Seattle National's biggest clients. The regime deposits a lot of drug cash there. Simpson is in Vietnam visiting with Hanoi leaders as we speak. He's meeting today with Prime Minister Vo Van Kiet and Communist Party Chairman Du Muoi."

"Ho?" Richardson asked.

"No sign of Trang Van Ho yet. Maybe he's lying low since Uyen Minh is there. But the play is being made by Simpson and Kwolski. Minh's gonna counter and immediately. The congressional hearings are in three days. Something will happen. McDermott and Decatur are stuck in the middle of a nasty drug war. Both sides don't want 'em to testify. We must anticipate their moves."

"I understand."

"I spoke to the chairman of the joint chiefs yesterday. Their investigation into the shredding of the embassy POW-MIA files has been completed. The executive order came from National Security Advisor Kwolski. Armstrong's CIA buddies executed it."

"So it's safe to assume the NSA's order was a result of Kuhn-Sah Duc's people stealing the UN records from the Bangkok embassy and delivering them to Jim Laramie."

"Yes. Kwolski didn't want any more sensitive data stolen. But Laramie in turn stole Duc's business transactions with Pacific Equity."

"How did he know?"

"Professor Robert Wallace tipped Laramie about Pacific Equity when he visited Southeast Asia. We broke into his E-mail after his body was found. He told the ranger about it."

"But it doesn't explain why Wallace met with Duc and Laramie."

"Kwolski manipulated Wallace to meet with 'em, told him about Pacific Equity concealing possible evidence of POWs after he returned from Moscow to discuss the La Mai document."

"That was risky considering his group is the one concealing the POWs."

"He didn't get where he is by playing it safe. Kwolski's ploy was dangerous but it paid off. It placed pressure on the White House and paved the way for the lifting of the embargo."

"I understand now. Wallace's knowledge of POWs and Duc's business arrangements exploited the existing rift between Duc and the White House as planned by Kwolski."

"Correct. Wallace unwittingly made two very powerful enemies, the CIA drug cartel because of discovering the La Mai document and the White House because of knowledge of Pacific Equity."

"So which one killed him?"

"It's not important. Counter intelligence says Duc informed Laramie of locations of imprisoned POWs in Vietnam. Duc hoped to use Laramie to expose the cartel's Achilles heel—the POWs—and eliminate the UN money that had hurt his heroin trade. But Laramie was savvy. By then he knew of Pacific Equity and stole Duc's records on the corporation."

❁ ❁ ❁ ❁ ❁ ❁

The telephone rang and rang. Stephen did not stir. It had been a long night. After visiting with Gordon Osato, he and Blake drove around Washington, D.C. for several hours until they were satisfied the tail was gone, then picked up the original records from a safety deposit box he had rented.

They traveled back to Stephen's apartment in Alexandria and stayed up all night preparing their testimony and reviewing the transactions and clients listed in Kuhn-Sah Duc's records and Armstrong's UN files.

The answering machine picked up and an excited voice greeted the slumbering journalist.

"Stephen, Stephen, pick up the damn phone. It's Malcolm. Big news man. Will ya pick up the phone, please!"

He turned over and looked at the digital clock: 6:15 a.m. Eyes still closed, he groped for the phone on the nightstand beside the bed. He picked up the receiver and put it to his ear.

"Yeah."

"Stephen, thank God you're there. Wake up pal. You're not gonna believe it. I can't believe it. Things are really goin' crazy."

"Jesus, Malcolm. It's six in the morning. I just got to bed. What the hell's so important?"

"Steve, Collin Simpson is dead."

Suddenly, his eyes peeled back the layer of sleep and opened widely. He jerked straight up in bed as if stuck with a hot poker.

"Did you hear me? Commerce Secretary Simpson is dead."

"Yeah, yeah, I heard you. What happened?"

"He was assassinated in Hanoi. Some right-wing extremist group is claiming responsibility. Someone planted a bomb in Hanoi's Trade Center Committee Building where he was meeting with Vietnamese leaders. The explosion also killed a guy named Trang Van Ho, who according to the international desk at the *Post,* was a former minister of South Vietnam before becoming an economic advisor for united Vietnam."

"God, I can't believe it. Someone must have found out about his deal."

"Found out about what deal?"

"Uh, nothing. I'm still asleep. Anything else?"

"Yeah, about the same time that bomb went off in Hanoi, a bank in Singapore was bombed. It did a lot of damage. I think most of the bank building was completely destroyed. And guess what?"

"It's that French bank that Corbett fingered in his article."

"Yeah. How did ya know?"

"Just a lucky guess. Do they know who did it?"

"Some Chinese nationalist group is claiming responsibility."

"Do they think the bombings are related?"

"Nope. Police authorities in Vietnam and Singapore told the *Post* they believe the incidents are separate and unrelated, conducted by completely different terrorist groups."

"Do you buy that?"

"Shit no! It's too coincidental."

"Me either."

"Pick up this morning's edition of the *Post.* The stories came over the wire service late last night but we got it in before the press run. It's scanty on details. More details are coming today."

"Okay."

"One other thing."

"Yeah?"

"Ted Mitchell."

"What about him?"

"He's gone."

"What da ya mean?"

"He left the newspaper yesterday on a sabbatical of all things. The boys at Metro said he was real nervous and jumpy. Said he had to get outta town and think about some personal matters in his life. Took a leave of absence and no one knows where he went or when he'll be back."

"Strange."

"I'll say but he's one strange dude. At least you don't have to worry about him writing more scurrilous stories about you and Blake for a while. Good riddance, huh?"

"Uh-huh. Listen, I've gotta go but I'll catch you later. Thanks man."

"Anytime. Hey, Tammy thinks you're real cute. We ought to go out more often."

"Tammy?"

"Yeah, our waitress at Planet Hollywood."

"Oh. The one in braces."

"Knock off the shit, Stephen."

"Listen, let me set you up with an older, more mature woman."

"Like who?"

"Michelle."

"Ha. Forget it pal. I'll stick to the youngsters. They're not as complicated. They don't want a BMW every Christmas."

"I'll see ya Malcolm."

Stephen hung up the receiver and paused for a moment to allow the shell shock to wear off. His mind was spinning in circles, trying to absorb what Malcolm said. He drew a deep breath, then jumped out of bed and hurriedly got dressed.

He reached under his pillow and withdrew a handgun. He shoved the pistol into the front of his trousers under the shirt tail.

He went down to the street corner of his apartment building and bought a copy of the paper. When he returned, he woke Blake and told him the news.

"God, what's going on?" the POW asked as he sat on the side of the bed, occasionally coughing, with his weary head in his hands.

"Someone found out about Simpson's deal with Hanoi and didn't want the trade embargo lifted."

"But who? The CIA cartel, American business and the Vietnamese government profit from lifting the ban. Who does that leave?"

"That's what bothers me. I don't know. According to the *Post* here, the assassination is being blamed on some right-wing Vietnamese group that opposes reestablishing diplomatic relations with America. They claim Western imperialism caused the Vietnam War and this same capitalistic imperialism will make Vietnam a economic colony of the United States. It doesn't sound right."

"You don't believe it was them then?"

"No. The assassination is related to lifting the embargo. But it wasn't done by this terrorist group."

"What about the bank bombing?"

"That's precisely why I don't believe it. It's no coincidence the French bank was bombed. Minh said $50 million would be deposited there from that United Nations Drug Control Program to help start a bank in Vietnam to finance American investment once the embargo was lifted. We know the records show that money from the UN program is being diverted by the CIA cartel toward heroin production. That French bank, according to Minh, also served as the off–shore account for Simpson to receive his lobbying fee from Hanoi. The two bombings are definitely connected.

"The *Post* says some Chinese nationalist group in Singapore bombed the bank," he continued. "I think both these terrorist groups claiming responsibility are just smoke screens, front groups paid to run interference. Whoever did these bombings hired those groups to take responsibility and muddy up the waters so the real killer couldn't be traced. But who would benefit from keeping the trade embargo in place?"

"For the life of me, I dunno," Blake said, rubbing his eyes. "It doesn't make sense. All the players would benefit. The Vietnamese government would benefit financially from American investment plus the POWs they're holding would be written off. American corporations would reap financial rewards like Gordon said. Those rouge CIA agents would benefit because the POW issue for all intent and purposes would be eliminated and the cartel could continue to reap drug profits."

"There's another player here we aren't seeing. Someone who has the power and influence in the Golden Triangle to order the killing of a top American official and bomb an international bank in two different countries but still cover his involvement. But who could have that much influence over there beside the governments themselves or the cartel."

"Maybe someone in the cartel double crossed another. You know, a kind of power struggle within the group. Maybe Kwolski had Simpson killed and wanted it all to himself."

"But why bomb the bank? It held the UN funds needed to finance American investment. The UN funds play a major role in the cartel's attempts to control poppy production in the Golden Triangle countries. No, the bank bombing changes the entire complexion of Simpson's assassination. There's something else here we're not seeing."

"Did Malcolm tell you anything else?"

"Yeah. He said Ted Mitchell took a leave of absence from the newspaper yesterday. Said he was real anxious to get outta town. Something tells me he knew what would happen to Simpson and felt like his life was also in danger."

"But why?"

"Maybe because the people he's working for are the same people that Simpson worked for. Trang Van Ho also worked for that same group and he died in the bombing. Minh told me Van Ho was the one who set up the Southeast Asian Economic Development Council and acted as middleman between Simpson and the Hanoi regime. Someone wanted them stopped. But who?"

The phone rang again. Blake got up from the bed and stumbled into the den. Stephen continued reading the *Post* story.

"Hello. Yeah, he's here. Hang on."

The POW came back into the bedroom with a disgusted look on his face.

"It's Richardson. He's ready."

Chapter Thirteen

The telephone rang in the office of Senator Walter Bainbridge, Washington State's senior representative. The senator's office was located on the second floor of the Richard Russell Senate Building off Constitution Avenue.

Bainbridge's congressional aid answered the phone and informed the caller that the 24-year senator was in an important meeting and could not be disturbed.

"Yes, he can be disturbed too. This is an urgent phone call. Please interrupt the meeting and tell the senator that Stephen Decatur wants to talk to him about the Golden Triangle. Understand? Make sure you tell him the Golden Triangle."

A perturbed voice came back. "Hold Mr. Decatur. I'll give him the message."

A few moments passed, then a dignified voice came over the line. "Hello. This is Senator Bainbridge."

"Senator, Stephen Decatur."

"Yes, Mr. Decatur. What can I do for you?"

"A lot. As you well know, Blake McDermott and myself will be testifying in front of your committee and the Senate Foreign Relations Committee. I'm sure you've reviewed the records I presented to the Justice Department."

"Why no Mr. Decatur. I haven't seen 'em. The Senate Select Committee on POW-MIA Affairs was waiting for you to personally present them at the hearing."

"Well, for your own information, the records contain incriminating evidence about Seattle National Bank and your own personal accounts there. You're a large stockholder so you should know the records reveal a paper trail back to Southeast Asia, in particular massive cash deposits from the Golden Triangle. Do you understand what I'm saying?"

"No. I'm afraid I don't. I'm a very busy man Mr. Decatur."

"Let's cut through the bull senator. Simply put, those bank records show an illegal laundering scheme for drug cash. You're own personal accounts reveal deposits of cash from the communist regime in Hanoi and other sources within Southeast Asia. Are you beginning to understand now?"

"Sir, you're violating federal privacy laws. Those accounts are exclusively private. This is an outrage."

"Excuse me senator but I don't think you'll prosecute. You've violated a few federal laws yourself. And the records prove that."

There was a long pause on the phone. "Hold a minute," came back the voice. Stephen heard murmuring in the background, then a door shut.

"I'm sorry. I had to ask my colleagues to leave. Now, what's your point Mr. Decatur? I have rights and I'm willing to fight it out in court. Is this conversation going anywhere?"

"Yes sir, it is. My point is this, Blake and I are willing to cancel our testimony in exchange for substantial compensation on your part. In other words, we're willing to cut a deal for the right price."

"Mr. Decatur, you must think I'm a fool. You're trying to blackmail me with false claims and extort money. How do I know you won't come back and ask for more money. What guarantees are there that you two won't still testify after being paid."

"We'll hand over the original records. The Justice Department has only copies. I think you're aware of that."

"What does it matter? That's of no value to me. You've already given the Justice Department what it wants."

"Please Senator, don't insult my intelligence. You and I know those copies at the Justice Department can easily disappear, especially with the help of your good friend, Marlin Kwolski. The JD hasn't leaked any of the records' contents to the press. No one knows what's in those records except you, me and the JD. And no one else will until Blake and I testify in 48 hours."

Again, a long pause.

"You don't want those POWs to come home and tell their story. The committee has looked the other way on the POW-MIA issue for years due to your influence. If Blake and I publicly announced we wouldn't testify, the press would have a field day. The media is already trying to make us look like fools, calling our claims outlandish and bigoted. So if we decline to testify, that would validate their claims and you would be off the hook. You'd have the original records and we would leave town humiliated."

"This all sounds interesting Mr. Decatur but. . ."

"Listen, the JD can easily dispose of the copies. The department certainly realizes the political downfalls of trying to pursue this issue. Even if we did renege and decide to testify, you have the originals. Without those, we have no proof, just hollow allegations."

"What do you and Mr. McDermott get out of all this?"

"Freedom plus two million dollars in cash tonight."

"Ridiculous. I don't have that kind of money and if I did, I certainly couldn't get it in a few hours."

"As I said, we've seen your bank records. You have plenty of cash on hand. Seattle National can wire you two million today with no problems. Are you really willing to let us testify and chance exposure? We're willing to cut a deal Senator. We don't want to be in the spotlight anymore. So what will it be?"

Stephen heard Bainbridge sigh, then he spoke. "Two million for the original records and no hearing, right?"

"Exactly. Meet Blake and I at Lafayette Park tonight at midnight."

❁ ❁ ❁ ❁ ❁ ❁

Light snow flakes littered the night air, drifting and falling silently upon the frosty ground. Lafayette Park took on the appearance of a cemetery that late at night—pallid, dreary and quiet.

A black limousine with tinted windows slowly crept beside the park as the halogen headlights illuminated the sheets of snowflake flurries. The limo stopped and turned the headlights off and on three times. Two figures approached the automobile.

A man in a brown trench coat got out of the back of the car and walked up to the two figures, shivering in the cold. White vapor exhaled out of their mouths as a conversation ensued.

"Have you got the records?" Bainbridge inquired.

"Have ya got the money?" retorted Stephen.

Bainbridge looked back at the limo and waved his hand. A large, muscular man got out of the driver's side, holding a brief case. He walked up to the senator and handed it to him. He then stepped back behind Bainbridge and watched Stephen and Blake.

"Here it is. Now give me the records."

"Open the brief case."

Bainbridge snapped open the case and lifted the top. Rows of green cash could barely be seen under the haze of the park's night lights. Stephen looked at Blake, who reached into his overcoat with his right hand. Bainbridge's burly employee reacted quickly to the POW's movement, reaching into his coat pocket and extracting a pistol.

"Whoa. Call your goon off Bainbridge. Blake's just getting the records."

The senator raised a finger. The thug lowered the gun and returned it to the pocket. But Stephen noticed he kept his hand there. Blake withdrew a file and held it by his side.

"Let me see it," Bainbridge hissed.

"Let me see the money."

❀ ❀ ❀ ❀ ❀ ❀

Bainbridge handed him the brief case and took the file from Blake while the goon watched intently. He took a penlight from his coat pocket and thumbed through the papers. After a few moments, he seemed satisfied and turned off the light.

"Well, you boys are more ambitious than I imagined. You really had me and the committee goin'. We thought you really intended to go through with it, testify and tell the truth, do your patriotic duty and all that noble crap. But you're just a bunch of common crooks like I thought, looking to make a fast buck."

"You should know Bainbridge. But tell us, who ordered the killing of Secretary Simpson? Was it you or Kwolski?"

Blake counted the stacks of cash in the briefcase while the journalist and senator exchanged words.

"I don't know what the hell you're talking about," he replied, handing the file to the armed thug.

"Knock off the stupid act Senator. Come clean with us. We've given you what you want. We pose no threat now."

"Give me what I want! Hell, this never belonged to you in the first damn place. I've given you two million dollars of my money for my own property. All you damned reporters are just alike, arrogant and presumptuous."

"Senator, you've got millions in drug cash stashed away according to those records. Two million is just a drop in the bucket for you. Now tell me, why kill Simpson? Was it another member of the cartel?"

"I don't know."

"C'mon."

"I told you, I don't know!"

"How long have you been involved in the POW cover-up for that CIA drug cartel?"

"Long enough to know troublemakers like you when I see 'em. I'm freezing my ass off out here. Let's go Manny." He signaled to the goon with a snap of his fingers.

"Wait until Blake finishes counting the dough."

"It's all there. You don't trust me?" The senator's wrinkled face broke into a grin.

"I trust you about as much as those POW families trust all that bullshit you throw at 'em at the committee hearings. How much of that drug cash does Hanoi and the cartel pay you in exchange for using the committee to cover–up the existence of American POWs in Vietnam?"

"More in one year than you two parasites will make in a lifetime. Now hurry up. My damn wife will be wondering where I am this late at night."

"I'm finished," Blake noted, closing the brief case. "It's all there."

Bainbridge began walking away, then stopped and turned around to the men again. He snapped his fingers at Manny, who withdrew the pistol and aimed it at them.

"Don't try to double cross me. You know I have very powerful friends, both in this town and Southeast Asia. Manny here expects ya to keep your part of the bargain about not testifying. If you decide to change your mind or go to the press, he's gonna visit you with some of my Vietnamese friends. You'll be missing in action too. Do I make myself clear?"

"Very clear. Your patriotism really warms our hearts Senator," Blake countered.

Bainbridge turned around, snow crackling under his feet as he stomped back to the limousine. The goon followed, opening the car door for him. They watched the black stretch job slowly pull out and disappear into the blurry night.

They looked at each other, then at the briefcase and began walking. A hunter green Ford Aerostar Van came around the corner and flashed its lights. The two men walked to the back of the van and stepped up inside.

One side of the van wall was installed with sophisticated communication equipment. Brad Richardson sat in front of the equipment wearing a pair of headphones, listening to the playback of a tape. Two agents were in the front seat. Blake handed Richardson the briefcase of money.

Stephen sat down and tore open his shirt. He pulled the tape from his chest and removed the wire, handing it to the FBI agent.

"So much for our prestigious federal representatives. There, was that enough?"

Richardson took off the headset and grinned, like the cat that swallowed the canary.

"Yeah, it was enough to nail 'em. The tape of that conversation combined with the records should put Bainbridge away for some time."

"Good because it almost got us killed. Bainbridge's steroid freak wanted to pump us full of lead."

"We'll get an indictment in no time. He really bought into those copies. I told 'cha he would. Bainbridge took those fakes like they were gold. I noticed he didn't let his guard down when you asked about Simpson."

"Maybe he did answer it," Stephen replied.

"How?"

"He said he didn't know."

"Well, of course."

"No. Maybe he really doesn't know."

"Hell, yes he knows. And he's gonna tell us more tonight."

"You gonna arrest him tonight?"

"Yep. The boys are waiting on him right now at his home in Reston. I called 'em after listening to the tape."

Blake removed his wire and tossed it over to Richardson.

"You guys don't seem that happy? We're getting one of the main men in the drug cartel. You should be glad."

"Sure. We just don't like being blackmailed into doing it."

"Don't hold that against me. It's not my fault that you two killed a deputy secretary of state and a journalist. That's a serious felony offense. You guys aren't exactly angels. Besides, you two wouldn't have done it for me without a little convincing."

"It was pure self-defense. They tried to kill us. It's more than you bums have done. Without us and our information, you'd still be busting counterfeiters instead of high ranking government officials. The glory boys at the bureau will claim responsibility when Bainbridge is indicted but without us, you'd have nothing."

Stephen began to button up his shirt. Richardson noticed a gun butt sticking out of his pants.

"Hey, I told you no damned guns! What if Bainbridge had seen it? You could have blown the entire sting operation."

"Shove it Richardson," Blake interjected. "We're not about to become sacrificial lambs so the FBI can look like their doin' their jobs. You guys don't mind getting us killed."

"What about the investigation into Uyen Minh's allegations?" Stephen asked. "Simpson's dead now. That ought to tell ya that Minh was on to something and was telling the truth about the commerce secretary."

"We're looking into it Decatur, okay? Let us do our job. These things take time."

"Well, Minh's out of the country now. He was suppose to testify with us. But he got scared because you guys are dragging your feet. How do we know the FBI isn't involved? Hell, CIA operatives in Asia are involved. Why not FBI agents?"

"Shut your damn mouth! I've heard all the bellyaching I can stand from you two." Richardson leaned over and poked Stephen in the chest with an index finger. "Minh's story is under investigation as we speak. As far as him leaving the country, it was his choice, not ours. Minh has his own agenda to carry out."

"What agenda?" he asked, pushing the agent's finger from his chest.

"Get the hell outta here."

"Paranoid bureaucrats," Stephen mumbled under his breath as he jumped out of the van.

"What'd you say?" Richardson retorted.

The journalist said nothing. Blake got out behind him, looked at the FBI agent for a moment, gave him the middle finger, then slammed the van door shut.

Brad Richardson entered Director LaCross' office for the second time in two days. He was quite shaken. The director had personally called him and requested he be in his office in fifteen minutes.

The FBI Director never called a special agent, the supervising officer did such menial chores. Something short of a national security breach must have occurred, Richardson thought, as he opened one of the double doors leading to LaCross' office. It was 6:30 a.m. The agent, distracted, didn't even notice the groping eyes of J. Edgar Hoover.

"Director LaCross. I got here as soon as possible, like you asked."

"We've gotta problem, Brad."

He never used an agent's first name, Richardson noticed, unless a major problem existed. It's funny how trauma brings people together on personal terms; then again, maybe the director wanted to pass the buck, dump it on someone else. His voice sounded depressed. Something was up, something really bad.

"I got word this morning from our CIA operatives in Southeast Asia."

Richardson was about to speak but the director interrupted him. "I know. You're in charge but this is an emergency. Uyen Minh gave 'em the slip over there. Somewhere between Hanoi and Bangkok, he substituted a double. He must have known he was being followed. Anyhow, they've lost him."

"How did they find out?"

"I became concerned when Simpson was assassinated and the Singapore bank bombed. I knew Minh was involved. I ordered the operatives to nab him immediately after we received news of the secretary's demise. They thought they intercepted him in Bangkok but it was a double. Christ, I can't believe how incompetent those CIA agents are. How could Minh substitute a double right in front of their damn eyes? Maybe the idiots are snorting that nose candy their fellow agents are running. I dunno. All I do know is intelligence blew it."

"Minh must have been tipped off. What do you want us to do?"

"We can assume that after Minh gave the operatives the slip, he met with his superiors and got his orders. We're trying to cover all the airports and harbors in Thailand, Laos and Vietnam but its impossible. He's gonna make his way back to the states. Intelligence doesn't know when he made the switch so he could already be here. I want you to increase surveillance of Decatur and McDermott immediately."

"Yes, sir."

"If Minh is on his way back, he may be goin' after 'em. But we don't know for sure. I was hoping those dumb–ass CIA agents would find out what he was up to, then we could prepare. But now, there's no telling. He could be here in the states or still back in Southeast Asia. Watch Decatur and McDermott. If Minh is back in town, those two will draw him out."

"Understood. By the way, Senator Bainbridge was arrested early this morning. I assume you were briefed on the operation."

"Yes. I understand the sting went well."

"Excellent. The tape is very damning evidence. Decatur and McDermott played their roles well thanks to the ballistic reports on Richard Armstrong and Paul Mathis. The senator will have an initial appearance in court today and bail set. Then it'll go to a preliminary hearing. I'm confident the case will be bound over for grand jury action. Our U.S. Attorney guarantees an indictment."

"Good. That tape of the undercover sting is our insurance policy. Senators as powerful as Walter Bainbridge have a way of slipping out of charges in this town."

"Not this time. It's airtight."

"We know Decatur retained the original records. Didn't he tell Minh that in Miami?"

"Yes, sir. He wanted Minh to look at 'em before the hearings began so they could prepare their testimony."

"That might bring Minh out in the open. With Simpson dead and the French bank demolished, they must feel pretty comfortable right now, in the driver's seat. The only thing left is the records."

❀ ❀ ❀ ❀ ❀ ❀

Walter Bainbridge collapsed in the study of his Reston, Virginia estate. He did not say hello to his wife when he returned home but walked straight into the study without a word.

He sat in his favorite recliner beside the window and stared out at the white blanket of snow covering the front lawn. He and his battery of lawyers had spent hours in the D.C. Federal Courthouse, listening to the charges against him during the arraignment process.

It was humiliating. The press swarmed over the courtroom like bugs on a dead carcass; the bureau boys had alerted them about their big catch. The FBI played the tape for his attorneys. Bainbridge knew he had slipped up and fallen into the FBI's trap, after all these years of teflon, non–stick criminal activity.

His worried wife knocked on the study door and asked if he was feeling well. He ordered her to leave him alone, at least for a little while. He had not told her; she would find out in due time.

Bainbridge walked to his desk and took a key from an ash tray lying on top. He unlocked the top drawer of the desk and pulled it out. Inside a revolver was removed.

The senator walked back to the chair, sat down and stared out the window.

Slowly, he raised the handgun to his right temple and cocked the hammer. The snow began to fall again, swirling in drifts. He looked at the plaques and awards hanging on the wall, proclaiming his magnificent record of public service to the state of Washington and the country.

He chuckled a moment. It was all quite funny, quite sick, an illustrious career ending like this. Bainbridge pulled the trigger and a shot rang out.

His wife ran down the stairs, startled by the loud popping noise. She entered the study and saw her husband slumped in the recliner in front of the window. His right arm hung down near the floor, grasping a smoking pistol.

The top half of his head was gone, splattered across the room; red mass stained the carpet, curtains and the commendations hanging on the wall.

Chapter Fourteen

Blake unlocked the apartment door just in time to catch the ringing telephone. He dropped a bag of groceries and scurried to the counter.

"Hello."

"Blake," the voice responded.

"Yes."

"This is Stephen."

"Yeah, buddy, where yah been? The VVA wants to meet again today. They've got some additional information to give us for our testimony tomorrow. I told 'em. . ."

"Just listen."

"Yeah, sure. Are yah alright? Yah sound funny."

"Meet me at the Oak Branch warehouse on 42nd, beside the Potomac River, pronto. Bring the records with you. It's important."

"The records. What's goin' on? Are yah in some kind of trouble?"

Stephen was gone. Another voice spoke on the other end of the line.

"Bring the original records or your comrade dies. Come alone. If you involve the authorities, you will never see him again. Do exactly as we say and Stephen Decatur will live. If you are not here in 30 minutes, he will die. Understand?"

"I understand." Click.

Blake reached under his shirt and pulled out the revolver. He checked the chamber: all six bullets were loaded. He snapped the chamber shut and walked over to the couch.

He slid one end of the couch away from the wall and kneeled. He pried up a piece of floorboard, then another until his hand fit below the floor. He withdrew the stack of files and placed the rotting floorboard back in place. He picked up the keys to Stephen's car and left.

The records meant everything—rescuing the POWs and punishing those guilty of hiding them. He lasted in Dach Lu, content with the sole hope of breaking out and finding the traitors.

It motivated him to the point of ignoring the beatings, the torture, the mental anguish and the stark realization that American government officials not only turned their backs on him but looked at all the POWs as nothing but a means to an end—a profitable end.

That was the worst slap of all. Not all of the Viet Cong's bamboo spikes, tiger cages or bull whips combined compared to that cold feeling of abandonment. How could he hand the records over when they were so close to exposing the conspiracy?

But Stephen's life was important, he reminded himself. Every individual is important.

He found the metal warehouse on 42nd Street facing the Potomac. It reminded him of the Thai refinery in the mango grove. Bad memories crept into his head.

He opened the warehouse door and walked through the back entrance of the dark building, clutching the records.

❁ ❁ ❁ ❁ ❁ ❁

The duct tape pulled his lips together, lacerating the tender skin around the mouth; it was uncomfortable and awkward. Stephen sat in the chair, arms tied over the back of the seat, motionless, unable to speak or move.

His legs too were bound as he squirmed and emitted muffled sounds underneath the silver tape. Uyen Minh walked between two armed men, one Vietnamese, the other American, and toward the bound victim, displaying the controlled displeasure of a host jilted by an invited guest.

Minh reached his hand to the face and ripped off the tape; the sting was so severe Stephen thought his skin peeled off too.

"The POW has ten minutes. If he's not here within that time, you're dead. Then we'll hunt McDermott down and kill him too. I should have never let an incompetent, street punk do the job. I'll get it done right. Then nobody testifies."

Minh smiled between nervous facial ticks; his mouth and lower jaw jerking in uncontrollable spasms.

"Who you are working for? The CIA drug cartel? The Vietnamese government? I don't understand," asked Stephen.

"Of course you don't," he replied, the enunciation marked by periodic twitching from the corners of his thin-lipped mouth.

"I was sent to infiltrate Trang Van Ho's Southeast Asian Economic Development Council and find out what Vietnam was planning with American officials. Because of my American education and fluency in Vietnamese, I was the perfect candidate to gain Ho's confidence as a business associate and accomplish the goal of sabotaging the secret agreement to lift the trade embargo between Simpson, Kwolski and Hanoi. But you see Mr. Decatur, I'm not Vietnamese. I am Laotian."

"Everyone in the Golden Triangle would benefit from lifting the embargo and normalizing relations between the two countries. The POWs would be history."

"Not everyone would benefit. The lure of lifting the embargo has powerful leverage with Vietnam and it must be stopped."

"You don't care about the POWs. What are you up to?"

Minh gritted his teeth into a macabre smile as the facial tick became more defined.

"I'm disappointed. I was told you we're clever, above average from the other ignorant Americans who populate your decadent country. Kuhn-Sah Duc expressed a grain of admiration for your tenacity. After all, you escaped the CIA web of intrigue and made it back to the states. Lord Duc does not often complement people, especially Westerners."

Stephen forgot about the stinging burn of the tape; the mention of that name struck him. Finally a crystal clear perspective came into focus.

"Of course, an agent for Duc's Golden Triangle network. I was told you left the country but not because you're scared. You're involved in the assassination of Simpson and the Singapore bank bombing."

"Yes. It was a bold and ambitious plan, worthy only of Lord Duc. I was aware of Simpson's itinerary prior to his departure thanks to Trang Van Ho. You see, the Southeast Asian Economic Development Council arranged his visit. Ho had not yet suspected my duel loyalty."

Minh paced back and forth across the dimly lit room.

"Before the Vietnam War, Lord Duc ruled the poppy with an iron hand. Then CIA operatives infiltrated Southeast Asia during the 1960s for intelligence gathering and began arranging their own deals to manufacture narcotics. The operatives recognized the potential of the poppy and its derivatives—opium, heroin, morphine—and exploited those resources."

Stephen struggled against the rope while carefully keeping his attention on the Laotian man.

"Both sides transacted business for many years. But that changed when the United Nations implemented its drug eradication program aimed at heroin producing countries like my homeland. Through manipulation and graft, the CIA operatives rose through the ranks of the American government hierarchy like Armstrong and Kwolski. They became powerful bureaucrats. They lured influential members of the government into their circles and promised them lucrative lifestyles in exchange for services rendered, like your Senator Bainbridge and Secretary Simpson.

"The American Imperialists swayed the governments of countries dependent upon poppy production to favor their cartel in exchange for infrastructure," he continued. "It was a win-win situation. The governments got free economic improvements paid by UN tax dollars of other countries while the CIA took more poppy territory. Duc felt betrayed by his government, his countrymen. The Southeast Asian governments had pledged their support to treacherous foreigners in exchange for some handouts. American colonialism had turned them against him."

"So the promise to lift the embargo would increase the power of the cartel over Southeast Asian heroin production."

"Yes. That was one of the conditions Trang Van Ho told me Simpson demanded in the agreement."

"What conditions?"

❁ ❁ ❁ ❁ ❁ ❁

"That Kuhn-Sah Duc relinquish what lands he had left in Vietnam and turn them over to the American

Imperialists. Lord Duc has fought a small war with the CIA over the years. The bloodshed and cost to innocent lives during the last 30 years has been incalculable. Peaceful peasants, who only wanted to grow their poppies for a modest sum of money, were caught in the middle of a war with both sides demanding loyalty. Farmers in Vietnam, Laos, Thailand, Cambodia and Burma were killed indiscriminately. Those farmers who opposed the CIA and favored Lord Duc were destroyed."

The journalist knew that time was ticking away. He hoped the Laotian would continue, forgetting that Blake had not arrived. He rubbed the ropes together behind his back and struggled to free himself; but the abrasive rope cut deeper into his wrists and his hopes of escape.

"The CIA utilized subversive tactics such as political assassinations and social strife to overthrow unfriendly governments. For example, the Khmer Rouge seized control of Cambodia after the collapse of South Vietnam in 1975. Lord Duc owned several large tracts of land there and arranged with the Khmer Rouge to retain his poppy fields in exchange for sharing profits with the regime. But Vietnam expelled the regime and occupied Cambodia for years. Duc found out the CIA cartel provided covert intelligence to the Vietnamese to assist them in the invasion and expulsion of the Khmer Rouge from power.

"More than one million Cambodians were killed in the holocaust that followed. Civil war has raged in Cambodia ever since though Vietnam eventually withdrew. The Vietnamese nationalized Cambodia's natural resources, thereby taking over Lord Duc's lands. The CIA renegades provided military and intelligence expertise for the invasion and pushed Duc out of Cambodia. We discovered Armstrong had cut a deal with Hanoi to take over and use POW slave labor from Vietnamese prisons to cultivate the poppy."

"The CIA edged Duc out of Cambodia," Stephen said, "by using the invading Vietnamese as a cover."

"Correct. But what enraged Lord Duc most was Armstrong's treachery in brainwashing local communities, with inflammatory propaganda against him, then equipping the peasants with arms. That's always been a CIA speciality I learned well, pitting one group against another, creating an invisible enemy, then secretly consolidating power while the groups fight among themselves. They tried to divide communities against him, create diversions, thereby weakening his position."

Stephen wondered if Blake would show; perhaps the demand for the precious records was too much to ask of a man tortured and written off as dead for 25 years. Minh looked at his watch, then at his two accomplices. His left cheek quivered as he spoke.

"Vo Van Kiet and Du Muoi knew they would get rich by skimming profits with Simpson from the revenue generated from American business investment. They readily agreed to pay Simpson his lobbying fee. Lord Duc's loyalists within the Vietnamese Communist Party found out and informed him. He had to stop it before it was too late, before his rightful property was stolen and his way of life eliminated."

"We'll testify and expose the cartel and the UN payments. But we need the records. Why take them?" Stephen asked.

Minh paced the floor, back and forth, considering the question. Stephen wanted to know but foremost, stall for time.

"Because of Pacific Equity."

"Part of that French company that owns the Singapore bank you bombed. I remember. Duc was doing some type of business with the corporation according to the records. But you destroyed the bank because of the UN money deposited there."

"The bank itself doesn't matter. We have others. Lord Duc is a large stockholder in Pacific Equity, along with President LaFleur."

"What. The president?"

"You Americans. So ignorant, so naive. You have no idea of the power and influence wielded by those who control your government. Americans can't see the forest for the trees. Do you really think your so-called representatives in Washington advocate the interests of American citizens. Hardly. They represent their interests, despite the fact it sometimes conflicts with the welfare of the society they pledged to uphold. It's the same way in my country. It's the same way in Vietnam."

"Minh, you're telling me the president has been a business partner with Kuhn-Sah Duc in laundering Golden Triangle drug cash through Pacific Equity?"

"Of course. Partners since 1964 when LaFleur met Lord Duc as a young Army intelligence officer during the war. It was LaFleur's business acumen and corporate connections that created Pacific as a branch of Equity International."

Stephen stared at the quirky Laotian, trying to determine if what he just heard was some sort of perverse joke; but no laugh, not even a smile appeared on the trembling face of Uyen Minh. Stephen smirked to cover his fear; fear that what Minh said might be true.

"Lord Duc's business associate returned to America after the war to fulfill his ambition. LaFleur moved up the ranks of American government. But on his way to climbing the pinnacle of social and economic supremacy, he realized the political expediency of backing the CIA cartel despite his ties to Lord Duc. He saw which way the wind was blowing as you Americans say so colorfully. The cartel was gaining strength in Southeast Asia due to UN money and its members played powerful roles in American government. Without their backing and cooperation, he could not hope to become president of the United States."

"Let me get this straight. President LaFleur helped build the Golden Triangle and is a partner with Kuhn-Sah Duc. You expect me to believe that?"

Still, no expression. "I don't expect anything of you. You're just a pawn, like the other 260 million people in this corrupt, imperialistic country. Just like the millions in Southeast Asia."

"If what you're saying is really true, why not expose Pacific Equity during the congressional hearings, if indeed the president is involved."

"Lord Duc still depends on technical and logistical support from Pacific Equity. But LaFleur has become too greedy. By lifting the embargo, the IMF loans he approved will finance business deals for Equity International in Vietnam, increasing stock value in subsidiaries like Pacific. The company is positioned to benefit from an estimated $600 million in loans from the International Monetary Fund. The Vietnamese bank the UN funds would have created belonged to Equity. The company is licensed to provide banking services in Vietnam. But without the embargo, Lord Duc can't use the POWs to expose the CIA cartel."

One of the accomplices motioned Minh, who abruptly smacked the tape back across Stephen's mouth. Someone was coming.

❁ ❁ ❁ ❁ ❁ ❁

Blake stepped away from the stack of crates and slowly climbed the metal staircase which led to a lighted office. The office, encased in glass, overlooked the entire warehouse floor.

Minh's men met him halfway up and provided a rough escort into the office where Stephen was being held. The two goons followed beside him like a pair of white and yellow bookends. They searched him and retrieved the revolver, handing it to Uyen Minh.

Minh took the records and meticulously scanned through them. He closed the folder and looked at Blake, face twitching in all sorts of contortions as excitement inside him grew. His mission was complete. The powerful drug lord of the Golden Triangle would award him handsomely for his loyalty.

"Excellent Mr. McDermott. You followed instructions and not a minute to soon. Your friend was about to be dropped into the Potomac with concrete shoes."

"You Vietnamese bastards got what you wanted. Now I expect you to hold up your end of the deal. Let 'em go."

Minh smiled and shook his head. "I was just lecturing Mr. Decatur on the stupidity of the American public. How gullible and assuming you are. I'm not Vietnamese nor am I an enemy. Appearances and reality tend to distort each other. Your assumption is correct. Vietnam is an enemy but so are your countrymen. The Vietnamese could never have imprisoned you in Dach Lu without the cooperation of American government officials."

"How do you know about Dach Lu?"

Ming waved off the inquiry as if it were an affront, beneath his dignity.

"I get paid to know. Unfortunately, due to extenuating circumstance beyond my control, I cannot honor our agreement. I must liquidate both of you. Liabilities outweigh your assets as Mr. LaFleur was so fond of saying at Pacific Equity board meetings. Please understand, it's nothing personal."

"That's what I hate about goddamned Southeast Asia, people tell you one thing and do another. They never honor their obligations."

"Just like the American government Mr. McDermott."

The two men grabbed the POW, leading him out of the office and down the stairs. While the three men descended the stairs, an eruption of noise echoed in the warehouse.

The American goon screamed, dropped his weapon and fell down the stairs. Blake struck the Vietnamese with his elbow and ran back up the stairs. Another hail of gunfire shattered the windows of the office.

Minh ran out, clutching the records and brandishing a gun, firing down into the warehouse as he fled downstairs with the stunned Vietnamese man. More gunfire was exchanged, striking propane tanks and igniting gas. A series of explosions rocked the structure, shaking the foundation. Rivers of fire splashed across the warehouse.

Stephen tipped over the chair and tried crawling across the floor but he couldn't dislodge the rope. He could barely move. The fire climbed higher and higher into the office.

❁ ❁ ❁ ❁ ❁ ❁

Brad Richardson pursued Uyen Minh up the fire escape unto the roof of the warehouse. The Vietnamese thug had died in a hailstorm of lead as a S.W.A.T team positioned below the staircase opened fire.

But the thug's boss responded by killing two S.W.A.T members and escaping to the rear of the building. The fire was engulfing the structure. Richardson could feel the heat permeating through the soles of his shoes as he pursued Minh across the roof. Portions of the ceiling were collapsing as fire ate through the support beams.

The Laotian ran to the edge of the roof and hesitated. The drop down was long to the roof of the adjacent building. He backed up and leapt across, falling head first onto the rooftop of the shorter building.

Richardson aimed and fired his pistol, striking Minh in the shoulder at he rose to his feet. The Laotian groaned, spun around and fired continuous rounds from the top of the shorter building.

The FBI agent ducked. Minh ran. Richardson had to leap across. The ceiling was falling in and fire rising. He backed up as smoke engulfed the warehouse, swallowed and began running hard.

He couldn't see the shorter building for a moment while airborne; in a split second, he emerged from a smoke cloud and saw the rooftop coming toward him at terrific speed. He landed with a thud, rolled and got to his feet. He looked around, spinning quickly in circles with the gun extended, hoping to anticipate the shooter, like he was taught at the academy in Quantico. No sign of Minh.

The roar of the fire became deafening as the warehouse ceiling totally collapsed, spewing flames and burning debris. The heat was tremendous, searing the agent's face though he was on top of the adjacent building.

He covered his face with an arm and back pedaled away from the blaze. The sound of a door shutting caught his attention. He saw a door leading downstairs into the building. It creaked open, because it was slammed too hard.

He raced toward it and entered, galloping down flights of stairs, the gun extended. He peered down the stairwell and spied a dark head descending rapidly. A burst of bullets erupted. Richardson ducked, falling on the steps. The bullets ricocheted, pinging against the wall and metal stairs. He got to his feet and continued the pursuit.

Minh ducked into a door, entering the second floor of the building. Richardson followed. The floor was dark but the agent could make out a floor space cluttered with offices, a perfect place for a criminal to hide.

❀❀❀❀❀❀

He stealthily crept in but was greeted with a flash of fire and rain of bullets. He jumped and rolled across what seemed like a book shelf. One bullet grazed his arm. Again, more shots. He rolled across the floor and desperately fired into the dark, hoping to hit a target.

Minh was too accurate for the darkness. Richardson couldn't see anything, yet he seemed to know precisely where the agent was located. He parked behind a desk and tried to gain his breath and composure. He felt his arm. A wet spot on the shirt sleeve stung.

He frantically reloaded the pistol and stared into the darkness. He spied an illuminated exit sign above a door. He thought he caught a shadow. He squinted and peered harder.

Yes, a dark figure moved slowly under the lit sign. It was Minh. Trained to observe unusual things, he noticed the head was distorted around the eyes. He strained harder to make out the face. Minh moved directly under the sign for a split second; there it was: night goggles.

Minh was wearing night vision goggles. Richardson knew he was a sitting duck in the dark. He observed a light switch beside the door, slightly illuminated by the exit sign. But Minh was standing near there.

He felt on the top of the desk—a tape recorder, perfect. He threw it across the room. Minh, his attention diverted, fired where it hit. Richardson leapt over the desk firing.

The Laotian tumbled across the floor, anticipating the shots, finger depressed on the trigger, spewing bullets everywhere. Richardson made it to the exit door and flipped on the light switch. An entire row of fluorescent lights in the ceiling burst on.

Minh screamed, tearing off the goggles. The flash of painful light caused by the goggles blinded him temporarily; he stumbled, firing with eyes closed.

Richardson ducked, then return the fire, striking Minh several times in his chest and face. The Laotian dropped the gun and fell across a desk. He walked up to the fallen man and felt a wrist for a pulse: nothing. He looked at the face. The lip was twisted upward in a grotesque shape; the facial tick frozen for eternity.

❁ ❁ ❁ ❁ ❁ ❁

The FBI agent walked up to the battery of police cars and ambulances stationed around the smouldering embers of what was the Oak Branch Warehouse.

The searing glow of orange reflected off the sky, producing a spectrum of colors against the skyline. He saw Blake McDermott receiving medical treatment for a leg wound. He walked up to him.

"What about Decatur? Did he make it out?"

EMS personnel wrapped McDermott's leg in a bandage and placed him on a stretcher. Blake did not say a word but pointed. Sitting on the curb was Stephen, his face blackened from smoke, rubbing his rope–burned wrists.

Richardson walked over to him and spoke.

"Are you alright?"

Stephen didn't say a word.

"It's okay. Everything is over. We got 'em. It turned out for the best."

Stephen quit rubbing his wrists and peered up at the FBI agent.

"The records?"

Richardson pulled a file from his coat.

"Minh?"

"Dead, in the next building. I got the records from 'em. Here you go."

The agent handed the journalist the records.

He placed the records under an arm and slowly rose to his feet. Richardson was about to speak when Stephen drew back a fist and struck him across the mouth. Stunned, he stumbled back and fell into the street.

The agent, propped up on elbows, wiped the red from the corner of his mouth with the back of a hand and looked up at him.

"What the hell was that for? After I just saved your neck and got the records back, this is how ya show your damned gratitude."

"Saved my neck my ass! You put our lives in jeopardy. You knew all the time that Uyen Minh was an agent for Kuhn-Sah Duc. You knew he entered this country to infiltrate the CIA cartel and stop the embargo deal struck between Hanoi and Simpson."

"It was classified. My hands were tied."

"Bullshit! Blake and I were the bureau's decoys. You watched us but not to provide protection like you said. We were followed in hopes Minh would show his face. You knew we would lure Minh out, then you could nab 'em. And we did just that."

Richardson rose to his feet and wiped off his arms. He withdrew a white handkerchief from a back pocket and dabbed the cut on his mouth.

"You needed us Stephen. Without us, you would've been dead. Justice couldn't have been served."

"You wanted Minh, not justice. You didn't give a damn about us. We were a means to an end. The bureau wanted to protect its interests. So you suckered us into your little conspiracy plot, and played us like a violin, using me and Blake. The bureau never intended to bust Simpson or President LaFleur, did it?"

Richardson didn't answer.

"You nailed Bainbridge because we helped. That counts for some PR mileage. Now you can brag at the press conferences about stopping government corruption. But you planned to lay low on the other big boys and just concentrate on the threats posed by Kuhn-Sah Duc."

"You got your damn precious records back for the congressional hearings. It contains evidence to nail all of 'em."

"No Brad. Not all of 'em. Some are untouchable, you know that. The FBI has known about the CIA cartel for years. But it looked the other way because politicians like Bainbridge control the agency's purse strings, which provides all the resources while the president appoints your director. But in the meantime, the bureau lost its objectiveness, its independence, its mission. The bureau has been circumvented like the United Nations, just a bunch of political hacks, answerable only to Washington insiders."

Richardson rolled the handkerchief up and threw it on the ground.

"We tried to help you."

"Hell no. You helped yourself. Another commendation, perhaps a promotion for killing Minh. More good headlines for the bureau."

Stephen stepped off the curb, walking toward the agent. The journalist braced for a parting shot as he stepped closer and closer with his fists clenched in anticipation. Richardson's eyes followed as he walked beside him, then past. Nothing happened.

He walked toward the ambulance where Blake was being treated and drew a breath of relief. He stopped, curious and turned around for a moment.

Richardson had not moved but stood there in the middle of the street, hands pressed against his hips, head lowered. He returned his gaze to the ambulance.

Blake, his coughing seizures aggravated by the smoke, gave a thumbs up sign as medical technicians loaded his stretcher into the ambulance.

Chapter Fifteen

The drizzle of snow drift covered Washington D.C. in a blanket of frosty white. The dreary winter day gave the nation's capital a look of bleak desolation. Congress had adjourned for a holiday. The beltway was deserted, except for crack pushers and drug gangs roaming its streets like predators scavenging for prey.

Stephen walked to the Mall and down toward Constitution Gardens where the Vietnam Veterans Memorial is located, a granite wall built on two acres and dedicated to honoring the 58,000 war casualties of the Southeast Asian conflict.

The bitter chill in the air made him shiver; he flipped up his coat collar and descended the steps toward the war memorial.

A lonely figure was reading the names of the Vietnam dead, running his finger down the sea of acquaintances engraved into the granite structure. Stephen walked up to Blake and looked at "The Wall."

"The VVA people told me about this memorial," Blake said. "The war was so long ago. I didn't realize we pulled out in 1975. The guards at Dach Lu use to tell us we had lost the war and our military left humiliated. They said we'd been abandoned but I never listened. I always thought they'd come back for us."

He pointed to a name. "Charlie Simmons, a buddy of mine. He was a pilot like me, got shot down in '69, I think. We never heard from him again. I recognize a lotta names here."

A young woman was also scanning the names a few yards away. She took out a pencil and sheet of paper from her purse and began a "rubbing," by placing the paper over a name and rubbing the pencil lead across it.

She stopped, looked at the tracing and put it back in her purse. No doubt a memento for family members unable to visit the memorial.

"I should be engraved on this wall. The government wrote me off long ago. Of course I'm not dead. But in Dach Lu, I didn't know I was alive either. Sometimes it was hard to tell. Might as well be dead I suppose."

"Blake, listen. . ."

"No Stephen. It's alright. I'm not feeling sorry for myself, just remembering the good ole' days. I look at all these names, too many to count, and I wonder why. Why? What happened to me over there? What happened when I got shot down? Everything changed. From there on, it got blurry, unreal, like I was living someone else's life, a nightmare."

The journalist stared at the polished granite, thinking about what he was saying. He tried to change the subject and sound positive.

"Hey, look what you've done for the POWs and all Vietnam Veterans. You testified at the congressional hearings, two straight months of pressure and stress, never cracked once under intense questioning. Some of those senators tried to make you out to be a criminal but you held your ground. Marlin Kwolski was indicted along with a slew of CIA, Defense and State department personnel. The Defense Department has located the POW prisons including Dach Lu and President LaFleur will meet with Vo Van Kiet to negotiate their release. Not bad for an Air Force pilot."

"I couldn't have done it without you. You were key to the testimony and evidence. Without the records, we would've been crucified."

"We both did it Blake. Look at it this way. Simpson is gone, Bainbridge is gone, Minh is gone, Trang Van Ho is gone, Armstrong is gone and Kwolski's goin' to jail. Not a bad day's work for a POW and unemployed journalist."

"Yeah but all my friends are gone too. I watched them die at Dach Lu one–by–one over the years. The only thing left of the friends I had before goin' MIA are here on this piece of granite. My parents are dead and gone. Never knew I was alive. Quang is gone." He looked at Stephen. "Mi Ling is gone."

The journalist looked down at the ground and kicked some pebbles. White vapor exhaled from his mouth as the cold wind circulated paper debris around the park benches.

"You're right. The POWs and MIAs will be coming home. We've done a lotta good. We accomplished our mission."

"You're the one that told me in the hospital not to think of ourselves but to do this for them, remember?"

"I remember." Blake tried to smile and sound upbeat. "So, what are you gonna do now? The hearings are over. We've done our patriotic duty. What next?"

"Well, I can tell you I'm not gonna cover any meetings in Southeast Asia anytime soon. Or Washington D.C. for that matter."

Blake's smile widened; he poked the black granite wall with a index finger. "Really, what will ya do now?"

"Take some time off, go home to Georgia and visit friends. No one's knocking down my door to offer a job. My free-lance career is down the drain. Nobody in the national media wants to hire me. I've been blackballed.

Those things I said under oath at so–called Vietnam Gate killed my career. Jesus! Those committees made me feel like I was facing the Inquisition. No metropolitan daily will take the chance of hiring me. But then again, small publications have heard of me too thanks to the televised coverage. I've been labeled a troublemaker, a malcontent. How 'bout you?"

"The Defense Department labeled me the same. We exposed too much. The Veterans Administration even tried to stop me from collecting benefits. I was due medical treatment because of my service and imprisonment. They denied me access to a VA hospital, said something about a possible court marshall because of my testimony. Can you believe that crap?"

"What happened?"

"Senator Jones stepped in and helped me out. I got the benefits. The Pentagon was just trying to scare me off. The minute Senator Jones mentioned talking to the chairman of the Senate Armed Services Committee about cutting their budget, they backed off. The VA is gonna provide medical treatment. The doctors at the VA hospital say I've got tuberculosis. I need treatment."

❀ ❀ ❀ ❀ ❀ ❀

"Good God, will ya be alright?"

"It's hard to say. The VA seems to think its pretty bad. Coughed up blood yesterday. But what the hell. I've beaten the odds before. Nobody thought I would make it back to America after 25 years in a death camp. And we eluded the CIA cartel, Kuhn-Sah Duc and the Vietnamese government. So far, I've been pretty damn hard to kill."

Stephen expressed a worried smile. "You're a fighter. You'll beat it. How's the leg?"

"It's fine. The pain from the bullet is gone. It's only fair that I get shot in the leg since you did. I mean, were partners right?"

"Right. I'm sure glad you came back and pulled me out of the warehouse before it collapsed. No thanks to the FBI. So what's next for you partner?"

"The VVA and some other veteran organizations want to hire me as a lobbyist on Capitol Hill. They think I can be very effective. You know, become a public speaker and tell about my experiences, push for more veteran benefits and services in Congress. Things like that. Can you see me as a damn congressional lobbyist?"

"That's great Blake. Yes, I can see you as a lobbyist. Telling your story would be an inspiration to other families of POWs and MIAs whose loved ones haven't come home. You could do some good in that position with your experience. I think you should accept their offer. Malcolm Whitaker told me you're in high demand across the country since the hearings. He told me people have been calling the *Post* wanting that POW who took on Congress to speak at their engagements. Vietnam-Gate may not turn out so bad for you after all. You're a hero."

"I'm no hero…just so hungry and tired I didn't give a damn anymore. The guys on this wall and those suffering in Vietnamese prisons are the heros. I was lucky. I escaped. But right now, I don't feel so lucky. I can't figure out what I escaped to. This isn't the same country I left. Things have changed."

"Yeah but Blake, you haven't changed. You've gotta message to tell America. A very important message. Even if America has changed. You need to get it out. Tell them about the Golden Triangle, tell them about the CIA, the poppy fields, the Vietnamese prisons, all of it. People need to know. Without that knowledge, we're bound to repeat the same mistakes."

"Do you want me to tell them about President LaFleur and Kuhn-Sah Duc too? I doubt people are ready to swallow that."

"Tell 'em everything."

Blake blew into his hands and rubbed them together.

"The Golden Triangle will continue ya know, killing people with heroin. There are still CIA operatives involved over there. I know it. You can never clean 'em all out. The spooks always find a way to creep back in. By the way, what did Senator Jones say about Pacific Equity?"

Stephen shook his head. "That information in the records has been designated national security and edited from the hearings. It will be many years before its declassified and released to the public."

"Figures. Some things are too hot to handle. Speaking of hot, where does the trade embargo stand?"

"Hard to tell. With the absence of Bainbridge, Senator Jones has persuaded the Senate Select Committee to endorse a proposal opposing the lifting of the trade ban since the POWs have been discovered. They drafted a letter to President LaFleur informing him of their decision. Right now with all the commotion we caused at the hearings, LaFleur will probably back off for a while and let the situation cool. But once the POWs are returned, who knows?

"I understand Equity International has begun digging that deep seaport," Stephen continued. "I heard some American oil companies are already drilling off shore near Vietnam in partnership with foreign petroleum outfits. Lifting the embargo could be sooner than we expect."

"Have you heard anything about the UN Drug Control Program?"

"I talked to the Senate Foreign Relations Committee yesterday. The entire foreign aid program will be evaluated for the upcoming fiscal year. Congress appointed a special prosecutor to conduct a criminal investigation of the U.S. Ambassador to the United Nations. All U.S. contributions to the UN Drug Control Program are suspended until the investigation is completed."

"How long will the investigation take? They've got the records. What else do they need?"

Stephen shrugged. "Maybe a year. Possibly longer. It's political. The wheels of justice turn slowly."

The snow stopped falling and the memorial was silent like a tomb. Evening was engulfing the gray sky. Stephen looked up and saw some stars peeking from underneath a cloud bank. The North Star shone bright white, diminishing its smaller blue companions.

"Well, my friend, I've gotta go." He reached out his hand. Blake grasped it with a strong shake.

"Take care. And Stephen...thanks for everything you did. I couldn't have made it without you. You were by my side the whole way. I'll never forget that. You're braver than a lot of pilots I knew."

Stephen saw the hurt in his red, watery eyes. Years of hurt.

"No Blake. Thank you. You saved my life. You showed me the way. I won't forget it. Partners, right?"

"Yeah, buddy. Partners."

Stephen let go of his hand and hesitated for a moment; he wanted to say something noble, something uplifting but nothing came out. He wanted to tell the POW how much he cared about him, how much his life meant to him. But the words stuck in his throat. Blake stared, anticipating a spoken word.

"Yeah?" he asked softly.

"Uh. Nothing." Stephen swallowed and smiled weakly. He began walking away.

Twilight slowly crept across the sky like an inky ghost. He stopped at the top of the steps and contemplated the situation.

Another name should be added to that polished granite wall: Jim Laramie. He died a long time ago in those jungles of Southeast Asia, Stephen thought, and never found his way out, until that night at Dach Lu.

He blew into his hands, stomped his feet and peered at the spectacle of the Lincoln Memorial across the Mall, now lit up as night began to descend. He looked back at the Vietnam Veterans Memorial.

The gaunt figure remained but he was on bended knees, touching the polished wall with one hand, his head lowered in the other. Those were his friends; they were gone.

Their sacrificial legacy engraved upon the black granite. His legacy died with them. He wanted to return and comfort Blake but he couldn't. There was nothing left to say. He heard the familiar cough between sobs.

A man in a wheelchair, wearing a black beret and army–issue green jacket, wheeled up to the memorial. Stephen watched as Blake rose to his feet and wiped his eyes.

He coughed some more and continued looking at the names, trying to regain composure. The disabled veteran moved closer and struck up a conversation. They shook hands and talked. After a few minutes, Blake walked behind the wheelchair and slowly began pushing the gentleman around "The Wall."

Stephen smiled and the pain in his heart faded, slightly. The Vietnam War would never end for them; though Saigon was an ocean away, the battle would continue on in their hearts and in their souls. The lost war had left an indelible mark on the American psyche, never to be erased.

Old soldiers do fade away, Stephen thought, but perhaps Blake's legacy wasn't finished yet. Not yet. He turned and walked away.

THE END

Photo by Kathy Riggs

Stuart Patray was born in Georgia in 1964. A graduate of Georgia Southern University with a Bachelor of Science degree in Journalism, he is a former newspaper reporter, editor and publisher. He continues to reside in Georgia.